MURDER at
ENDERLEY
HALL

BOOKS BY HELENA DIXON

Murder at the Dolphin Hotel

HELENA DIXON

MURDER
at
ENDERLEY
HALL

bookouture

Published by Bookouture in 2020

An imprint of Storyfire Ltd.
Carmelite House
50 Victoria Embankment
London EC4Y 0DZ

www.bookouture.com

ISBN: 978-1-83888-065-1
eBook ISBN: 978-1-83888-064-4

Murder at Enderley Hall is dedicated to Mr Cox. Mr Cox was my English teacher when I was at senior school and he always believed I would write books one day, saying he wanted to be recognised as the one who spotted me early on. He encouraged me to write and explore. So, Mr Cox, this one is for you.

Torbay Herald 10th June 1933

Notorious jewel thief captured

Residents and guests in Torquay can rest easy in their beds following the arrest of Laurence Holland, a notorious international jewel thief. The thief was arrested following a tip-off from Captain Matthew Bryant of Torbay Private Investigation Services. Gallant Captain Bryant, a Great War hero, worked closely with the police to effect the arrest following a series of thefts at various luxury hotels in and around the Torquay area. Captain Bryant was also involved in the apprehension of those involved in a series of diabolical murders in Dartmouth earlier this year. Torbay Private Investigation Services are based in Fore Street in Torquay.

Auction of valuable ruby

The auction of a large and fabulous ruby belonging to the Maharajah of Ethsindi occurred last week in New York. It went on to sell for twenty thousand pounds, a record sum for an uncut stone. The ruby is believed to have been one of the largest found in the last century. It was missing for several years in mysterious circumstances before finding its way back to the Maharajah. A substantial reward was given to the anonymous finder by the grateful former ruler.

CHAPTER ONE

Summer, Dartmouth 1933

Mrs Treadwell pursed her lips and perused the letter her granddaughter, Kitty, had presented to her. Kitty Underhay was at breakfast with her grandmother and great aunt Livvy in her grandmother's private suite at the Dolphin Hotel. Livvy had fallen on the stairs at her home in Scotland a few weeks earlier, fracturing her foot and her shoulder. Now she was staying at the Dolphin to rest and recuperate before returning home.

The sky beyond the leaded bay window was bright blue and cloudless and the morning sun was already heating the air coming through the open top lights. Livvy shared a smile with Kitty as her grandmother read the letter of invitation from Kitty's father's family once again.

'I don't know, my dear. The choice is yours. If you wish to go and stay with these people, then I suppose the hotel can spare you for a week.' Her grandmother dropped the letter down on the table, narrowly missing the marmalade.

'I think Kitty could probably use a little holiday after the terrible events of the past few weeks. After all, it's not every day that one gets caught up in a murder,' Livvy remarked, peeping at her sister over the brim of her china teacup. She winced a little as she stretched out her injured foot, which was still encased in layers of strapping.

Kitty felt her great aunt's comment was something of an understatement considering there had been three vicious murders, an arson attack, a burglary and an attempt on her life. All of which related to her long-estranged father, Edgar Underhay, who until then, she hadn't seen since she'd been four.

It was due to her father's influence that the invitation to stay at Enderley Hall now lay on the table before her. Edgar, keen to make some amends for his lengthy absence and roguish ways, had prevailed upon his estranged sister, Lady Medford, to recognise Kitty as her niece. She wasn't certain what he had done to persuade her aunt since the two were not on speaking terms. Whatever he had done though, it seemed to have worked.

Hence, she was now the recipient of a carefully worded invitation to stay with her aunt, uncle and cousin Lucy for a week in the country at their estate near Exeter.

'It would be nice to meet them, at least. If we don't suit one another then I can always make an excuse to curtail the visit,' Kitty said. She was curious to know more about this side of her family that she hadn't known existed until recently. She knew very little about her father's family.

Her grandmother looked unconvinced.

'Lord Medford is highly thought of, my dear. He did great things during the war you know, supplying munitions and inventing several materials which greatly aided the war office,' Livvy remarked gently.

'I know, but Edgar Underhay is not exactly reliable. Who knows what he may have said to his sister to lead her to extend this invitation? After all that business with the ruby – which nearly got Kitty killed – is this an invitation to be trusted? We knew nothing at all of the connection until the other week.' Her grandmother eyed the letter with suspicion.

'I am rather curious to meet them and learn more of my father's family. And Lucy did kindly send a telegram to urge me to accept before the invitation even arrived.' Kitty spread butter on another triangle of toast and avoided catching her grandmother's eye.

The sense of restlessness that had pervaded her spirits before the previous dramatic events had begun to return of late, leaving her feeling trapped and bored.

The older woman sighed and appeared to accept defeat. 'Well, I suppose you had better meet them. They do at least appear to be respectable. You are looking a little peaky and it would be nice for you to be in company.'

Livvy tapped her good foot against Kitty's ankle under the table. 'Do you think you ought to take a maid, my dear? Such a grand house, you could borrow my Esther.'

Kitty didn't care for the idea of being accompanied by the rather dour-faced Esther, with all her complaints of lumbago and insomnia. 'I'm sure Aunt Hortense will have enough servants and I am very used to managing for myself.'

Her grandmother sniffed and drew herself up. 'I wouldn't want them to think we couldn't afford to keep a servant. You are not a charity case.'

Kitty could see that if she wasn't careful, she would be lumbered with Esther. 'What if I take Alice to accompany me?' Alice was a young chambermaid at the hotel. At sixteen years old, she was the eldest of eight children from a poor family. She was a bright, chirpy little thing and Kitty enjoyed her company. She would probably like the excitement of a visit to a big house and a break from her usual routine.

'I suppose that would be acceptable and she can be spared for a week,' her grandmother said, her pride mollified.

Kitty saw Livvy trying to hide a smile.

'You should get a new dress or two as well, Kitty, show off that lovely neat figure of yours. A good many young women would envy your excellent complexion and natural blonde hair. It's all the thing I understand and I expect there will be more society there.' Livvy winked at her. 'What a shame that nice young Captain Bryant is not included in the invitation.'

'Livvy! Matthew is a friend, that's all, as well you know,' Kitty reprimanded her aunt as her face heated at the implication.

Captain Matthew Bryant had stayed at the Dolphin previously in her grandmother's employ to protect both Kitty and the Dolphin when the murders had taken place. His parents were old acquaintances of her grandmother's and Matt had recently left his post with the government and had been at a loose end. He had ended up rescuing both Kitty and her father from the killer, placing himself in considerable danger to do so.

Since then, he had moved to a small, modern house in nearby Galmpton and opened his own business in security and private investigation. He was currently engaged in solving a series of jewel thefts from guests at a premier hotel in Torquay. Although roughly a decade older than Kitty's twenty-three years, his status as a war hero and widower, and financial stability, rendered him as quite a catch in local society. As Grams and Livvy seemed all too aware.

While working with Matt to solve the murders that had taken place only a few weeks ago, Kitty had come to realise that there were parts of his past that still haunted him. Things he had seen and done during the war, and a terrible personal tragedy that had widowed him at a young age. She wished he would open up more to her about his past, but she knew that he struggled with anything that he considered to be a weakness.

'I'd better send a reply to Aunt Hortense accepting her invitation and tell young Alice that we are going to take a trip, then.' Kitty touched the corners of her mouth with a linen napkin and, rising, retrieved her letter from the table.

She knew she would be barely out of the room before her grandmother and great aunt would be discussing her visit and what her father's family might be like.

*

'People are beginning to talk,' she said to Matt later that afternoon when he arrived at the hotel to take her to tea at Dartmouth Castle tearooms. Despite the dapper cut of his suit, he always had a slightly rakish look to his tall, wiry frame.

'Define "people".' He grinned at her as she collected her gloves and handbag. The dimple in his cheek flashed and his dark blue eyes twinkled at her.

'Very well, my aunt Livvy, then.' She smiled back at him as they stepped out of the cool of the oak-panelled hotel lobby into the bright sunshine of the embankment.

Light sparkled on the rippling water of the River Dart as it made its way towards the open sea at the mouth of the estuary. Dartmouth Castle, with its grey stone tower, stood guard on one side of the river, and the smaller matching Kingswear Castle sat on the opposite bank. Both buildings guarded the river mouth and the towns beyond, as they had done for centuries.

Matt offered her his arm and she rested her hand lightly on him. The muscles of his arm bunched under her touch and she was relieved that his shoulder seemed to be recovered from the injuries he'd received a few weeks earlier when grappling with a murderer. It was hard still for her to believe those horrific events had taken place in such a peaceful spot.

'And does it bother you if your aunt Livvy makes assumptions?' he teased.

Kitty laughed. 'We both know it doesn't. I'm happy to have your friendship. And I can't wait to hear all about your latest case. I saw in the paper there had been an arrest.'

They walked happily together along the steep thirty-minute walk around the cove at Warfleet up to the castle. The tearooms were busy, and they had to wait a few minutes whilst a waitress cleared a table for them.

'Oh dear, we've been sighted,' Kitty murmured as a familiar female figure waved an imperious hand at them from a table across the restaurant.

Resigning themselves to their fate, they crossed the room to say hello to Mrs Craven, former mayoress of Dartmouth and a close friend of Kitty's grandmother.

'Captain Bryant, how lovely to see you again. And you, Kitty.'

Kitty knew Mrs Craven had never really cared for her, and now probably cared even less after she had been attacked and burgled by thieves looking for a valuable gemstone that Kitty's missing mother, Elowed, may have left in her care.

'You appear to have made a good recovery, Mrs Craven,' Matt said.

'No thanks to that ruffian who attacked me. I felt quite nervous about returning home.' The feather in her hat quivered indignantly.

Kitty struggled to imagine the formidable Mrs Craven being nervous about anything. She was a sturdy lady with a stern expression who was on any committee of note within the town.

'I trust your grandmother and Livvy are both well?' She turned her attention to Kitty.

'Yes, thank you. I think Aunt Livvy is recovering very well. She has even been able to walk short distances with her cane these last few days.'

'I hope Doctor Carter has sanctioned that. Livvy was always impetuous, much like your mother. I shall call on them tomorrow morning before lunch.'

'I'll pass the message on,' Kitty promised, relieved to see that their table was now ready for them.

'Not so fast, young lady. Any news on that disreputable rogue of a father of yours? In America by now, I suppose?' Mrs Craven's tone told Kitty exactly what she thought of Edgar Underhay. Not that

Kitty could really blame her. Her father was, by his own admission, a ne'er-do-well, which was why her grandmother was so wary of Kitty meeting up with that side of her family.

'I expect so, his ship sailed some days ago.' She had seen the report in the *Herald* about the auction of the Maharajah's ruby in New York. It was unlikely to be coincidental that her father had just such a stone in his possession when he had boarded the ship.

Mrs Craven sniffed. 'If you ask me, the trouble with your father is that he was always hoping his ship would come in, preferably laden with gold, jewels and peacocks. I can't think what your mother ever saw in him, and I suppose now we'll never know.'

Kitty sucked in a breath and counted to three in her head. 'I'm sure I'll hear something from him shortly. He promised to follow up some information to try and trace what may have happened to my mother.' Mrs Craven had no idea how close to the truth her remark had come.

Mrs Craven arched her brows. Elowed, Kitty's mother, had vanished without a trace in 1916. Despite offers of rewards, numerous investigations and appeals, no new clues had ever been found and the leads had all petered away.

'We must go to our table, Mrs Craven. It's lovely to see you looking so well.' Matt took Kitty's arm and steered her away before she and Mrs Craven could come to blows.

'Insufferable woman. I wonder now how I could have ever felt sorry for her when she was in hospital.' Kitty took her seat at the table. She drew off her white cotton gloves and placed them neatly on top of her handbag before returning her attention to the menu.

'Do you think your father will contact you? I saw the report of the auction,' Matt asked after they had given their order for sandwiches, tea and scones to the waitress.

She gave him a sharp look, then shrugged. 'I'd like to think so, but who knows? Everyone knows my father is not reliable. I'll be interested to meet his sister, my aunt Hortense, when I stay at Enderley Hall.' She wondered if her aunt would be anything like her father. She got nervous butterflies in her stomach every time she thought about meeting her previously unknown family.

'Hobnobbing with the great and the good, eh?' Matt grinned at her. 'Lord Medford moves in the highest circles. I heard that he is developing new materials for the Ministry of Defence. There are even rumours of a secret laboratory at Enderley.'

'Then it's a good job I'm not a spy.' She smiled at the waitress as she set down their order. 'Anyway, enough of me. How goes the detecting at Torquay Private Investigation Services?' She poured them both a cup of tea.

'The lesson is: never trust a tennis coach. We caught him red-handed with Lady Cronshaw's diamond brooch. Our friend, Inspector Greville, made the arrest.'

'A success, then.' Kitty raised her teacup and chinked it gently against his. 'And are you settled in your house now?'

'Very nicely, still a lot to do. I even have a housekeeper, Mrs Milden, a respectable elderly widow of the parish who "does" for me. I have even taken up golf at Churston on the course near my house. You would admire my domesticity.'

'Hmm.' Kitty was not deceived by the twinkle in his eyes.

'I also have transport.'

She was instantly intrigued. 'That sounds exciting, tell me more. I didn't see a car at the hotel.'

'That's because it's a motorcycle.' He laughed at her puzzled expression. 'I always used to have a motorcycle during the war and just afterwards. I've purchased a Sunbeam, they did quite well last year at the TT races. You could come for a spin some time.'

Her heart gave a flutter, whether of excitement or fear she wasn't certain. 'Then tongues would most definitely wag. You could always ride over and visit me at Enderley Hall, it's not terribly far away. I suspect my cousin, Lucy, would like it.'

'I may take you up on that. I confess I'd like to see the place. Your aunt is well known as a keen horticulturalist and the gardens are supposed to be spectacular.'

Kitty placed her cup back on its saucer. 'Now I know you're becoming domesticated. You will be asking for tips for your roses next,' she teased.

After Matt had escorted her back to the Dolphin, Kitty went in search of Alice to inform her of her temporary change of employment.

She discovered her hard at work in the linen store under the tutelage of Mrs Homer, the housekeeper, organising and counting linen.

'I'm sorry to disturb you, Mrs Homer, but I need to speak with Alice for a minute.'

The housekeeper, who wasn't too enamoured of her newest chambermaid, considering her far too pert, was only too happy for Kitty to take Alice. She clearly thought that the young lady was in for a reprimand for some misdemeanour.

Kitty took Alice to a quiet corner of the corridor.

'Is everything all right, miss?' the girl asked, her grey eyes wide with apprehension. 'If it's about room twenty not having any towels this morning, that weren't me, miss.'

'No, it's not about towels. You aren't in any trouble, Alice.'

The girl's scrawny shoulders relaxed and she let out a breath.

'I have a proposal for you. I have been invited to stay with my uncle and aunt, Lord and Lady Medford, for a week at their country house near Exeter. My grandmother and great aunt both feel that I should take a staff member with me as my maid and I wondered if you would like to accompany me?'

The girl's face lit up with excitement. 'Me, be a real lady's maid, like in the films, miss?'

Kitty was amused by her enthusiasm. 'Yes, well, I suppose so. You would have to take care of my clothes, run small errands and look after things for me.'

Alice clapped her work-reddened hands together in delight. 'In a real, big posh house, miss?'

'Yes.' Kitty reached out a hand to straighten the white lace collar of the girl's uniform. 'I think we'll have to tidy your dress a little before we go.' Alice was a slender little thing and the uniform was a poor fit.

Alice immediately attempted to smooth her wayward auburn hair back into a bun before twitching her apron straight. 'I can take it in, miss, I'm good with a needle. I'll talk proper and everything like in the films, miss. In the films sometimes, they lady's maids is French.'

'You don't have to be French, Alice.' Kitty bit back a smile, hoping Alice wouldn't attempt a French accent whilst they were at Enderley.

She looked a little disappointed at this pronouncement. 'I could maybe have a little lace cap though, miss?' she suggested, her eyes hopeful.

'I'll see what I can do,' Kitty promised and left the little maid to return to Mrs Homer and the linen store. She was quite excited about the trip herself, although this was tinged with apprehension about how she might be received.

CHAPTER TWO

Kitty's grandmother insisted that she and Alice travel by car rather than train. 'I don't want your father's family to think you are some kind of charity case. Heaven knows what nonsense Edgar may have told them. You will go in Mr Potter's motor taxi.'

Alice bubbled with suppressed excitement as she supervised the loading of the luggage into the boot of the car with all the importance of her new position. Kitty had insisted on buying her a new pair of shoes and some new stockings as part of her uniform. The longed-for lace cap was carefully starched and stowed in the luggage. Consequently, Alice was enjoying herself enormously as she took her seat next to Kitty in the back of the car.

Kitty was glad of the maid's excitement as it took the edge off her own nervousness at the thought of meeting her father's family for the first time.

'Cor, this is better than the omnibus or the train, miss.' Alice wiggled on the leather seat to get a better view from the window. 'I in't ever been in a car before.'

They had travelled up the hill now, out of Dartmouth and into the open farmland that lay between there and Exeter. Mr Porter was driving at a steady, if unexciting, pace and Kitty tried to settle back and enjoy the journey. Her cousin, Lucy, who was a similar age, had sent her a telegram ahead of her aunt's written invitation urging her to make the visit. The message had done much to make her feel as if she would be welcomed by Lucy, at least. So why did she have this annoying sense of anxiety? Just the idea of going into the unknown, she supposed.

'Will there be lots of staff, miss? Other lady's maids?' Alice asked.

'I expect Lady Medford will have a maid, and possibly my cousin, Lucy. I don't know who else is to be part of the house party though, or if it's just to be family this week.' She glanced at Alice, who appeared to be considering the matter. 'You will be fine, Alice. Just mind what Lord Medford's butler and the housekeeper tell you and remember you are there to look after me. Don't be afraid, you will be absolutely splendid. We are both going to have a marvellous adventure.'

The grin returned to Alice's face at Kitty's vote of confidence. Enderley Hall was situated to the other side of Exeter near Crediton, along a country lane not far from the small village of Newton St Cyres and only fifty miles from Dartmouth. Kitty joined Alice to peer through the window for their first glimpse of the house.

The long gravel driveway was lined by an avenue of trees; sheep grazed the fields around them as they approached. The house itself was a large, red-bricked building of much greater antiquity than Kitty had expected. The leaded windows were set deep in their stone mullioned frames and the great number of chimneys rising above the grey slate rooftop gave testament to the grandeur of the manor. The frontage of the building appeared dark and forbidding even in the bright sunshine.

Kitty took a deep breath and placed her hand discreetly on her diaphragm in a bid to still the nervous flight of the butterflies stirring within her. Alice, too, appeared awed by their surroundings as Mr Potter stopped the motor car in front of the house.

'Cor, it's as big as the Dolphin – but not so friendly-looking,' Alice said.

Kitty remained frozen in her seat as Mr Potter alighted and came around to open her door. The house loomed over them, the windows blank and soulless. In the distance the rooks cawed in the trees. She suppressed a shiver.

Alice had already scrambled free and was at the boot ready to supervise the unloading of their bags. The large oak front door of the hall opened and a tall, distinguished manservant with greying temples came towards the car. He was rapidly overtaken by a young woman in a tweed skirt and cream silk blouse. She had wavy dark hair and bright eyes, and was accompanied by a small scruffy brown and white dog of indeterminate parentage.

'Come on, Mr Harmon.' She urged the servant before turning and beaming at Kitty. 'Oh, I'm so happy you've come. I'm your cousin, Lucy. Welcome to Enderley Hall.'

'It's lovely to meet you,' Kitty managed to find her voice as she eased out of the car only to be swept up in an exuberant hug.

'Muffy, do stop barking!' Lucy addressed the dog. 'I can't believe I have a cousin.' She released her and stepped back to study her face. 'You're awfully pretty; you must look like your mother. I can't see any of Uncle Edgar in you.'

'Perhaps, knowing my father's reputation, that could be considered a good thing.' Kitty smiled as her comment drew a peal of laughter from Lucy.

'You could have a point. Mother despairs of your father and Papa absolutely refuses to allow him to visit.' She linked her arm through Kitty's. 'But we read about your adventures in the paper after Uncle Edgar sent his telegram to Mother, and I insisted you come to stay. Oh, I'm so thrilled to meet you. You're just in time for luncheon. Come inside and meet the others. Mr Harmon or Mrs Jenkinson, the housekeeper, will show your maid your room and sort your luggage.'

Kitty was given little choice but to accompany her cousin and Muffy the dog inside the house, leaving Alice to manage. Once inside, a maid relieved her of her hat and coat and showed her to a large downstairs powder room in which to freshen up. The cool water running on her hands helped to calm her thoughts somewhat before she rejoined her cousin in the large square hall with its black and white tiled floor and massive oak staircase.

Lucy led the way to a sunny drawing room furnished in the latest style. An ornate Italian marble fireplace dominated the room and fresh flowers were arranged on a couple of the side tables. 'Mother, look who's here,' Lucy sang out as they entered the room.

A tall, elegant woman with grey hair turned from her position by the French doors where she had been contemplating the stone balustraded terrace. Her face paled and her hand moved to her throat to touch the strand of pearls encircling her neck as Kitty entered.

'Lady Medford, thank you for inviting me.' Kitty moved forward to greet her, wondering what it was about her appearance that had apparently startled her aunt so much.

'Please, call me Aunt Hortense. You are family, after all.' She appeared to swallow hard before moving forward to place a cool kiss on Kitty's cheek. 'Welcome to Enderley Hall.'

Lucy had headed to a well-stocked drinks cabinet near the marble fireplace. 'I was saying to Kitty that she doesn't look much like Uncle Edgar.'

A hint of colour reappeared in Aunt Hortense's cheeks. 'No, no she doesn't. You must favour your mother, my dear.'

'Yes, I believe so,' Kitty agreed, finding herself fumbling for an appropriate response.

Lucy handed her a glass. 'An aperitif before lunch, Kitty darling.' She glanced at the ornate French clock on the mantelpiece. 'Where on earth are Rupert and Daisy? They must still be on the tennis court.'

Kitty clasped her glass and tried not to reveal her bewilderment.

'Friends of Lucy's from London. She invited them,' Aunt Hortense observed drily as she too accepted a drink from her daughter.

Just then, a short, rotund elderly woman panted her way into the room and addressed Lady Medford. 'I found your spectacles, dear. They were in the library where you'd been looking at the horticultural catalogues with Mr Henderson.' She proffered an embroidered spectacles case to Lady Medford before peering myopically at Kitty, who was standing next to Lucy.

'Kitty, darling, this is our lovely Nanny Thoms. She was my nanny, but she helps Mother now and is our darling family friend. Nanny, this is Kitty.'

'You must be Edgar's girl. Lovely to meet you, dear.' She squinted at Kitty. 'My eyes aren't what they were I'm afraid, but you do seem very familiar, as if we've met before.'

Lady Medford stood suddenly, draining her glass as a gong sounded from the direction of the hallway. 'Where are the others? It is lunchtime already.' Kitty realised she was quite famished, and she hoped someone would remember to offer Alice something to eat.

Lucy linked arms with her once more. 'You'll meet Papa at dinner tonight, he rarely leaves his work to take lunch with us. He's terribly busy at the moment, some government thing. Aubrey, his secretary, will be there, though. He has quite the pash on Daisy, you'll see, he's completely moonstruck.'

They were joined as they entered the dining room by a tall, skinny, solemn young man with round spectacles whom Lucy introduced as Aubrey, Lord Medford's secretary. A slim young woman with bleached blonde hair in the latest Jean Harlow Hollywood style arrived as they were being seated, together with a tall, fair-haired good-looking young man in a striped blazer.

'Kitty, may I introduce my friends, Daisy and Rupert Banks.'

'Delighted.' Rupert kept hold of her hand for just a fraction too long as he studied her face.

'We've heard so much about you from Lucy. A secret cousin, it's so exciting.' Daisy took her seat at the table and earned herself a cold stare from Lady Medford.

'Will Viola be joining us?' Lady Medford asked as she adjusted her napkin across her lap.

'She's having sandwiches, doing a tricky bit on the mural apparently. Something to do with flaking.' Rupert rolled his eyes.

'Frau Fiser, Viola, is doing some conservation work on the mural that leads from the head of the stairs into the long gallery. It's perfectly hideous and would be better painted over but Papa insists it has to stay,' Lucy explained to Kitty.

'It's very valuable and part of the history of the house.' Aubrey frowned and blushed as if concerned he had spoken out of turn.

'You must take Kitty to look at the family pictures in the gallery after lunch, Lucy. She might like to see the portraits of the Underhays,' Lady Medford said.

'Well, they are certainly better looking than some of the Medford ones.' Lucy giggled.

'No Mr Henderson today?' Daisy enquired.

'He is visiting a nurseryman on my behalf to source some hardier plants for the new beds he is designing for me as part of the new garden plans. He'll be back in time for dinner.' Lady Medford signalled the servants to begin serving.

Kitty was seated to the right of her aunt who was at the head of the table. The place settings were quite formal for lunch with the silver cutlery perfectly placed on the crisp, white linen cloth. Lucy was to her left, with Rupert opposite her. She wondered if anyone had noticed Muffy the dog sneaking in to lie under Nanny Thoms's chair. She was conscious of a frost in the air around the table but was relieved that it did not seem to be directed at her.

'Quite a turn up for the books, eh, finding out you had a cousin, Lucy?' Rupert said as he dived into his lamb cutlets. He had a deep, pleasant voice, and like his sister, was well-spoken.

'Uncle Edgar has been rather persona non gratis for quite a while,' Lucy said.

'Your father threatened to shoot him.' Lady Medford gave a small, rather unladylike snort.

'My father does appear to have that effect on people. I hadn't seen him myself since I was four until he suddenly reappeared a few weeks ago,' Kitty said.

'Gosh yes, I read all about it in the papers. You poor thing, being caught up in a murder, how ghastly.' Daisy's eyes grew wide as she gazed at Kitty. 'Did they discover what became of the ruby?'

Kitty gave a small shrug. 'No, no one knows.' That wasn't strictly true, but she wasn't about to share any information. It would appear that Daisy, at least, had not made the connection with the report in the paper of the auction in New York.

'Quite a surprise for you then, having your father reappear. I thought the paper said something about your mother having gone missing in nineteen-sixteen? If I may enquire?' Rupert took a sip from his glass.

'Sadly, yes. The war was on and the police were short of manpower. At first it was assumed she had gone to visit friends. With so many being displaced and moving around it was hard to trace people. My grandmother employed private detectives and made several appeals, but she has never been found.'

'Oh, poor you,' Daisy said.

Nanny Thoms had a frown puckering her forehead. 'Wasn't that when we went to London? Nineteen-sixteen? Lord Medford was doing some very important work for the government in munitions.' She stared at Kitty. 'You do look so familiar, my dear.'

'Nanny, are you feeding that wretched dog?' Lady Medford demanded.

Nanny Thoms immediately looked guilty and rested her hands on the tablecloth. Kitty suspected quite a bit of Nanny's lamb had disappeared under the table.

'Well, I am absolutely delighted to have a cousin. I always longed for a sister, so having Kitty here will be so much fun.' Lucy beamed at her.

Kitty hoped she was right. It certainly looked as if it would be an interesting week at Enderley with such a diverse group of people.

CHAPTER THREE

Daisy and Rupert tagged along in accompanying Kitty, Lucy and Muffy the dog upstairs to the long gallery.

'This part of the house is one of the oldest bits. It dates back to Tudor times, but of course Papa's ancestors added on all sorts of stuff, including commissioning this dreadful mural.' Lucy waved an expressive hand at the artwork which started near the top of the stairs and covered the wall and ceiling as they entered the long gallery. A colourful classical scene featuring various Greek gods and goddesses in a pastoral setting lay before them. It was clear that extensive cleaning and restoration work had been carried out, with only a small portion remaining to be restored.

A trestle table stood to the side covered with a variety of pots, brushes and bottles. There were various magnifying devices and lights. A thin woman in her forties, garishly dressed under her smocked coverall, scowled at their party as Muffy bounced happily towards her, wagging her tail.

'How am I expected to work with all these interruptions?' the woman demanded.

'Frau Viola Fiser, this is my cousin, Kitty Underhay,' Lucy performed the introductions, ignoring Viola's obvious annoyance at their party's appearance in the gallery.

'Humph.' Viola glanced at Kitty. Muffy sidled up to the art conservator, wagging her tail. 'Oh, do take that wretched beast away. It keeps trying to steal my brushes.' She made ineffectual shooing motions at the dog.

'Darling Muffy, she really likes you, Viola.' Lucy smiled indulgently at her pet. 'We're going to show Kitty the Underhay family portraits that Mummy brought back from Ireland.'

Viola sniffed disparagingly. 'They are very ordinary. There are much better pictures in the collection.'

'Yes, but they aren't of Kitty's family, silly,' Lucy said.

'Oh, but Frau Fiser is an art expert,' Rupert drawled, earning a glare from Viola. Kitty sensed an underlying current of ill-feeling between Rupert and Viola and wondered at the cause.

'Bad Muffy!' Daisy reproved the little dog as, tired of Viola ignoring her, Muffy seized a small brush and scampered away down the gallery drawing a frustrated scream from Viola.

Lucy seemed to judge it advisable to make a swift exit, leaving Viola to her work. Rupert set off in pursuit of the dog, leaving Daisy to dawdle along with Kitty and Lucy.

Huge diamond-leaded windows with coloured lights showing the family crests dominated the exterior wall of the long gallery. The interior wall was wood-panelled in dark oak with a suit of armour at the midpoint. Pictures had been hung at various intervals; portraits interspersed with landscapes of the park. Glass-topped curio tables and oriental cabinets stood at the sides, filled with bits and pieces collected by various generations of Medfords.

'You might like these.' Lucy halted in front of one of the glass-topped cases housing a collection of miniature portraits. 'See anyone you know?' she teased.

Kitty studied the contents of the case. The portraits appeared to span a considerable time period from bewigged Georgian gents to stern Victorian matrons. 'Oh, there is father.' She spotted Edgar. It had clearly been painted when he was a young man, possibly around the time he had met her mother. He was quite dashing, and she could see why her mother had fallen in love with him. 'Oh, and there is Aunt Hortense.' Lady Medford had also been captured as a young woman, with rosy cheeks and dark hair.

Daisy cast a cursory glance at the cabinet before ambling off to look out of the window.

'Sweet, aren't they? Granny Underhay had them painted when they were in their twenties, Uncle Edgar is three years older than Mother. Granny was from Boston, you know. The marriage quite restored the Underhay family fortunes as she was something of an heiress. Come on, I'll show you Granny and Grandpa's pictures. Grandpa looks very fierce in his.' She led the way to where two huge matching portraits hung.

'There was a fire at the house in Ireland, so Mother brought some furniture and some pictures back here for safe-keeping.'

Grandpa Underhay was a rather stern individual with an impressive set of mutton chop whiskers. Granny Underhay had the same look about her as Lady Medford. It was a surreal moment for Kitty to be face to face with images of grandparents she had never had the opportunity to meet. She stared at their faces and wondered what they had been like. Would they have liked her? Or she, them?

'Oh dear.' Daisy's comment drew them away from the portraits to join her at the window.

'Oh no, Mother and Mr Henderson will have a perfect fit,' Lucy said as Muffy raced along the terrace below them with what appeared to be a small tree in her mouth. Bits of mud seemed to be flying everywhere as Rupert and one of the gardeners attempted to catch her.

'Rupert is useless,' Daisy declared as her brother allowed Muffy to evade capture once more.

'We had better go and get her before Mother sees the damage.' Lucy led the way down the stairs at the far end of the long gallery and out onto the terrace via a small side door.

'Muffy, drop that! Come here!' The little dog dropped the tree and yapped at Rupert before trotting towards Lucy looking extremely pleased with herself as the gardener retrieved the plant.

'That animal is a liability.' Rupert's face was flushed with exertion and he didn't look terribly happy. 'Your mother already doesn't care for me so I expect I shall get the blame for not preventing the damage this time too.'

Lucy appeared unfazed by his outburst. 'You do talk rot. You should stop talking about communist principles at the dinner table and offering her that wretched newspaper to read if you want her to like you more.'

Daisy sniggered. 'Lord Medford didn't appreciate your debate either last night, and poor Aubrey didn't know where to put himself.'

'People need to be informed about the struggles of the working man and the need to combat fascism,' Rupert said indignantly.

Kitty wondered what work Rupert did. He hadn't struck her as someone who had a hard manual job, or even a job at all.

'Rupert, darling, I know you mean well, but I don't think you represent the average working man.' Her cousin echoed her thought.

'Mock me if you will, but you'll see. I thought you understood what we were trying to achieve.' Rupert stalked off along the terrace, leaving Muffy to gaze mournfully after him.

'Oh dear, I think I hit a nerve.' Lucy sighed, a small frown puckering her forehead.

'He'll get over it. He always does,' Daisy said.

'What work does Rupert do?' Kitty asked.

Daisy smiled. 'Well, if you ask him, he'll say he's a creative. He writes poetry and paints. He's an admirer of the surrealist school, all lines and things.'

'Is he any good?' The question slipped out before she could stop herself.

Lucy and Daisy exchanged a glance. 'He thinks he is,' Daisy said. 'Frau Fiser disagrees.'

When Kitty returned to her room to change for dinner, she discovered that Alice had been busy. Her clothes had all been unpacked and her dresses pressed and hung.

'Thank you, Alice, you've done a splendid job.' She admired the maid's handiwork. Alice flushed with pleasure at the compliment. 'Thank you, miss.'

'I hope they are looking after you?' Kitty asked.

'Oh yes, miss. Cook gave me a lovely dinner and Mr Harmon, the butler, is ever so nice. Mrs Jenkinson is a bit quiet, but she seems nice as well.'

Kitty was relieved to hear that the girl had been treated kindly. The notion of having a maid still sat somewhat uncomfortably with her. She was more than used to taking care of herself with just a little help from one of the hotel maids for special occasions.

'This is a lovely room, miss, and I've got me own bed just in here, look.' Alice led her through a doorway into a small dressing area containing a cot bed with a small nightstand. 'So, if you need me, I'll be right here.'

Kitty was oddly comforted by the idea of having Alice close by. The day had been quite overwhelming so far with new people, and she still had to meet her uncle. For all the times she had wished to escape from the Dolphin, now it had happened, she felt a little lonely. There was also still an odd feeling that she had been unable to shake off ever since her arrival. She couldn't even say what it was exactly, but something in the atmosphere at Enderley was making her uneasy.

Her bedroom was nice, not too large, and light and bright despite the midnight blue heavy velvet drapes at the window. The walls were papered with a cheerful yellow with small landscapes hung on the walls. On the dressing table, a glass vase held some yellow roses which added a delicate scent to the room.

'The lav is across the landing, miss, and the bath has hot water in the taps. There's scented bath salts and everything. Would you like me to run you a bath, miss?' Alice asked.

Kitty smiled at the girl's eagerness to please. The small lace cap Alice had longed for to mark her new status was perched a little tipsily on top of her auburn hair and her eyes were sparkling at the idea of a bathroom with so much luxury. 'That would be lovely, Alice, thank you.'

A little later, bathed and dressed in a dark green fitted satin gown of Alice's choosing, Kitty made her way to the drawing room to join the rest of the party for pre-dinner drinks.

Butterflies danced in her stomach at the thought of meeting her uncle, Lord Medford, and the mysterious Mr Henderson. She hoped Rupert had recovered his temper and that Viola would be a little more sociable. Part of her envied Alice, who could hide herself away and not have to make small talk with strangers. She took a deep breath and squared her shoulders. After all, she talked to people every day at the Dolphin. She could do this.

The hum of chatter met her in the hall as she approached the sitting room door. It was slightly ajar, so she slipped inside as unobtrusively as possible.

CHAPTER FOUR

'Ah, Elowed, just in time for drinks.' Nanny Thoms beamed at her.

Kitty's stomach plummeted floorward. 'I'm sorry, what did you call me?' She must have misheard her.

Nanny Thoms's round pleasant face crumpled into a bewildered frown. 'I'm sorry, dear?'

'You called me by my mother's name, Elowed.' Kitty sank down onto a nearby chintz covered sofa, thankful that no one else in the room seemed to have noticed her entrance.

'Your mother? Oh yes, of course, that's who you look like.' Nanny Thoms's expression brightened as if she had just solved a particularly difficult puzzle.

'But, when did you meet my mother?' Surely that wasn't possible. Her father had said that his sister hadn't known about his marriage or Kitty until he'd sent her a telegram a few weeks ago just before his return to America.

'Now then, let me think. She came here once, years ago, during the war, to see Hortense. Such a pretty little thing.'

'Here? My mother was here?' Kitty found it hard to believe what she was hearing. No wonder her aunt had looked so shocked at her appearance. It must have been as if the past was repeating itself. How could her mother have been to Enderley? And why didn't her aunt want her to know?

Lucy came over with a cocktail glass in her hand and gave it to Kitty. 'Do have a drink, darling, you look quite pale. Is everything all right?' She glanced at Nanny Thoms.

'Oh yes, perfectly fine. It's been a busy day,' Kitty rushed to answer and flashed a smile of reassurance at her cousin. She needed time to process this information. She wanted to ask Nanny Thoms more questions. When exactly had her mother been to Enderley and why? Why had her aunt Hortense denied knowing about her? Was it guilt that had prompted the sudden outburst of hospitality? So many questions were buzzing in her brain and she suddenly wished that Matt was there with his cool, calm logic to help her work it out.

Nanny Thoms seized upon Lucy's arrival as her chance to slip away. Kitty took a deep breath and tried to recover her wits. She glanced around the room as she sipped her drink. Rupert was lounging near the marble fireplace, waving his hands around as he talked to Viola, who was wearing a garish orange gown with mustard accessories. Aubrey was seated next to Daisy, his face peony pink as she smiled at him. Her aunt, resplendent in black velvet, was deep in discussion with a tall, bluff ex-military type man in his mid-fifties. Nanny Thoms had moved close by, listening to their conversation. Kitty guessed the unknown man must be Mr Henderson, the landscape designer.

At that moment the door opened and two more men entered. She recognised her uncle immediately from his portrait in the long gallery. A short, somewhat rotund man, he reminded her of a well-to-do grocer, like Mr Finch, the Dolphin's supplier, rather than a scientist and leader of industry, though he was dressed in expensively cut evening wear.

The man accompanying him was also faintly familiar, but she wasn't sure why. He was in his mid-forties with steel grey hair and an unmistakeable air of authority. Lady Medford abandoned Mr Henderson to cross the room to greet her husband.

'Hortense, darling, this is Sir Horace Blunt. Horace, may I present my wife, Hortense.'

Kitty tried to look as inconspicuous as possible as Lucy bounced off the sofa and was also introduced to Sir Horace.

'Papa, you haven't said hello to Kitty yet.' She tugged Kitty to her feet.

Lord Medford turned his attention to her. 'Edgar's girl, eh? Read about you in the paper, terrible business. You were very brave, I understand. Welcome to Enderley.' His gaze was shrewd and assessing. She shook his hand and was also presented to Sir Horace.

'Aubrey. Where the dickens is Aubrey?' Lord Medford suddenly demanded as he attempted to peer around his wife.

At the sound of his name, Aubrey abandoned Daisy and hurried to his employer's side.

'Ah, there you are. Sir Horace wants to see our progress after dinner, in the library.'

'Yes, um, very good, sir, everything is ready. I'll fetch the file from the laboratory safe after dinner.'

Dinner turned out to be a much more formal affair than lunch and Kitty was glad she had followed Alice's suggestion and worn a formal gown. The dining table groaned with crystal glassware glistening in the light from the candelabra and the silverware sparkled. Muffy had been banished to the kitchen and Lord Medford headed the table. Sir Horace was clearly the guest of honour and Kitty was relegated to sit between Mr Henderson and Rupert, with Viola opposite. Nanny Thoms was again at the bottom of the table, along with Daisy.

Mr Henderson seemed to be of a taciturn disposition, and Rupert still sulky from the afternoon. His mood probably not being helped by Viola glowering at him across the table. Kitty decided her best chance of any social interaction must be with Mr Henderson, even though she knew little of gardens or gardening.

'You are assisting my aunt in improving the gardens then, Mr Henderson?'

He dragged his attention away from his soup as if noticing her for the first time. 'That's correct, Miss... um...'

'Underhay, Kitty Underhay. I'm Lord and Lady Medford's niece,' she supplied helpfully.

'Ah yes, of course, Thomas Henderson. Yes, her ladyship wishes to make more of the walled garden and to reduce some of the more labour-intensive aspects of the grounds.' He dove back into his soup bowl.

'I suppose it must be difficult to maintain such a large estate; it takes a lot of manpower,' Kitty persevered, ignoring the faint scoffing sound emanating from Rupert.

'Indeed, and of course, a lot of damage was done during the war with the shift from ornamental beds to more food production. It's taken a lot of work to restore the tropical house.' Mr Henderson set down his spoon and gazed mournfully at his now empty bowl.

'In the art world too, the war changed many things,' Viola chipped in. 'Many terrible things occurred, and are happening again.'

The conversation, such as it was, paused as the bowls were cleared and the second course served.

Kitty noticed Sir Horace and her uncle had their heads close together, deep in murmured technical conversation with Aubrey looking somewhat forlornly, as if left out, at them across the table. Her cousin was talking to her mother, whilst at the other end of the table, Nanny Thoms was advising Daisy on how to remove a stain from a satin evening glove.

Once everyone was served, Mr Henderson turned his full attention back to his dinner, eating like a man half-starved. Viola, on the other hand, picked and pecked at her food in between sniping at Rupert. Kitty stifled a sigh and wished Matt were present to enliven the affair.

It came as something of a relief when dessert was finished and the party withdrew. Lord Medford, Aubrey and Sir Horace to the library, to discuss her uncle's work. Rupert and Mr Henderson went for a game of billiards, and the ladies moved to the drawing room for coffee.

'Oh, what a nuisance. Nanny, I've left my spectacles again. Do be a dear and fetch them for me,' Lady Medford requested as she seated herself before a small worktable and fetched out her embroidery.

Lucy ignored the coffee in favour of mixing herself another drink from the bar. Viola buried her nose in a large book on Venetian glass, alternately reading and making notes in a small leather-bound notebook. Meanwhile, Daisy leafed through a publication of Parisian fashion before tossing it aside and announcing her intention of going to watch the billiards match.

Kitty wished she had thought to bring something with her to occupy her time. She didn't fancy Daisy's magazine and instead wandered over to the French doors to look out at the darkened garden as her cousin sorted through the gramophone records for some music. The stars appeared particularly bright and the moon fat and almost full. She made out the shape of a fox slinking along the edge of the terrace where the light from the library window spilled out onto the stones.

Nanny Thoms panted back into the room. 'They were on your dressing table, dear.' She handed the glasses to Lady Medford before taking a seat nearby and reaching for her knitting bag.

Kitty moved away from the window to rejoin the group. 'I didn't know my mother had visited here.' She waited for her aunt's response, keen to learn if Nanny's information had been correct.

Nanny Thoms's needles stopped their busy clicking and Kitty saw her aunt had pricked her finger, sucking at the wound before the blood could fall and stain her work. Nanny immediately began clucking about fetching a dressing.

'Oh yes, she may have done once. I had quite forgotten,' her aunt said, and Kitty knew from her expression that she was lying.

'Nanny Thoms said she came here during the war. It must have been when I was small, before she disappeared.'

Lucy's eyes widened in astonishment. 'Mother, you said you didn't know anything about Kitty when Uncle Edgar's telegram came. You never said you had met her mother.'

'It had slipped my mind,' Lady Medford snapped, waving Nanny Thoms away. 'It was very brief and a long time ago.'

'When did she come here?' Kitty persisted.

Nanny Thoms screwed up her round face in thought. 'I am sure it was summer. She had been given a lift from the station in the village on the mill cart. She stayed overnight and Lord Medford's carriage took her back to the station after breakfast the next day.'

'My husband was away from home at the time, in London on war work. We were packing, preparing to join him. It was most inconvenient.' Lady Medford sighed.

'Why did she come?' Kitty's heart rate accelerated as she tried to take in all this new information about her mother.

Nanny Thoms looked as if she were about to answer but a glance from Lady Medford silenced her.

'She came for advice about your father. My brother, as usual, had disappeared and she had received no response to her letters for some time. She recalled him mentioning my name and came to see if I had any news or information.'

'Mother! Why didn't you tell me anything about this when Uncle Edgar sent his telegram about Kitty?' Lucy asked.

'It was a long time ago, Lucy. There was a war on.'

'But you know how much I wanted a cousin.' Lucy glared at her mother.

'Oh, do be quiet, Lucy dear,' her aunt snapped.

'So, it was the summer of nineteen-sixteen? Around the time she disappeared?' Kitty asked.

Her aunt appeared uncomfortable. 'I can assure you that she boarded the train at Newton St Cyres safely. I don't know where she planned to go next. We did not have that kind of conversation.'

'You look so much like her. Same colouring and eyes. Gave me quite a turn when you arrived,' Nanny Thoms mused, earning herself another harsh look from Lady Medford.

Kitty couldn't believe her mother had visited her aunt and not mentioned that she had a child. However, her aunt's countenance indicated that she knew a lot more than she was prepared to say with Lucy and Viola present. For Kitty was certain that Viola was listening closely to the conversation despite pretending to be immersed in her book. Further questions were prevented by the arrival of Daisy and Rupert.

'Is Mr Henderson not joining us tonight?' her aunt asked.

'Retiring early, he said.' Rupert flung himself down on the nearest vacant chair. 'Daisy, old girl, fix a fellow a drink, would you?' He flashed a smile at Kitty.

His sister frowned at him but moved to the bar trolley to pour two whiskies; one for Rupert and one for herself.

'What was that? Something moved.' Viola jumped up and clutched her chest as she peered anxiously at the window.

Rupert followed her gaze. 'Nothing, there is nothing there. Honestly, not this tosh all over again.'

'It is not "tosh" as you call it. There are people watching me, watching all of us.'

'Tosh,' Rupert repeated.

'I tell you there is someone out there, watching us.' Viola's gaze darted back to the window.

'There was a fox there earlier,' Kitty said.

'See, a fox. Just a fox.' Rupert took a sip from his drink.

Viola closed her book with a snap. 'I think I too shall retire; I won't stay where people do not take me seriously. I have warned you all. Good evening.' She stalked out of the room clutching her notebook.

'Bit frosty in here, isn't it?' Rupert observed, taking another swig from his glass.

Kitty wondered if she could make her own excuses for the evening. It occurred to her that Rupert was a little the worse for wear and she could see her aunt was not amused either with Rupert or with Viola's bizarre histrionics.

'Muffy! Bad dog!' Lucy gave a cry as her dog sneaked into the room and promptly stole a ball of pale pink wool from Nanny Thoms's bag before dashing away into the hall with Lucy in pursuit.

'Oh really, that naughty animal. Nanny, you'd better go after them,' Lady Medford commanded. The old lady immediately put down her knitting and followed after Lucy.

Her cousin returned shortly afterwards with the remnants of the ball of wool. 'Naughty Muffy, she is the most dreadful little thief.' She returned the yarn to Nanny's bag.

Kitty took the opportunity to make her excuses and slipped away. As she climbed the stairs the faint rumble of masculine voices reached her from the library, and she surmised her uncle and his group would be retiring late.

CHAPTER FIVE

Alice woke Kitty the next morning with a tray of tea carefully deposited on her bedside table.

'There's a right to-do going on downstairs, miss,' Alice informed her as she swished open the curtains to let in the bright summer sunlight.

Kitty pushed herself upright and arranged her pillows behind her head. Alice lifted the tray onto her knees and poured her tea through a silver strainer into a white china cup decorated with fat pink roses. 'Why? What's happened?'

'Mr Aubrey, your uncle's secretary, is tearing about all over the place. Some papers have gone missing from out the safe in his lordship's study. Lord Medford is yelling at everybody, and that government man that came yesterday, Sir Horace, is organising people to search the house.'

'I presume these papers must be important,' Kitty mused and took a sip of her tea.

'Yes, miss, something to do with defence of the country, Mr Harmon said. I think Sir Horace wants to search the bedrooms too.' She said the latter in a scandalised hush.

'Gracious, they must be important then. But, was the safe opened? Is it a burglary? Surely my uncle would have called the police.'

'I don't know, miss, Mr Harmon and Mrs Jenkinson are quite flustered. I don't think its burglars, miss. Cook says as it's someone in the house.'

Kitty hurriedly finished drinking her tea as Alice selected a dress from the wardrobe. 'I think I had better go down and find out what's happening. It sounds quite serious.' She could only assume that the missing documents related to her uncle's research and must be the ones he had been sharing with Sir Horace in the library. The bad feeling that had haunted her since they had first arrived at the house now appeared justified.

She had barely finished dressing when there was a knock at her door and Lucy appeared.

'Kitty, have you heard?'

Alice discreetly withdrew to the dressing room as Kitty opened the door wider to allow her cousin inside the bedroom. Lucy took a seat at the end of Kitty's bed. It looked as if she had been preparing to go downstairs and had been disturbed. Her hair was done, and make-up hastily applied, but she still wore her peach satin pyjamas with a matching wrapper.

'Alice said some papers are missing.'

'Sir Horace is organising a full-scale search of the house, including everyone's rooms. Although I think it might prove impossible to find Papa's missing papers in a house this size.' Lucy's cheeks had a pink tinge.

'Yes, but I can only assume Sir Horace will be especially thorough in my room, given my father's reputation.' Kitty knew her father and uncle were not on good terms and it was an entirely understandable supposition that she should be suspect. Even if she had absolutely no idea what the papers might be about and didn't know her way around the house to be able to steal and hide anything even if she were that way inclined. Which, of course, she wasn't.

'Oh, Kitty, please don't think that anyone believes that you might be involved with Papa's papers going astray. This is so embarrassing and hardly a nice welcome for you, especially after finding that Mother hadn't said anything about your mother's visit here during the war.' Lucy was now crimson.

'With my father's reputation and record, it's quite understandable that my room should be one of the first on the list to be searched.' She heard Alice give an indignant gasp from behind the door to her sleeping quarters. 'Uncle was still in the library when I came to bed, and Alice has been with me ever since, except when she went to make my tea this morning, and I believe the papers were already gone by then. As for my mother visiting here, perhaps your mother will remember more about it in the next few days.'

Lucy looked as if she were about to cry. 'Oh, darling, please don't be offended. I'll speak to Mother. I know you wouldn't be interested in Papa's inventions. I haven't even had the chance to show you the rest of the house or his laboratory yet.'

Kitty hugged her cousin. 'I'm not upset, truly. I'll finish getting ready and go to breakfast, and you may tell Sir Horace to search away.'

Relief flashed across Lucy's face. Kitty closed the door behind her as she scurried off to find her father and Sir Horace.

'Fancy thinking as you might have stole some stinky, old papers.' Alice popped back into the room, her eyes bright with indignation.

'Unfortunately, my father is hardly a man of spotless morals and my uncle doesn't know me, remember?'

Alice sniffed. 'Well, he should know better. You and Captain Bryant was in all the newspapers catching that murderer. Lord Medford should know as you would never do anything dishonest.'

Kitty finished getting ready to go down for breakfast. 'Stay here, Alice, please. Don't leave this room until after Sir Horace has completed his search.'

The maid stared at her for a moment before realisation dawned. 'In case somebody tries to plant something in here, miss? Like in the pictures?'

Kitty nodded. 'Perhaps, but either way just to be aware of what is happening. I'm going to breakfast and to make a telephone call. Keep your eyes and ears open.'

'Yes, miss.'

Mr Henderson was seated at the dining table, shovelling scrambled egg into his mouth from the huge mound on his plate. Viola sat opposite, nibbling delicately on a triangle of toast as she radiated distaste at her dining companion's table manners.

Kitty murmured 'good morning' to them both and helped herself to kedgeree from one of the large silver covered dishes on the sideboard.

Viola dabbed at the corners of her mouth with a napkin. 'I suppose they are searching your room also?'

Kitty smiled at the maid who deposited a pot of tea in front of her. 'Of course. Have they searched yours?'

Viola gave a dainty shudder. 'We are all outsiders, of course they will suspect us first. Although I doubt anyone will listen when I remind them that I thought I saw someone outside again last night.'

Mr Henderson broke off from his breakfast. 'Rubbish, you are always imagining someone is prowling about the grounds up to no good. Got to check on everyone.'

Kitty sipped her tea. 'What are the missing papers about?'

'Something Medford was working on. Presume it's to do with defence as Sir Horace is here. He works in government procurement.' Mr Henderson returned his attention to his scrambled eggs.

'I know nothing of Lord Medford's business interests. I am an artist. I care only about art and its restoration and preservation, and I tell you there is a prowler in the grounds. Ever since I came to this country I have been followed.' Viola made an expansive gesture with her arms, causing her bead necklaces to clatter and her scarves to float around her.

Rupert drifted into the dining room, looking somewhat the worse for wear, with his sister hot on his heels.

'Daisy, be a good girl and rustle up some coffee.' He sank down on the nearest vacant dining chair.

'Bad head?' Kitty enquired.

'Please do not give him any sympathy. He's brought this on himself.' Daisy took the seat opposite her brother and slid a plate of eggs and bacon in front of him.

Rupert groaned and half-heartedly stabbed at his bacon with a fork. 'Sir Horace turfed me out of my room. Something about missing papers.'

'They've already searched my room. It's quite shocking to be treated so.' Daisy poured herself a coffee. 'I wonder what's happened. All the servants are upset and running around the house peering under cushions and shaking books.'

'Probably that ass, Aubrey, has put them away in the wrong drawer,' Rupert said.

'He locked them in the safe. He said they were valuable. You know how conscientious he is.' Daisy glared at her brother.

'My guess is, he made a mistake and doesn't want to admit it.' Mr Henderson wiped his mouth with a napkin before draining his cup of tea.

Daisy's eyes sparked. 'Aubrey is not the kind of man to make mistakes.'

Rupert winced at the increased volume in his sister's voice. 'Steady on, Daisy. I'm sure they'll discover they have misplaced the papers,' he soothed.

'It was most likely burglars – spies,' Viola suggested.

'No sign of a break-in, and who would know that Lord Medford had something worth showing to the Ministry of Defence? If those papers are missing, then it has to be an inside job. Maybe even a servant.' Mr Henderson stood. 'Better get on, her ladyship will be waiting for me in the rose garden.'

Viola smoothed her scarves and straightened her cardigan around her bony shoulders. 'Now perhaps they will find the prowler in the grounds. I too need to return to work on the mural.'

Rupert groaned.

Kitty finished her breakfast. She had a telephone call she wanted to make. The business of the missing documents bothered her. She hated feeling that she was somehow under suspicion and she had a nasty feeling that the papers were unlikely to be recovered easily. Viola's talk of an intruder was also disturbing.

Lucy met her in the hallway with Muffy trotting at her heels. 'Sir Horace is searching the bedrooms now. Mr Harmon has taken one of the footmen and they are searching the attics. Mrs Jenkinson is in the maids' quarters. Everywhere is in uproar; it's awful. I don't understand what could have happened.'

'Is there really no sign of a burglary or break-in?' Kitty asked.

'None, and who would know of Papa's work and its significance? It would have to be someone on intimate terms with the family. Papa never speaks of his work and neither does Aubrey. It would have to be someone knowledgeable about the laboratory and the technologies father is exploring.'

'I'm sure it will be resolved soon.' Kitty spoke with far more conviction than she felt. 'Go and take some breakfast. Things always appear worse on an empty stomach.'

A wan smile twitched the corners of her cousin's lips. 'Perhaps. I'm sure Muffy is ready for her sausages and egg.'

The little dog's ears perked up at the mention of food and her tail swished happily as she trotted after Lucy as she continued to the dining room.

Kitty was looking around the hallway when Mr Harmon descended the staircase looking somewhat dishevelled. 'Mr Harmon, I wish to make a call. Is there a telephone I might use, please?'

'Certainly, Miss Underhay. The telephone here in the hall is at your disposal.' He indicated a padded velvet seat next to a small lacquered cabinet in the Chinese style with a telephone on top.

'Thank you.' She took a seat and dialled, holding her breath as she waited for the connection. 'Matt?'

'Hello, Kitty, how is life with the great and the good?' His bright, familiar tone cheered her, filling her with comfort.

'Matt, there is something dreadfully wrong here. Do you know a Sir Horace Blunt?' She kept her voice low as various members of the household passed her by. Matt's father was well connected, and she knew from her grandmother that he had many friends and acquaintances in high places.

'I know him by reputation, but I believe my father knows him quite well. Something to do with defence procurement for the government, I believe. Why do you ask?' Matt's tone became sharper.

'He's here at Enderley. And overnight some valuable papers of my uncle's have gone missing, something about a defence project that my uncle is involved with. Sir Horace is searching the house for them; it's something to do with the laboratory. But there is something not at all right here, Matt. I can't explain what is making me so uneasy. My cousin and aunt have been more than kind, but there are secrets.' She faltered to a halt.

'Secrets?'

'My mother was here just before she disappeared. My aunt doesn't wish to speak of it but Nanny Thoms rather let the cat out of the bag. It's hard to explain, but there is an odd atmosphere within the house and one of the house party keeps mentioning a prowler in the grounds.'

'Let's take it one thing at a time. I take it these papers of your uncle's must be of vital government importance for Sir Horace to be searching the house. Have the police been called?'

'I don't believe so. They seem to think it was an inside job. Matt, there is something dark afoot here. I'm so glad Alice is with me.'

'Hold tight, old thing. Father may well have some connections that can assist us. Let me make some enquiries and I'll come to you.'

Kitty released the breath she had been subconsciously holding. 'Thank you, Matt. I'll look out for you.'

'I should be with you after lunch. Be careful, Kitty.'

She ended the call reassured that he would be with her soon. She considered herself plucky enough, but she would be happier with Matt by her side. She didn't want to think too deeply about why that might be.

What her uncle and Sir Horace would think about her involving Matt, she had no idea. Perhaps she could allow them to believe his arrival was due to his affection for her rather than to investigate if necessary.

Sir Horace's endeavours proved fruitless with no sign of the missing documents. Kitty stayed out of the house, contenting herself with a walk in the grounds accompanied by Lucy, Daisy and Muffy. Rupert pleaded the need to deal with some urgent correspondence and remained inside while Viola was hard at work on the mural.

Mr Henderson, her aunt and Nanny Thoms were in the walled garden inspecting the old hot beds.

'There is Papa's laboratory.' Lucy indicated a large, low stone-built building that looked as if it might have been some kind of farm building for the house at some point.

'What does he do there?' Kitty asked. The building certainly appeared secure, with metal bars over the windows and a sturdy door.

'Something to do with valves and materials.' Lucy shrugged. 'Papa never really talks about his work. Aubrey is the only other person who goes inside, and he never talks about what they do there, either. During the war Papa developed lots of ideas there that assisted in our victory; that much I have picked up.'

'Such a fuss over some beastly papers.' Daisy threw a ball for Muffy to retrieve.

'Poor Aubrey is beside himself. He's blaming himself for not returning the papers to the safe in the laboratory rather than the one in Papa's study at the house,' Lucy said.

'It was late and dark. Who would have thought something would happen? It wasn't as if he left them on the library table for someone to help themselves. And I can tell you it doesn't help with Viola imagining prowlers hiding in every shadow.' Daisy took up the ball and threw it again as the girls turned to walk back towards the house.

Kitty shivered despite the sunshine. Rooks cawed to each other overhead. The eerie feeling of something bad about to happen pressed down upon her.

CHAPTER SIX

The party for luncheon was somewhat depleted and rather subdued. Lady Medford and Mr Henderson were dining al fresco in the garden with Nanny Thoms. Lord Medford, Aubrey and Sir Horace were at the laboratory and Viola was taking a working lunch upstairs.

'How is the head?' Daisy took a place next to her brother.

Rupert scowled. 'It would have been much better without that infernal blighter Sir Horace Blunt giving a fellow the tenth degree when he can see a chap is under the weather.'

'What's happening now?' Lucy asked as she slipped Muffy a titbit under the table.

'Dashed if I know. Lots of telephone calls and Sir Horace and your father are still interrogating the servants, I think. Mrs Jenkinson has a face like a smacked fish.'

'Have they called the police?' Kitty asked.

Rupert shrugged. 'They didn't confide in me. Seems unlikely though if those papers are so top secret and hush hush.'

'They could call in Scotland Yard.' Kitty was conscious of something shifting in the air at her innocent suggestion.

'Maybe,' Rupert agreed. 'I wouldn't worry your lovely head about it.'

Daisy changed the subject to the idea of a croquet match after lunch and the moment passed. Dessert had just finished when Mr Harmon appeared at the dining room door.

'Excuse me, Miss Underhay, there is a… erm, gentleman to see you.'

Colour stole up her cheeks under the astonished gaze of the others. 'I'll come straight away.' She rose and placed her napkin on the table before hurrying along the hall to see Matt's tall, rangy figure divesting himself of goggles, cap and long leather motoring coat.

'I'm so happy to see you.' Her heart unexpectedly speeded up at the sight of his familiar face.

Matt handed his things to one of the maids and strode towards her. 'I came as soon as I could. I made some calls first, so your uncle and Sir Horace are expecting me. Sir Horace has invited me to join the investigation.'

Kitty tried to suppress the slight feeling of annoyance that Matt would be allowed to investigate openly what might have become of the missing documents, while she would probably be sidelined because of her sex and lack of connections.

Lucy and Daisy appeared in the hall. Her cousin and her friend were both bright-eyed with curiosity. Muffy hurtled towards Matt and began to enthusiastically sniff at his shoes.

'Kitty, are you going to introduce us?' Lucy asked as she smoothed her dark curls and smiled at Matt.

'Captain Matthew Bryant, may I present my cousin, Lucy Medford, and her friend, Miss Daisy Banks.'

Matt duly shook hands with both girls. 'A pleasure to meet you both.'

'You're the one who helped Kitty catch that murderer!' Daisy said. 'Are you here about the missing papers?'

'You'll have to excuse me, ladies, I need a quick word with Kitty, and then I have to see Sir Horace.' Matt flashed one of his most disarming smiles in Daisy's direction before taking Kitty's arm to steer her out of earshot of the two girls.

'How are you? Tell me what you've found out so far?' he asked as soon as they were sure no one could overhear their conversation.

Kitty quickly ran through everything she knew about the missing documents and the inhabitants of the house, while Matt listened attentively.

'I believe Sir Horace and my uncle are over at the laboratory. Do you want Mr Harmon to call them or will you go over?' As she spoke there was a tentative cough from the doorway and Aubrey appeared. Kitty was shocked at the rapid change in his demeanour since last night. He was pale and haggard, his shoulders stooped as if the cares of the world had landed on him.

'Captain Bryant?' He stepped forward and offered his hand. 'I'm Lord Medford's secretary, Aubrey Mountford. He and Sir Horace are expecting you.'

Matt shook hands with Aubrey and, with a tiny smile of apology to Kitty, accompanied him from the room.

Lord Medford and Sir Horace were in the study. Both men wore serious expressions. Sir Horace was seated at the dark, imposing desk that dominated the room. Lord Medford paced up and down in front of the window as if trying to burn off the frustration and rage that emanated from every pore as he walked. Aubrey performed the introductions and Matt was conscious of Sir Horace's swift, assessing glance.

'I take it you're aware of our problem?' Sir Horace said.

'Yes, sir.'

'It's a bloody disgrace. Stolen from under our noses, from my own safe. In my own house. This material is very sensitive, you understand. You're aware of the issues in Europe? We need to be prepared and this information could be disastrous in the wrong hands.'

'Indeed, sir. Could you talk me through the sequence of events last night?' Matt asked.

Lord Medford huffed and puffed before blustering his way through a recitation of the evening's events. His account tallied with the one Kitty had given him.

'Aubrey, you placed the documents in the safe?' Matt asked as he examined the small black metal safe set in the wall behind a forbidding portrait of a woman who he assumed must be one of the Medford ancestors.

'Yes, I was the last to leave the study. I put the documents inside and locked the safe, then I came out and locked the study behind me.' Aubrey looked wretched and Matt guessed that he had borne the brunt of Lord Medford's displeasure.

'Who has keys to the safe and to this room?' Matt could see no sign that either the safe or the study door had been forced.

'Aubrey, obviously, and myself.' Lord Medford flung himself down on a large overstuffed red leather armchair in a corner of the room.

'Where do you both keep your keys?' Matt asked.

'Mine are in my jacket pocket. I have a ring with the laboratory keys.' Aubrey fumbled in his pocket and produced his key ring. Matt examined it closely, looking for any trace of wax or soap to indicate if an impression could have been taken.

'And you, sir?' Matt turned to Lord Medford after he'd returned the keys to Aubrey.

'The safe key is locked in my desk drawer and I have the key to the study in my pocket.' He brandished the study key.

'Was the desk drawer open this morning?'

'No, it was still locked,' Sir Horace said.

'Was the key inside?' Matt could see no sign of damage to the desk drawer.

Lord Medford got out of his seat and unlocked the drawer. Matt examined the safe key carefully.

'If you look closely, sir, I think there are some traces of wax and on the desk key. I believe your thief has taken an impression of both keys at some time, probably waiting for just such an opportunity.'

'This was pre-planned?' Lord Medford's normally florid complexion paled.

Sir Horace took the keys and studied them. 'Then our culprit merely needed to open the study if they had possession of the safe and desk keys. This confirms that it cannot be a random act. It must be a member of the household.'

'With respect, sir, the lock to this room is not complex.'

Sir Horace nodded slowly, his expression grave. 'Then we must consider opportunity.'

'What time did you retire?' Matt asked Aubrey.

Aubrey's shoulders sagged as if tired of recounting the information. 'Sir Horace and Lord Medford went upstairs shortly after one. I placed the papers in the safe, locked it and then came out and locked the study. When I reached my room, my bedside clock said one fifteen.'

'Did any of you see any other members of the household when you retired?'

Sir Horace shook his head. 'No, everyone else had gone upstairs when we came out of the study.'

'Although thinking about it now, I'm not sure if I heard something upstairs before we went up,' Lord Medford said.

'Aubrey?' Matt asked.

'I've thought of nothing else all day and I didn't see or hear anything out of the ordinary.' The man's face was wretched.

Matt turned his attention back to Lord Medford. 'What kind of sound did you think you heard, sir?'

'Maybe a door closing, very quietly. I didn't give it any thought at the time. It could have been someone using the bathroom.'

'Aubrey, you found the safe open and the documents missing this morning?' Matt asked.

'Yes, I came downstairs early to prepare for Sir Horace and Lord Medford to continue work after breakfast. That was about seven thirty. The study door was closed but when I tried the key, it was already unlocked.'

'And you are quite certain you locked it?' Sir Horace asked.

Aubrey's pale face flushed brick-red. 'Yes, sir. I tried the door after I turned the key, it's a habit.'

'What did you do next?' Matt enquired.

'I was concerned. I thought perhaps Lord Medford had come downstairs before me. But when I opened the door I saw the safe standing open and the papers were gone.'

'Aubrey alerted me immediately.' Lord Medford glared at Matt.

'We instigated a search straight away but with no clues to guide us and a house the size of Enderley…' Sir Horace left the statement open. Matt could see the difficulties.

'Do you have suspicions of anyone? Any information at all could prove relevant.'

'Rupert Banks is peddling a load of provocative political tosh about workers' rights. Damn communist,' Lord Medford muttered.

'The artist woman, Viola Fiser, what nationality is she?' Sir Horace asked.

'Austrian, I think, but she has some connections with Germany. Keeps wittering on about seeing intruders watching the house,' Aubrey said.

'She is internationally renowned in the art world. She's Jewish, however, and unfortunately after recent events abroad she's now quite paranoid,' Lord Medford blustered, clearly perturbed at the suggestion that he may have inadvertently invited a potential spy into his home.

'Has anyone left the house or visited the house since the papers were stolen?' Matt hoped that they would say no. If the papers were still somewhere on the premises, then there was a chance they could be recovered without any damage.

'I have spoken with various people; the house is under surveillance. The chief constable has been informed. No one can get in or out without being observed. Tradespeople, post, everything. Our thief may have his or her prize, but we must ensure they are isolated. If Viola Fiser is correct and there is someone hiding in the grounds, we'll soon flush him out.' Sir Horace's tone was grim.

'The information is too technical and the formula too complex to be dictated over a telephone. We cannot emphasise enough the importance of recovering those papers to the future security of the nation.' Lord Medford glanced at Sir Horace.

'The backgrounds of all the guests are of course being investigated?' Matt knew the government man would have taken steps already. His earlier conversations with his father and various civil servants had intimated as much.

Sir Horace nodded. 'I think for today we have done all we can. We must use tonight to watch like cats at a mouse hole and see what emerges.'

When Matt came out from the study, he spotted Alice, Kitty's young red-headed maid from the Dolphin loitering in the hall. She waited until Sir Horace and Lord Medford had gone before approaching him.

'Miss Kitty is in the rose garden, sir. You goes along the terrace and down the steps a way.' Alice beamed at him and, her message safely delivered, retreated back towards the servants' corridor.

He smiled to himself as he followed Alice's directions out into the late afternoon sunshine. He passed the French doors leading to the sitting room, and the library and study windows. The billiards room was located on the other side of the hall, next to the dining room.

The scent of the roses teased him as he walked down the stone steps into the rose garden. A gravel path led him past the first rose bed and under a covered walkway draped in trailing lavender wisteria flowers.

The sound of voices just out of sight made him pause in his tracks.

'For heaven's sake, Rupert, you are such an ass. What did you think you were going to achieve? It's not something you can return. If Sir Horace finds out about it then he's bound to think the worst.'

He recognised Daisy's voice as she remonstrated with her brother.

'It's not something I asked for or expected and no one was hurt.'

'But Lucy was involved. Her father will not be pleased if he discovers she was there.'

'You should be worried about yourself, sister dear. You weren't in your room all of last night,' Rupert replied.

'Oh, do shut up!' Daisy retorted.

The voices faded and he guessed they had moved further away. That was definitely an interesting conversation and it seemed as though both Daisy and Rupert might have some insight on the whereabouts of the missing papers. He wondered what Lucy may have been involved in. Could she have been implicated somehow?

CHAPTER SEVEN

Kitty was seated inside a small, rustic, rose-covered arbour. The rose pattern on her dress matched the delicate pink of the flowers surrounding her. She leapt to her feet as soon as she saw him approach.

'Come and sit down. Tell me everything,' she commanded.

He followed her into the arbour and took a seat on the bench next to her. She listened to all the information. 'What next?'

'I think Sir Horace intends to try to flush the thief out somehow.' He went on to share the conversation he had just overheard.

'Interesting! I can't believe Lucy would be involved in taking her father's papers, though.' Kitty frowned, clearly puzzling over what he'd heard.

'It seems unlikely, but we cannot rule it out. Remember, you do not know your cousin very well yet,' Matt cautioned. He listened as she in turn told him what she'd found out about her mother's visit to the house in 1916.

'It sounds as if Nanny Thoms knows more than she's said already,' he observed.

'I know, but I'm not sure if she'll tell me, especially if my aunt is present.'

'Let's hope your aunt will tell you more when she has had time to recall the events.'

'I hope so. This is the first positive lead I've had in years, even if it's all rather vague at the moment.'

Matt smiled at her. 'I'm sure she will, but until then it would seem we have two mysteries on our hands.'

*

Alice reached down the dress she had prepared for Kitty to wear to dinner. 'Did Captain Bryant find you in the garden, miss?'

'Yes, thank you, Alice.' She stepped into the gown and waited for Alice to fasten the tiny satin-covered buttons at the back of her frock.

'Cook was saying, miss, that she was working here back when your mum came. She wasn't Cook then of course, she was a kitchen maid. She said the missus was all put out and flustered, especially as your mum had to stay over and she wanted her gone before the master come back.' Alice fastened the last button and indicated for Kitty to sit so she could tidy her hair.

Kitty's heart raced as Alice began to carefully comb her hair into place. 'Does she remember why my mother came here?'

'She says she heard your mum was after your dad. She and her ladyship was at it hammer and tongs, Cook says. Your mum was angry, and the missus wouldn't tell her anything or give her no help.'

'I'd like to speak to Cook if I could, while I'm staying here.' Her fingers shook as she picked out a necklace for Alice to secure around her neck.

'I'll ask her for you, miss. She said it fair gave her a turn when she set eyes on you when you was out in the garden. You look so much like your mum. She said missus had told Nanny Thoms not to say anything but Cook says she thinks she'd forgot as she was here then too.'

'I see. Thank you, Alice.' She surveyed herself in her dressing table mirror. Her cheeks were pink and there was a steely glint in her eyes. 'Did you learn anything more about the missing documents from the other staff?'

'No, miss.' Alice shook her head.

'What do they say of the other house party members?' Kitty asked.

Alice looked flustered as she began to sort out the clothes Kitty had discarded. 'I dunno, I don't like to say.'

'It could be important. It might help us find who stole the papers. They are very important to the safety of the country. It's not gossip; you are doing your duty, Alice.'

The girl blushed. 'Well, they say as Miss Daisy is sweet on Aubrey, his lordship's secretary, but as how she hasn't got any money and he hasn't got enough to marry her yet. His mother apparently don't look well on his marrying. Miss Viola, the foreign one, is highly strung, keeps picking at the food like they'm trying to give her poison and of course with her having a German surname… She keeps on too about seeing people watching her. She had Mr Harmon and the gardeners on a wild goose chase a bit ago looking for some bloke she reckoned was a-peering in the windows. Mrs Jenkinson weren't none too pleased about it, nor Mr Golightly, the gardener. Mr Henderson is a queer one, they says, as he keeps looking at maps and digging holes everywhere and he hasn't got no breeding. Mr Golightly don't care for him much either. Mr Rupert is here to keep an eye on his sister. He keeps giving everybody this newspaper about workers' rights and flirting with the maids. They did think as he was sweet on Miss Lucy but she in't having none of it.' The maid came to a breathless halt.

'Well done, Alice. If you hear or see anything that strikes you as odd do tell me or Captain Bryant.' Her eyes met Alice's in the mirror. The maid nodded. 'Right, I'd better go downstairs for dinner.'

The rest of the party were gathering in the drawing room for pre-dinner drinks. Matt had been cornered on the sofa by Lucy and Daisy. Both girls looked pretty in pastel gowns; Muffy lay at Lucy's feet. Sir Horace was in conversation with Lady Medford and Nanny Thoms. Rupert and Aubrey were by the drinks trolley. There was no sign of Viola, Lord Medford or Mr Henderson.

'Miss Underhay, may I offer you a drink?' Aubrey asked.

'A sherry would be lovely and please do call me Kitty.'

He handed her a glass. She noticed his gaze kept drifting to Daisy who was chatting and laughing with Matt in her usual flirtatious way. A diamanté clip sparkled on the side of Daisy's blonde hair and her cheeks were rouged. A tiny spear of jealousy prodded at Kitty as she sipped her drink.

There was an air of tension and she could see Sir Horace keeping a subtle surveillance on his fellow guests. The others drifted into the room shortly before the gong sounded for dinner, Viola in mauve chiffon and Mr Henderson in a slightly shabby dinner suit.

Matt appeared at her elbow to escort her down the hall to the dining room. 'Your cousin and her friend are delightful company,' he murmured.

'Yes, I noticed.' As soon as she'd spoken, she wished she'd sounded a little less acerbic. Annoyingly, the corner of his mouth quirked, and she suspected he was amused at her expense.

She was seated between Matt and Rupert with Daisy opposite her. At least she should have some conversation this evening. Sir Horace was seated between Lucy and Viola, something which appeared to be making Viola extremely agitated.

Kitty placed her napkin on her lap as the watercress soup was served.

'Any luck with finding the papers, Sir Horace?' Rupert enquired.

'We have some clues to follow up, so we're hopeful of their recovery very soon.' Sir Horace's tone was bland.

'Well, that's marvellous. I dare say they were simply misplaced. Or picked up by mistake, so easy to do, isn't it?' Nanny Thoms twittered and slipped a morsel of bread to Muffy who had sneaked in under the table.

'Oh no, this was a deliberate theft, Nanny Thoms,' Lord Medford said.

Nanny Thoms flushed and appeared flustered. 'Oh no, surely not. I mean, I'm sure the person must have made a mistake.'

'The papers were taken from a locked safe in a locked room,' Lucy pointed out.

'Yes, but perhaps it was not properly locked,' Nanny wittered.

'I can assure you, it was secured,' Aubrey said stiffly.

Viola scowled into her soup. 'So long as you do not automatically assume it is some poor servant or immigrant who has committed this culpable act.'

'Not at all, Viola,' Lord Medford assured her. 'We are certain the servants were not involved, they have all been with us for some time. However, there is no evidence of an intruder.'

'There was someone outside the window,' Viola insisted.

'Even if that were the case, we virtually have proof that the papers were taken by someone in the house party.'

The implications of his remark seemed to sink in as the empty soup bowls were collected and replaced with dinner plates. After initial shocked exclamations, conversation sank into murmurs about passing the salt or the tenderness of the chicken.

The aura of gloom continued through dessert until dinner was finished and they adjourned back to the drawing room for coffee. The men appeared to be in no mood for port and joined in the general company, although Rupert and Mr Henderson soon departed as usual for the billiards room.

Daisy placed a record on the gramophone and soon persuaded Aubrey to sit with her. Lucy joined Kitty and Matt while Viola paced about the room wringing her hands. Sir Horace sat with Lord and Lady Medford. Nanny Thoms resumed her knitting, scolding Muffy who attempted to steal her wool as soon as she opened her workbag.

'Is Sir Horace right? You might get Papa's papers back soon?' Lucy asked in a low voice as soon as they were seated.

Matt raised a shoulder. 'We have some information we're working on.'

Lucy appeared troubled, nibbling her lower lip nervously. 'It is certain that it is a member of the house party?'

'It would seem so,' Matt murmured.

Viola flung herself down onto the chair opposite them.

'I do not like all this whispering in corners. People giving me the side-eye like I am the thief. Or that I lie about what I have witnessed.'

'I'm sure no one thinks you are a thief or a liar, Viola dear.' Lady Medford's voice cut over the dance music.

'I am going upstairs, I cannot relax in this atmosphere of suspicion.' Viola clattered from the room in a jangle of glass beads and mauve fabric.

'Oh dear, poor Viola has a persecution complex, I'm afraid. Foreigners are so temperamental. Nanny dear, do go after her, offer her some tea or warm milk or something,' Lady Medford suggested.

Nanny Thoms immediately replaced her knitting in her workbag and lifted it out of Muffy's reach before tottering off after Viola.

'Poor Nanny, Mother bullies her dreadfully and Nanny never seems to mind,' Lucy said. Muffy flopped down at her feet and began to tug at the toe of her shoe. 'Wretched dog. I'd better take you outside.'

Lucy rose and Muffy bounded off ahead of her as they left the room. Lord Medford and Sir Horace followed her into the hall. Aubrey appeared to be sunk in gloom despite Daisy's attempts to brighten his mood with gramophone music.

'Is it always this much fun?' Matt whispered.

Lady Medford glared at him and set her pile of gardening catalogues to one side. 'My husband informs me that you are a private detective?' She aimed her question at Matt.

'That's correct, Lady Medford.'

'Hmm, and you were the person who rescued my niece from that murderer?'

Kitty bristled at the idea that she had needed rescue.

'I helped Kitty, yes. To be fair, she had done quite a lot of damage to one of the miscreants before I got there.' His lips twitched as he glanced at Kitty.

'You are a veteran of the Great War, I believe?' her aunt continued with her interrogation. Kitty knew opening up the subject of the war would irritate Matt. He disliked talking of his experiences, tried not to use his military title and still suffered the effects of his campaign. She knew too that he had suffered some deeper, more personal loss from the war. She had never discovered the full details for the subject was too personal but she had recently found out that he had been widowed.

'Yes.' He didn't offer to expand.

'You were a captain?' Her aunt appeared to not take the hint.

'Yes.'

'Sir Horace spoke highly of you and your war record. He said you had recently resigned from a government position.'

Matt shifted uneasily in his seat. 'That's very generous of him. I decided upon a change of direction so came to work for Kitty's grandmother initially while I established my business.'

Her aunt pursed her lips. 'Then let us hope that you will be able to recover my husband's documents quickly. You realise the importance to the nation, of course?'

'Certainly, Lady Medford.'

Apparently satisfied, her aunt gathered her magazines together. 'Very well, I'm glad you understand the situation. I think I will retire for the evening. Good night, Kitty, Matthew.'

'And then there were four,' Kitty murmured, glancing across the room to where Daisy and Aubrey were deep in conversation.

'I think your aunt and Mrs Craven must be related,' Matt said.

Kitty grinned. 'I had thought the same thing. She is quite formidable, isn't she? Not at all like my father in looks or ways.'

'What did you think of the dinner conversation this evening?' Matt's voice was low and she had to lean in to hear.

'Nanny Thoms appeared somewhat rattled. Do you think she might know something or suspect something?' Kitty murmured.

'I'm not sure. I think Sir Horace plans to talk to her in the morning. A little time may work on her conscience and her memory. She appears somewhat scatty.'

The gramophone music ended and Daisy jumped up to turn it off. Aubrey stood and left the room without wishing them good night. Daisy watched him leave as if undecided about following him.

'Is everything all right, Daisy?' Kitty asked.

Daisy smiled a bright, fake smile that didn't meet her eyes. 'Aubrey is terribly upset over the theft. He blames himself because the papers were taken from the study, even though I've told him that's ridiculous.'

'Oh dear.' Kitty had seen how seriously Aubrey took his responsibilities in just the short time she had been staying at the house.

'Please excuse me, I'd better go after him.' She closed the door behind her as she left.

Kitty realised she was alone with Matt in the sitting room. It had been a long time since they had been together with no one else around them. Not since the terrible events of a few weeks ago. It felt strangely intimate and just a little too pleasant for her peace of mind.

'Do we have any other leads?' She placed the empty china coffee cup she'd been holding back on the tray. She expected that one of the servants would be along to clear it away soon. It had grown late and the shadows in the corners of the room had deepened, leaving mellow pools of light from the lamps.

Matt sighed. 'Not much, except whoever did this had clearly done some groundwork, getting keys cut. It was just unfortunate that Aubrey used the study safe last night instead of the lab safe. Although I suspect that would only have delayed the theft until another night.'

'Do you think the culprit may have keys to the lab too?' Kitty asked.

'It's something to consider. Luckily there seems to be far better security there. I can't help thinking our thief had been waiting prepared for an opportunity.'

A shiver ran along her spine. 'It's not a nice thought that we have a thief, and most probably a traitor, amongst us.'

Matt's expression was sober. 'We need to move carefully. Whoever has those papers has a lot to lose; they could be dangerous if cornered. The documents would have a limited commercial value. Their real value would be to a foreign government.'

The sitting room clock chimed the hour. 'Eleven already.' Kitty placed a hand over her mouth, stifling a yawn. 'I think I'm going to turn in.' The rustle of the silk of her skirt seemed loud in the quiet room as she stood.

'I'll walk you upstairs, I'm going to have an early night too. I take it Alice will be waiting for you?' Matt opened the sitting room door for her.

'I expect so. I'm so glad she's with me, especially now this has happened. Ever since we arrived at the manor, I have felt that something was out of kilter.' She kept her voice low as they walked along the dimly lit hall to the main stairs.

'It's not been the greatest introduction to your family, has it? Discovering they know something that might relate to your mother's disappearance and then having a thief in their midst, all within hours of your arrival. Hardly the restful holiday your grandmother wanted for you.' He fell into step beside her on the broad oak staircase.

'Not an auspicious beginning, I agree. Perhaps things will seem better in the morning,' she said as they halted at the door to her room.

'I hope so. Sleep well.'

Her heart gave a crazy little skip as his lips brushed her cheek and he quietly wished her good night before turning towards his own room at the far end of the landing.

CHAPTER EIGHT

It was still dark when Kitty was woken by a strange noise and Alice shaking her arm. 'Miss Kitty, wake up!'

The bedside lamp was turned on and she blinked at the sudden light. Alice was at her bedside in her white cotton nightgown, her red hair in a braid.

'What on earth?' She suddenly realised the noise she could hear was a woman screaming from another part of the house.

'Something's going on, miss.'

Kitty scrambled to sit up, swinging her legs over the side of the bed. 'Pass me my dressing gown.' She toed her feet into her house shoes.

Alice handed her the robe and pulled her own flannel dressing gown on before seizing the poker from beside the fireplace. 'I'm coming with you, miss.'

Together they ran out onto the landing and towards the direction of the screams. 'Servants' stairs, Miss Kitty,' Alice said as they hurried along. They opened the baize door leading to the staircase in the servants' area.

Ahead, the lights were on and she could see a group of people in night attire huddled around an object on the floor at the foot of the steep, narrow stone stairs. Her heart pounded in her chest as she realised the crumpled form was a female body. The screaming seemed to be coming from a sturdy young under-housemaid who was being hastily hustled away from the scene by Mr Harmon.

Matt was already with Sir Horace and Lord Medford at the foot of the stairs. He lifted his head and his gaze locked with hers and he gently shook his head in warning. Kitty realised Alice was close behind her on the narrow staircase and her thought was to shield her young maid from the sight.

'It seems there has been an accident, Alice. Matt is there with Sir Horace and my uncle. I fear there is nothing we can do to help.' She turned around and steered her maid back up the couple of steps and through the baize door to the landing where they encountered Lucy and Daisy.

'What was that frightful row? What's going on?' Lucy asked. Like Alice and Kitty, she and Daisy were also wrapped in their dressing gowns.

'It seems there has been an accident and someone has fallen down the stairs. It's being dealt with.' Kitty placed a warning hand on Alice's arm.

'Oh, how ghastly. Are they hurt? A servant, I suppose?' Daisy looked surprisingly young without her make-up, her face pale without her rouge.

'I'm not sure. I think Mr Harmon and my uncle are dealing with things.'

Lucy yawned. 'Oh, it's so early. Six o'clock. I'm going back to bed.' The others mumbled agreement and departed towards their various bedrooms.

'Who was it, miss? What happened?' Alice asked as soon as they had reached their room and closed the door.

'I don't know for sure, Alice. I think someone may have been badly injured or even killed in a fall on the stairs. I couldn't see who exactly it was, I think it was a woman.'

The little maid's face paled and she sank down on the corner of Kitty's bed, still clutching the poker. 'Not Cook, miss? Or one of the housemaids?'

'I don't know, Alice. I have a bad feeling about this, but I didn't want to alarm the others, especially my cousin.'

Colour started to return to the maid's face. 'Do you think you know who it is, miss?'

Kitty swallowed and sat next to Alice on the bed. She had glimpsed the woman's grey curls and she had a horrible feeling that the fall victim might be Nanny Thoms. But why Nanny Thoms would be using the servants' stairs she wasn't sure. Had the elderly woman slipped, or had she been pushed? The thought made her feel sick to her stomach.

'You're shivering, miss. Hop back under the covers a minute and I'll get a bit of a fire going in the grate.' Alice, ever practical, assisted her into bed and set to work at the small fireplace, where kindling had already been placed.

Under Alice's skilful fingers a small blaze was soon dancing in the hearth. A few minutes later there was a soft tapping at her bedroom door. The maid straightened her dressing gown and at a nod from Kitty opened the door. Matt slipped into her room.

'You saw what appeared to have happened?' Stubble was dark on his chin and he, like herself, was clad in his night attire and a plaid dressing gown.

Kitty nodded. 'Was it Nanny Thoms?'

Alice gasped.

'Yes.' He looked tired, dark shadows lay under his eyes.

'I take it that you think it may be suspicious?' Kitty asked.

'Sir Horace and your uncle have requested Inspector Greville and Doctor Carter attend. Sir Horace was insistent the chief constable send men who were reliable and discreet so I suggested them. Father added his weight behind my suggestion. Apparently, the local doctor is unwell and the local police lack the expertise and discretion. For now they are keeping everyone away. Lady Medford has yet to be told.'

'And Lucy?' Her cousin would be heartbroken.

He nodded. 'I must go. I just wanted to forewarn you.'

'Yes, thank you.' He slipped out of the room and Alice closed the door quietly after him.

Kitty hugged her knees and shivered under the covers despite the heat that had begun to warm the room from the fire.

'Nanny Thoms. You were right, Miss Kitty. But who would want to hurt an old lady like her?' Alice asked.

'I don't know. Matt said last night he thought that whoever had taken my uncle's papers could be dangerous if cornered. He suspected that Nanny Thoms might know something from the way she spoke at dinner last night. He and Sir Horace had intended to talk to her this morning.' From Nanny Thoms's behaviour and comments at dinner, Kitty had wondered if she'd been protecting someone. But, if so, who? It could only be one of the family surely. Either Lucy or her aunt. She wouldn't have cared as much about any of the others, but neither Lucy or Aunt Hortense had any need to steal the papers.

'What will happen now, miss?'

'I'm not sure. Do you remember Inspector Greville from before?'

Alice smiled. 'Yes, miss. He was always very nice. Likes his cakes and biscuits.'

Kitty grinned. 'Yes. I assume Sir Horace has asked him to investigate rather than a local man who may not have as much experience. I think my uncle is expecting him shortly. My poor aunt and cousin will be terribly upset. Nanny Thoms has been part of the household since Lucy was a baby, and I think before that.'

Alice perched herself on the edge of the small tapestry-covered fireside chair and held out her hands towards the flames leaping in the grate. 'It's awful. Everyone likes Nanny Thoms. She was ever so kind and a bit scatty, but she was devoted to your aunt and Miss Lucy. Are they sure it couldn't just be an accident? Those stairs is a bit dark at the top and terrible steep. If she was going down them without her glasses it would be easy to miss a step – and her an old lady.'

'Inspector Greville will hopefully be able to decide that.' She hoped it was an accident, but her instincts told her that it was unlikely. For Nanny Thoms to have had such a dreadful accident just when Matt and Sir Horace planned to question her was a coincidence too far.

Inspector Greville arrived shortly before breakfast. Matt had been looking out for the car and hurried outside with Sir Horace to greet him.

'Captain Bryant, our paths cross again.' He shook hands with Matt. 'And, Sir Horace, a pleasure to meet you, sir.' The inspector was his usual lugubrious self, tall and thin with a rather depressed moustache. Like Matt, he was also a veteran of the Great War.

'Thank you for agreeing to manage this investigation. Lord Medford will join us shortly; Lady Medford and her daughter are greatly distressed by the death of Nanny Thoms.' They walked together along the terrace and around to the tradesman's entrance at the rear of the house. As they walked, Sir Horace explained the circumstances of Nanny Thoms's death. The inspector's face was grave when he learned of the missing papers.

'You have not moved the body, I hope?' he asked, pausing at the entrance.

'No, sir. The butler, Mr Harmon, has kept the staff at bay and ensured nothing was disturbed until you arrived.' Matt led the way inside the house to the stairwell. Nanny Thoms still lay on the red quarry-tiled floor; a small, sticky pool of blood had oozed from the wound on her temple onto the floor.

'Nasty head injury. She must have died instantly.' The inspector looked at the narrow stone stairs with a shrewd eye. 'Came from top to bottom, it would appear. You don't believe it was an accident even though Nanny Thoms is elderly and may have missed her step?'

'I think Nanny Thoms may have seen or heard something which could have led to the recovery of Lord Medford's papers. She appeared very perturbed during dinner.'

'The housemaid found her?' Greville's moustache looked even more morose as he considered the position of Nanny Thoms's body. The woman was dressed in her nightgown and robe. Her house shoes were on her feet. The inspector looked at the soles of her shoes.

'There appears to be a good grip on her slippers,' Greville observed.

'Her glasses are here but appear to have been broken in the fall.' Sir Horace indicated Nanny Thoms's wire-framed spectacles, their lenses shattered, lying a short distance away from her body.

'Very well.' The inspector indicated that the examination of the scene was complete and that the body could be moved. 'I would like to speak to the maid who found her.'

'The girl is in the housekeeper, Mrs Jenkinson's, room. She was hysterical when she found the body. Her screams roused half the household,' Sir Horace said.

'This is Gladys, Inspector.' Mr Harmon, the butler, showed them to the housekeeper's room which was situated off the kitchen. The room was small and comfortable, with chintz-covered furniture and an oak dresser and coffee table.

Gladys was a sturdy girl with untidy brown hair and work-roughened hands that were nervously twisting and pleating her apron. Traces of tears were visible on her cheeks and her eyes were red-rimmed from crying.

'Now then, Gladys, this gentleman is from the police. You need to pull yourself together and tell him all you know.' Mr Harmon fixed the young housemaid with a steely gaze. The look appeared to have a settling effect on the girl.

Greville folded himself into a seat opposite the maid. 'When did you find Nanny Thoms?' His tone was fatherly.

'I gets up early 'cos I does the fires, see, sir, so I'm up at cock crow. I gets dressed an' runs downstairs to fill the scuttles and to start laying the fires. It's chilly first thing, see, and Missus likes a warm house even though it's summer. I does the drawing room and some of the main rooms.' The girl paused to blow her nose on a grubby handkerchief. 'I comes down from the top floor and goes through the door to go down the back stairs.'

'Was the stair light on or off?' Greville asked.

'Off, sir. I switched it on myself and then I'd only gone a step when I sees her lying on the floor. I run down and her head… her head was all bloody.' She started to sob.

'There, there.' Greville placed an avuncular hand on her shoulder as Cook carried in a tray of tea replete with a plate of biscuits.

Inspector Greville poured the girl a cup of tea and ladled sugar into the liquid with a heavy hand before helping himself to a biscuit. He munched for a moment while Gladys sipped her tea and recovered her composure. 'And you screamed?'

'It was the shock, so 'orrible.' The girl shuddered. 'I keep seeing her face, all surprised, like.'

'Who arrived first when you screamed?' Matt asked.

The girl sniffed and put down her cup to wipe her nose again. 'Mr Harmon was there quick. His room is nearby, see. Then Mr Aubrey and Mr Henderson, then you, sir, before Miss Kitty and her maid, Alice, come to the top of the stairs.'

Mr Harmon had reached the scene before Matt had made it down the stairs and had been trying to bundle Gladys away to try and calm her down. Aubrey too had clattered down the stairs in his pyjamas and dressing gown. Henderson, however, had appeared from the direction of the kitchen and was dressed for the garden in moleskin trousers, shirt and tweed jacket.

'You didn't hear anything?' the inspector asked Gladys when she took up her cup again.

The girl shook her head. 'No, sir.'

'Thank you, Gladys, you've been most helpful.' The inspector helped himself to the last biscuit on the plate then rose. 'I think I need to speak to Lord Medford.'

'Had Nanny Thoms been dead for long when you got there?' Greville asked as they walked down the cream-walled servants' corridor back towards the main part of the house.

'Her skin was cold, so the fall wasn't recent,' Matt confirmed. 'She must have been there for a while.'

'Small hours of the morning probably, then. I'm sure the doctor will confirm your impression on his examination. She is unlikely to have gone down those stairs in the dark so who turned off the light, I wonder?'

Mr Harmon showed them into the library where Lord Medford came to join them. He appeared tired and drawn. 'My apologies, gentlemen, my wife and daughter are naturally extremely distressed over Nanny Thoms's unfortunate accident.' He shook hands with the inspector and offered him and the others a cigarette from the monogrammed silver case he carried in his pocket.

'You are inclined to believe this lady's death is an accident, sir?' Greville asked as he accepted the cigarette and a light from Sir Horace.

Lord Medford flung himself down onto the overstuffed green leather chesterfield and lit his own cigarette. He blew out a plume of smoke as if considering his answer before meeting the inspector's gaze. 'No; while I want to think Nanny fell on those stairs, common sense makes it an unlikely scenario.'

'It would seem that our thief is also a murderer, then.' Sir Horace shoved his hands in his trouser pockets as he paced the room staring at the bookshelves as if they might contain the answer to their present conundrum.

'And may be one of the house party,' Matt added.

CHAPTER NINE

The group gathered for breakfast were both small in number and in a sombre mood. Lucy and Lady Medford were absent, and Sir Horace, Lord Medford and Matt were with Inspector Greville elsewhere within the house.

Kitty helped herself to scrambled eggs from the silver serving dishes on the sideboard and took her seat at the dining table. Aubrey was staring at his bowl of porridge without eating much. Daisy nibbled at a piece of toast while Rupert sipped his coffee. Viola had a cup of hot water and a tiny triangle of toast. Of all the people in the room, she appeared the most composed.

'Is Mr Henderson not joining us?' Kitty asked, suddenly realising he was missing. It was unlike the man to miss a meal.

'He ate earlier. He has gone out to dig some test beds for Lady Medford,' Viola said with a disparaging sniff. She eyed Kitty's plate of egg with distaste. 'My nerves are in pieces with such happenings, and now the police are here. I understood this was a respectable house. I cannot stay here. I told everyone; I warned them about the man in the grounds.'

'Do you really think they will let you leave?' Rupert asked, looking up from his coffee cup.

Viola jumped up from her seat, bumping the table and causing some of Rupert's coffee to spill out onto the saucer. 'Nonsense! I am a free citizen. I have committed no crime. It is insupportable that I could be forced to remain here. If that woman has been killed by the person who stole the papers then we all could be in danger.' Her gaze darted around them all as if she suspected them of wishing to kill her.

'Viola, that's rot. I'm sure the police will find poor Nanny Thoms's death was just a terrible accident. Why would anyone want to kill a harmless old lady?' Daisy asked.

'Because she knew something,' Viola hissed, leaning forward and thrusting her face towards Daisy.

'Oh, don't be ridiculous, Viola. What on earth could Nanny Thoms have possibly known?' Rupert abandoned his spilled coffee.

She turned her attention to him, clutching dramatically at the multiple strings of garish glass beads she wore around her neck. 'Because she knew who had those papers, that's why.'

'You do talk utter tosh, Viola. How could she know? She would have told Lord Medford immediately. You know how loyal she was to the family.'

'That's why she wouldn't say. Don't you see? It could be a family member who had those papers.' Viola straightened up, a satisfied smirk on her lips.

'Mad, barking mad,' Rupert announced.

Aubrey got up from the table. 'Stop it! Stop it, all of you! A woman is dead.' He marched out of the room, banging the door behind him.

'Now look what you've done.' Daisy rose from her seat and immediately followed after him.

'Oh dear.' Rupert refilled his cup from the silver coffee pot. 'It's going to be a long day.'

Viola scowled at him. 'I suppose I must get on with my work. The arts may soothe my senses, as much as they can be soothed with a murderer amongst us.' She flounced from the room.

Kitty put down her knife and fork, having lost what small appetite she had had for her breakfast. 'You shouldn't upset her.'

'Dear, sweet, innocent Kitty, you should be thanking me. You realise that you are one of the family that darling Viola thinks may have pinched the papers?' Rupert took a sip of coffee, his gaze meeting hers over the brim of his cup.

'Me? But I only met my family a couple of days ago.'

Rupert raised his eyebrows. 'Precisely my point.'

Kitty found Lucy in the sitting room, cuddled up to Muffy. Her eyes were red from crying.

'Lucy, I'm so sorry.' She took a seat on the sofa next to her cousin.

'What did poor Nanny Thoms ever do to anyone? She was just a sweet old lady. It must be a dreadful accident. It must be.' She pressed a crumpled and sodden lace handkerchief to her mouth.

'Why was Nanny Thoms using the servants' stairs?' Kitty asked.

Lucy sniffed. 'I don't know. She usually used the main stairs as they were better for her. I suppose she must have been going to the kitchen, perhaps to get herself something to drink.'

'Did she often do that?'

'It was a habit she had. She sometimes had indigestion and couldn't sleep so she would go and make herself warm milk to settle her stomach. She used to make a cup for me when I was younger.' Lucy dashed a tear from her cheek.

Kitty sighed. 'Did everyone know she did this?'

Lucy shrugged. 'Probably; she told everyone who would listen about her insomnia.' She blew her nose. 'You think someone pushed her down those stairs, don't you?'

Kitty handed her cousin a clean, dry handkerchief from her pocket. 'I think it's possible. Did you see Nanny Thoms at all last night after you took Muffy out?'

Lucy shook her head. 'I walked Muffy along the terrace, then she spotted a rabbit and took off. I was outside for an absolute age trying to persuade her to come back inside. I went straight to bed when she did come in, I was so tired.'

'Did you see any of the others?' She stretched out her hand to stroke Muffy's soft fur.

'Rupert came out onto the terrace for a smoke. I saw his face as he lit his cigarette but that was just after I set off after Muffy.'

The little dog turned her head and licked Lucy's face when she heard her name.

The door to the sitting room opened and Mr Harmon entered. 'Miss Lucy, your mother is asking for you.'

'Thank you, Mr Harmon, I'll be right there.' Lucy patted her eyes dry and shooed Muffy off the sofa before smoothing the crumpled cotton of her dress.

'I'd better go. I'll see you later.' She gave Kitty a wan smile and followed Mr Harmon out of the room with Muffy at her heels.

Kitty wondered how Matt might be faring with Inspector Greville and her uncle and if he had learned anything to advance the case. She was about to stroll out into the garden for some air when Daisy appeared.

'Have you seen the policeman yet? They are interviewing everyone.' Daisy dropped down onto the sofa. 'Poor Aubrey feels as if everything is his fault, which is plainly ridiculous. He thinks if he had taken those wretched papers to the laboratory safe rather than the study then Nanny Thoms would be here now. I've told him that's nonsense, but he won't listen. Now that policeman is with Sir Horace and your boyfriend, asking him all kinds of questions.'

'Matt is not my boyfriend, and I'm sure the police will want to talk to everyone about where they were last night.' Kitty was aware that her cheeks had heated at the inference that she and Matt might be walking out together.

'Well, I have nothing to hide. I was with Aubrey until I went up to my room. That was well after midnight.'

'Did you see anyone else?' Kitty asked.

Daisy tossed her head. 'No, we were talking in Lord Medford's study. I thought I heard the door to the library open and close at one point; the door has a squeak.'

'I expect that would be my uncle and Sir Horace,' Kitty said. 'I think they were talking in there until quite late.'

'If it wasn't an accident, then what do you think Nanny Thoms knew about your uncle's papers?' Daisy asked.

Kitty had been pondering the same question. 'Maybe she didn't know anything. Maybe she saw something or heard something or perhaps she didn't know anything at all, but the killer simply thought she did.'

Rupert entered the room and came to sprawl on the armchair opposite the sofa. 'What are you two lovely ladies up to? Nattering away as thick as thieves in here.'

Daisy hurled a cushion at her brother. 'Have you been interviewed by the police yet?'

Rupert yawned and took out a cigarette from his pocket and lit up, blowing out a thin plume of smoke before answering his sister. 'Not yet. Have you?'

'No, they're still interviewing poor Aubrey, I think.'

'Aubrey is the most dreadful ass.' He smirked at Daisy.

'I suppose Inspector Greville will talk to everyone in turn,' Kitty said.

Brother and sister both turned to look at her. 'Do you know the inspector?' Daisy asked.

Kitty nodded. 'He arrested the murderer in that case Matt and I were caught up in at the Dolphin.'

'So, you have an in, Kitty dearest,' Rupert drawled, blowing out another thin plume of smoke.

'Hardly; Inspector Greville is a pillar of integrity. I'm sure I shall only know as much as any of you.' She kept her fingers crossed as she spoke. Inspector Greville probably wouldn't say much to her about the case but she hoped that she and Matt might make some headway on things themselves.

Aubrey came to join them as she finished speaking. Kitty felt sorry for him as he took a seat next to Daisy. His complexion was a sickly shade of white and dark circles lay heavy under his eyes. He took off his glasses to rub his face with a weary hand.

'The inspector would like you to go to the library, Rupert.' His tone was dull.

Rupert extinguished his cigarette, screwing it down into the heavy glass ashtray on the small side table next to him.

'Better go and confess my sins,' he joked as he walked away. No one laughed. Aubrey leaned forward and held his head in his hands. Kitty couldn't help wondering if Aubrey had perhaps made some small omission that was now laying on his conscience.

'Are you all right, Aubrey?' she asked.

He shook his head slowly. 'I feel responsible, Miss Underhay. Your uncle trusted me with securing the formula and plans.'

'But this theft had clearly been long-planned. The thief would have found some way to get hold of the papers; they are both determined and ruthless.' Kitty met Daisy's stricken gaze.

'Kitty is right, Aubrey. You must not take this all upon yourself.'

'I wish I could feel the same, but I cannot forgive myself,' he said.

CHAPTER TEN

Matt glanced up as Rupert swaggered into the library. For all the man's attempts at insouciance, it was clear he was nervous.

'Mr Banks, please take a seat. We just have a few questions for you if you would be so good.' Inspector Greville indicated the dark green leather chair opposite his own.

Rupert took a seat, crossing his legs and picking an imaginary thread from his trousers as he did so.

'Mr Banks, as you are aware, some valuable documents were taken from Lord Medford's safe in his study the night before last. I understand that evening you were in the drawing room until late in the evening, is that correct?'

Rupert took out his cigarette case and extracted a cigarette. 'Yes, I was with my sister, Daisy and some of the others.' He paused to light his cigarette. 'I'd had a few drinks, so my memory is a tad hazy, but I think I retired at the same time as the rest of the party. Viola and Henderson had already gone up.'

'Was Nanny Thoms present in the drawing room that evening?' the inspector asked.

Rupert frowned, screwing up his face in thought. 'Yes, when Daisy and I arrived there seemed to have been some kind of discussion going on with the lovely Kitty.' He gave Matt a quick sideways glance. 'Lady Medford appeared rather put out with Nanny T, I recall. Oh, Nanny Thoms went after Lucy and that blasted dog of hers at one point. Think it had pinched her knitting and run off. Dog's a menace.'

'Thank you. And last night I believe you were playing billiards with Mr Henderson again, until late in the evening?'

Rupert took another drag from his cigarette. 'Until about ten thirty actually. Henderson's something of a billiards fiend, has his own cue and everything. He likes a bit of a wager on a frame. Henderson said he was getting up early to dig some test beds for Lady Medford so he called it a night. I went out to the terrace to take the air and have a last smoke before bed.'

The inspector made a series of incomprehensible squiggles in his notebook. 'Did you see anyone else during this time?'

'Lucy was running around the garden in the dark after her dog. I think Lord Medford and Sir Horace were in the library as the light was on. I could see it on the terrace as the curtains were open.'

The inspector continued to take notes. 'Once you had retired for the night, did you get up at all for anything?'

Rupert extinguished his cigarette. 'Nothing at all. I'd had a drop of whisky and went out like a light. Never even stirred through that girl caterwauling.'

'Thank you, Mr Banks.'

Rupert jumped up at the dismissal. As soon as he had left the room, Lord Medford protested. 'You never asked him about his political sympathies and that rubbish he keeps spouting about workers' rights. Been trying to stir up my staff. Blasted commie nonsense.'

'All in good time, Lord Medford,' the inspector soothed.

'Captain Bryant, do you know anything about the discussion Miss Underhay had with Lady Medford?'

Matt sighed. 'I believe Nanny Thoms had said she remembered Kitty's mother visiting Enderley shortly before she vanished back in nineteen-sixteen. Kitty had been previously unaware of this. As you may remember, Inspector, Kitty has been looking for information regarding her mother's disappearance for a long time.'

The inspector's eyebrows rose slightly at the information, but his tone was noncommittal. 'I see, yes, thank you.'

'What's that? Hortense has never mentioned the girl's mother coming to the house. I had expressly forbidden contact with that dreadful brother of hers.' Lord Medford's complexion turned a slightly deeper shade of puce.

'I doubt it is of any import, sir. It was a long time ago,' Matt soothed. Kitty would not be happy if her uncle were to prevent her from learning more about her mother's brief stay at Enderley all those years ago.

'We ought to talk to that gardener chap, Henderson. He is the only one so far who has been up earlier than everyone else. He could have seen or heard someone,' Sir Horace said as he paced about the room.

'I agree. Everyone else so far seems to be intent on convincing us that they were all tucked up in bed when the papers were taken and when Nanny Thoms had her unfortunate accident.' The inspector frowned as he studied his pages of scribbled notes. 'Mr Henderson is out in the gardens somewhere. I expect he will appear for lunch as I'm led to believe he is a man who likes his food. And we'd better talk to Banks's sister, Daisy. I gather she and your secretary are sweet on one another?' The inspector addressed his question to Lord Medford who was staring somewhat glumly out of the window.

'What? Um, I suppose so. Lucy met Daisy in London and they became friends. Not too keen on them myself, especially her brother. Hot-headed young fool, flirts with the maids and pays too much attention to my daughter.'

'Did Daisy know Aubrey before she came here?' Matt asked.

'Dashed if I know. Not something I talk to my secretary about, his love life.' Lord Medford sounded affronted by the question.

'I'll ring for a tray of tea and ask Mr Harmon to send Miss Banks in to see us.' Sir Horace suited his action to his words.

Daisy arrived at the same time as the tea tray. She was a pretty girl in a rather obvious way. Her hair was fashionably blonded and she wore rather more make-up than Matt found attractive. Kitty wore very little in the way of cosmetics, just a dab of powder and some lipstick. Daisy took the seat her brother had recently vacated and Inspector Greville poured her a cup of tea.

'Miss Banks, thank you for coming. We need to ask some questions to establish where you and other members of the party were during the evening Lord Medford's papers were taken, and also when Nanny Thoms met her death.' The inspector handed her a cup before helping himself to a biscuit.

Daisy simpered and took a sip of tea, leaving a smudge of red lipstick on the rim of the cup.

'Now, Miss Banks, I believe you are a friend of Miss Lucy Medford?'

'Yes, we met in London at a club and we hit it off straight away. We knew each other slightly through mutual friends.' Daisy appeared relaxed as she answered the inspector's question.

'Did Miss Medford befriend your brother at the same time?'

A frown line creased Daisy's forehead. 'I think Rupert was at the club, but I don't really remember. They do get along frightfully well.'

The inspector smiled gently under his moustache. 'Did you know Mr Aubrey Mountford at that time too?'

Pink spots of colour appeared on Daisy's cheeks. 'I'd bumped into Aubrey a few months before. I'd broken the heel on my shoe getting off an omnibus and Aubrey very kindly came to my rescue. It was raining and I dropped my bag. He took me to tea, and we became friends.'

'Were you aware that he was in Lord Medford's employ when you befriended Lucy?'

Daisy's eyes widened in alarm. 'Well yes, he told me he was a secretary for Lord Medford when we met.'

Lord Medford looked as if he were about to erupt into speech, only a hand on his arm from Sir Horace restrained him.

'You followed him here to Enderley?' the inspector asked.

She slammed her cup back down onto her saucer, spilling some of the tea. 'That sounds so awful! He wanted me to come and Lucy kindly invited us. Aubrey needs me to be near him. We intend to be married.' Her colour mounted higher into ugly patches of red beneath her foundation.

'And how does your family view your engagement? I notice you are not wearing a ring.'

Daisy immediately covered her left hand with her right, hiding her fingers. 'All right, it's an informal engagement. Aubrey has yet to tell his mother, and my brother does not approve, although he does not forbid the match, but financially he considers it imprudent.'

Inspector Greville continued on more neutral lines to confirm that she too had not left her room or seen anyone the night Nanny Thoms had died.

Lord Medford exploded into speech the moment Daisy left the room. 'Brazen hussy, set out to seduce Aubrey and taking advantage of my daughter's good nature. Wastrels, the pair of them. Probably in it together.'

Matt pondered all they'd learned that morning. The inspector's line of questioning with Daisy had certainly opened a new train of thought. Had Daisy deliberately targeted Aubrey and ingratiated herself into a friendship with Lucy so she could steal the papers, aided and abetted by her brother? It seemed an outlandish notion, but when it could affect the future of the nation, nothing could be ruled out.

'I suggest we break for a short while to gather our thoughts. It will be time for lunch shortly, we can reconvene afterwards with Mr Henderson,' Sir Horace suggested.

Inspector Greville asked to use the telephone and Matt headed outside onto the terrace, relishing the fresh air after being in the library for so long. His experiences in the trenches had left him with a dread of enclosed spaces, and although the library was a large room, the book stacks towering over them still made him feel twitchy and uncomfortable.

'Hello, how are things? Daisy did not look happy after her interview with Inspector Greville.' Kitty stepped outside to join him.

'Shall we walk?' They strolled along the terrace away from the house towards a more secluded spot where they were unlikely to be overheard. Once certain there was no one nearby, Matt told Kitty what he'd learned.

'Daisy does appear to genuinely care for Aubrey,' she said thoughtfully. She told him what she'd learned too while she'd been talking with the others throughout the morning.

'It will be interesting to discover what Mr Henderson has to say. Has Inspector Greville spoken to Viola yet?'

Matt shook his head. 'No, and of course Lady Medford is too distressed to answer any questions at the moment.'

They turned and strolled back towards the house. It was pleasant to feel the sun warming his skin and to smell the scent of the roses blooming in the garden. He stole a glance at Kitty. She too appeared to be enjoying the brief respite from the tense atmosphere inside the manor. He couldn't help thinking of the contrast between Kitty's natural good looks and Daisy's painted features.

His wife, Edith, had never favoured cosmetics. Like Kitty, she had only used powder and lipstick. She had been a keen and clever needlewoman and had made many of her own clothes and those for baby Betty. He suppressed a sigh and tried to refocus himself in the moment.

Muffy came racing up to them as they neared the house, her stumpy tail wagging with excitement. Lucy panted up the steps towards them, her face flushed with exertion. 'Wretched dog. She's been stealing again. I just chased her all around the garden to try and get Mother's spectacles back before she could bury them in one of Mr Henderson's test beds.'

'Oh dear, naughty Muffy.' Kitty tried to hide a smile as she petted the little dog.

Lucy glanced at her wristwatch. 'I need to go and freshen up, the gong will sound for lunch in a few minutes. I don't expect it will be terribly good. Cook always struggles when something has upset the household.' She ran inside the house with Muffy trotting after her.

'At least Lucy seems a little better now. She was dreadfully upset earlier,' Kitty said.

'Do you regret coming to stay here?' Matt asked.

She shot him a glance. 'A little. It's not exactly been the visit I'd hoped for. Now with poor Nanny Thoms, I don't know if I'll ever find much more out about my mother's visit here. Alice said Cook might know something but…' Her words tailed away and she gave a graceful shrug of her shoulders.

The gong resonated from inside the house.

'Lunch. Is Inspector Greville going to be joining us?'

'I'm not sure. He was making telephone calls as I came out. I believe he has arranged to base himself at the Railway Engine public house in Newton St Cyres while the investigation is ongoing. There is no police station in the village and the constable lives some half mile away. Lord Medford obviously invited him to stay at the manor, but he declined.'

Kitty raised her eyebrows at this news. 'It's not far away I suppose, and he must have his reasons. Sir Horace is here on the spot, isn't he?' She led the way along the hall to the dining room where the others were already taking their seats.

'Mother is taking a tray in her room. The inspector and Sir Horace are dining with Aubrey and Papa in the library,' Lucy said as she shook her napkin out onto her lap.

'I suppose dear Viola is having a working lunch yet again,' Rupert drawled. 'Has she been investigated by our resident policeman yet?'

'Really, Rupert.' Daisy glared at her brother.

'Well, if anyone is behaving oddly, it's Viola. All this tosh about seeing intruders and people spying on her. She's the most likely person to have shoved Nanny Thoms down the stairs. She's so paranoid.'

Mr Henderson mumbled what sounded like agreement whilst busily eating his lunch. Lucy rolled her eyes, though whether at Henderson's poor table manners or his agreement with Rupert, Matt couldn't be sure.

'I think Inspector Greville wishes to talk to a few people after lunch.'

As soon as he spoke the attention of everyone around the table was fixed on him.

'He's seen Daisy and me. Lucy, you've been seen?' Rupert placed his cutlery on his empty plate.

'Yes, he asked me a few things about the night Papa's papers were taken as well as last night.'

'Dashed inconvenient if I have to hang around for long. Got a lot to do.' Mr Henderson wiped his mouth with his napkin.

'The interview didn't take long. Unless, of course, you've a lot to say?' Rupert raised an eyebrow.

Henderson dropped his napkin on the table. 'The first thing I knew was when that girl started screaming her fool head off. I was outside getting my kit together and came dashing back in when I heard the commotion.'

'I'm surprised you didn't go out via the servants' stairs, Mr Henderson. Surely it would have been quicker than the main staircase?' Kitty turned a seemingly innocent face towards him.

Henderson flushed an ugly shade of red. 'I had some equipment in a cupboard in the hall that I needed to collect. I am entitled to use the main stairs, you know.' He rose from the table and turned to Matt. 'Tell the inspector I'll be in the rose garden when he wants me.'

He marched off leaving behind an awkward silence broken by Lucy declaiming mournfully, 'Oh dear, he must be upset, he didn't wait for dessert.'

CHAPTER ELEVEN

Kitty went to sit with her aunt and cousin after lunch whilst Matt met up with Inspector Greville.

'Doctor Carter just telephoned. There are suspicious bruises on Nanny Thoms's shoulders and upper back consistent with being pushed or hit. Apparently, the old lady took some kind of medication, aspirin or some such that thins the blood, so she was more prone to bruising. The marks match the shape and position of a palm print.' The inspector sighed and gazed around the empty terrace where he and Matt were standing.

'Definitely murder, then?' Matt asked.

'It would seem so.'

'Mr Henderson appeared very twitchy during lunch.' He told the inspector of Henderson's response to Kitty's question about the stairs.

'Hmm, interesting. Let's leave him to sweat a little longer. Could you ask the artist woman – Frau Fiser, is it? – to come to the library first?'

Matt decided to find Viola himself rather than asking a servant. He doubted if she would be very pleased at having to leave her work to attend an interview with Inspector Greville.

He soon discovered he was correct.

'This is most inconvenient. I have work to do here and I must press on while the light is good.' Viola scowled at him as he made his request.

'I'm afraid the inspector insists that you attend. I'm sure this won't take long,' Matt soothed as Viola peeled off the brown smock she wore to protect her clothes.

He could see how much work she had done, cleaning and restoring the mural. It was much cleaner and brighter, revealing details that must have previously been hidden by years of dust and grime.

Viola marched down the stairs in front of him, her glass beads tinkling with every indignant step. Matt followed and closed the door behind her after she'd entered the library. Lord Medford had returned to work at his laboratory with Aubrey, leaving Sir Horace to sit in during the remaining interviews.

Inspector Greville rose to greet Viola, ushering her to a chair opposite his before resuming his seat. Matt tried to appear unobtrusive in the far corner of the room by the window.

'Frau Fiser, please take a seat.'

Viola sat, spreading the garish mustard skirt of her dress daintily over her knees and straightening her beads. 'I hope this will not take long. I am employed on an important project by Lord Medford and I must make the most of daylight hours.'

'Not at all. This is just a matter of establishing the facts.'

Viola fidgeted in her seat, twiddling the corner of her bright green cardigan between her fingers. She inclined her head graciously. 'Of course, I'm happy to help if I can.'

Matt's eyebrows rose. He'd never seen Viola behaving in such a calm, reasonable manner.

'You have been here for a few weeks now?'

Viola nodded. 'Restoring the mural is a complex job. I was the first of the house party to arrive. Miss Lucy Medford and her friends arrived a few days after me and then Mr Henderson. Miss Underhay only arrived a couple of days ago.'

'The night Lord Medford's papers were stolen you retired to bed early?' The inspector opened his notebook.

'Yes, I dislike staying up late. I like to retire at a reasonable time as I have trouble sleeping. Besides, I was angered that no one in this house takes me seriously. I have been telling people for days now. You know I have seen someone watching this house?'

'Yes, I also understand that no one else has seen this person despite extensive searching. Did anyone come upstairs after you that evening?' the inspector asked.

'I was in my room alone, Inspector.' Viola bridled, obviously insulted that he had dismissed her concerns.

'I meant, did you hear anyone else come upstairs, any doors opening or closing, voices?' the inspector enlarged.

'No, nothing. I went to bed, put on my eye mask and took a mild sleeping draught. I have difficulty sleeping, as I told you. My nerves are bad.'

'And last night? I understand Lady Medford was concerned that you might be upset so she sent Nanny Thoms to offer you some hot milk.' The inspector appeared to consult his notes.

'Yes, I had been in my room for about thirty minutes when Nanny Thoms knocked on the door and offered me a cup of cocoa. I had been upset. She'd been to the kitchen and made it for me. It was a kind thought; I took the cup from her and she left.'

'What time was this?'

Viola frowned as if trying to recall the event. 'It must have been around ten.'

Matt realised that Viola may have been the last person to see Nanny Thoms alive. The idea appeared to strike the inspector too.

'Did Nanny Thoms say where she was going when she left you?'

Viola fidgeted. 'She said she had to go and find her workbag. She was afraid Lucy's dog would get it. That animal steals everything. She couldn't recall where she'd left it.'

'I see. Did you see or hear anything else after Nanny left you? Think carefully, Frau Fiser, you may be the last person apart from the killer to have seen Nanny Thoms alive.'

Colour leached from Viola's cheeks. 'Murder, it was murder, then? I knew it. This place is not safe. There are secrets, people creeping about. Faces at the windows spying on me.' Viola's voice increased in volume and she clutched at her beads.

Inspector Greville leaned forward, 'You've mentioned this before and no one else has reported seeing anything untoward. Can you describe these faces at the window?'

'I am a foreigner here, Inspector, but you must be aware that even in my own country, Austria, and others abroad there are things happening. Terrible things, my own husband…' She paused and swallowed hard. 'Suspicion everywhere. I am being watched. It was a man's face, pale and ghastly, distorted through the glass.' She hissed the last part of her speech from between clenched teeth and shuddered violently.

'Frau Fiser, please be calm. Now, who do you think is watching you?' Greville's tone was mild.

'It was a few weeks ago. After dinner I went to the library to find a book and there was a face against the glass, the same man's face, watching me. I'm sure. It could be someone from my country. My husband was murdered, you know. I have enemies.' She shuddered again and clutched at her throat.

'Did anyone else see this face?' Sir Horace asked, strolling over to join the conversation.

Viola's eyes darted from side to side like a trapped animal. 'No. I screamed, naturally, and Mr Harmon came to my aid but there was no one to be found.'

'Probably a tramp,' Sir Horace said.

'This house is dangerous, I am on my guard,' Viola declared.

After she had gone the three men gathered around the library table while Sir Horace rang the bell for the maid.

'I agree with that ass, young Banks, on very few things, but I think he may have a point regarding Frau Fiser's sanity. She certainly has a bee in her bonnet about this so-called prowler.' Sir Horace sighed.

A young maid entered the room and the inspector dispatched her to the garden to request Mr Henderson's presence.

'Paranoid, certainly,' the inspector said. 'And she has a point about things abroad being somewhat unsettled, especially as I believe Lord Medford said she was Jewish. Things do not look good in Germany and Austria. It'll be interesting to find out what did happen to her husband.'

'Dash it all though, man, does that make her a spy? It seems unlikely.' Sir Horace proffered his cigarette case to the others before lighting up a cigarette.

'Do you think there was a man at the window?' Matt asked.

'Probably a tramp or a poacher,' Sir Horace said.

'Probably, but it may be wise of us to keep an open mind for now.' Inspector Greville reviewed his notebook. 'Let's hear what Henderson has to say for himself.'

Thomas Henderson arrived for his interview, somewhat crimson in the face and minus his muddy boots which he had left in the entrance hall. Matt noticed an ill-made darn on the heel of his sock as he took his seat opposite the inspector. His trousers were spattered with soil and he brought with him the scent of cut grass and earth.

'Thank you for coming, Mr Henderson, we appreciate you are a busy man,' Greville soothed.

Henderson's ruddy features relaxed and he seemed mollified by the policeman's approach. 'Well, it's a big job this, you know. Lady Medford wants the entire garden remodelled. It's not that straightforward. The rock is very close to the surface in places, quite unsuitable for what she wants.'

'Hence your use of maps and the test beds?' the inspector asked.

'Precisely; one has to do a great deal of preparatory work in these matters. It's about making the grounds less labour-intensive.'

'The evening Lord Medford's papers were stolen, I believe you retired early?'

Henderson scratched his head. 'Yes, I believe I did. Lady Medford had been running me ragged over the planting themes. Been up early and dealing with nursery men and things so I was tired.'

'You didn't see or hear anyone after you retired to bed?'

'Had a drop of whisky and went out like a light, I'm afraid.'

Greville scribbled in his notebook. 'And last night?'

Henderson shuffled on his seat. 'Played a couple of games of billiards with Rupert Banks, then went upstairs. I had to be up early today. A lot to do.'

Sir Horace perched on the edge of the library table corner. 'And again, did you see or hear anyone?'

Henderson shook his head. 'Maybe a few doors opening and closing but I sleep very soundly. Sign of a clear conscience.' He gave a self-deprecating laugh like a seal barking.

'You were up early this morning?' the inspector asked.

'Five thirty. I wanted to dig the last few test beds before meeting Lady Medford after breakfast.'

Matt noticed a subtle change in Henderson's body as he spoke, his frame somehow was more rigid and his voice a little rougher. The upper-class accent he affected sliding slightly to betray more working-class roots.

'Talk us through what you did, saw and heard up to the point when Nanny Thoms's body was discovered,' Sir Horace said.

'Alarm went off at five thirty. Went across the hall to wash and shave, dressed.'

'You don't keep a man?' Sir Horace intervened.

'No. Must have been just before six when I went downstairs.'

The inspector's pencil stilled for a moment. 'The main stairs? You didn't use the servants' stairs?'

Henderson's cheeks turned a shade darker. 'Main stairs. My boots had been left in the porch, where they are now. There's a small closet where Lord Medford permits me to keep some of my equipment. The rest of my things are in a shed by the lake in the grounds.'

'Did you see anyone when you went downstairs?' Sir Horace asked.

The man shook his head. 'No one.'

'Did you go to the kitchen for a cup of tea before leaving the house? Or go through the servants' corridor?' the inspector asked.

'No. I have a spirit stove in my shed with tea and a tin of biscuits. Cook dislikes people using her kitchen.' Henderson sounded sulky and Matt guessed that Cook must have been displeased by Henderson helping himself from her pantry.

'Did you see Gladys, the maid? Or hear anyone else moving around either inside or outside the house?'

'Nothing. I put on my boots and collected my tools. I'd walked around towards the back of the house when I heard that girl screeching like a mad woman. Naturally I rushed inside to see what had happened and found everyone gathered around Nanny Thoms.'

'Frau Fiser said that a few weeks ago, shortly after you arrived at Enderley, there was an incident with a face at the window.'

Mr Henderson snorted. 'Stupid woman jumps at her own shadow. Forever imagining things, seeing faces and the like. She was hysterical, claiming she had been followed and was being watched. We all went outside and looked round the grounds, and no one was there. That wasn't the only time she had us on a wild goose chase like that either. One time it was over a new scarecrow in the bottom field. She's forever saying she's seen something and getting everybody rushing about the place.'

The inspector closed his notebook. 'I take it then that you set no credence in Viola's concerns?'

'Load of old hogwash, if you ask me. I tell you the woman is paranoid.' He started to stand to take his leave.

'Do you know if Nanny Thoms shared these worries of Viola's? Did she ever indicate she was worried about being watched? Or seeing strangers?' Matt asked.

Henderson's expression changed; his eyes bulged, and the tips of his ears pinked. He sat back down and glowered at Matt. 'Not to my knowledge. The old lady used to follow Lady Medford about collecting up stuff she'd lost and fussing over everybody. She would accompany Lady Medford and join in sometimes in discussions about the planting schemes. She never mentioned taking Viola's paranoia seriously.'

'Thank you, Mr Henderson.' Inspector Greville shook his hand and Henderson took his leave.

'Well?' Sir Horace asked once the door was closed.

'You think he was telling the truth?' Matt asked.

'No, I'm sure like some of our other interviewees, there were matters that he was withholding from us. I am not sure, however, how important some of those facts might be.'

CHAPTER TWELVE

After sitting for an hour with her aunt and cousin, Kitty decided to walk around the side of the house to the servants' area. Perhaps Cook might have time to answer her questions about what her mother may have been doing at Enderley shortly before she disappeared. Now Nanny Thoms unfortunately could no longer help her, she really wanted to speak to Cook about her mother.

She stepped through the back door onto the rear porch, wiping her feet on the mat before entering the white-washed scullery. The sound of voices and scrabbling noises came from further inside the house. The door stood slightly open leading to the kitchen and Kitty peeped through the gap to see who was about.

Muffy immediately bolted past her, a string of sausages hanging from her mouth.

'Oi, come back here! Dratted dog.' A sturdy housemaid, wiping her hands on a sacking apron, narrowly missed cannoning into her. Kitty recognised her as Gladys, the girl who had discovered Nanny Thoms's body.

'Oh, miss, I'm so sorry.' The girl skidded to a halt, her eyes round with surprise at Kitty's unexpected appearance.

'I was looking for Cook. I didn't mean to intrude.'

'Of course, miss. It just threw me, what with Miss Lucy's dog stealing from the pantry again. Them sausages was for Mr Golightly's supper.' Gladys looked as if she was about to cry.

'Oh, poor you. You've had the most terrible day.' Kitty felt sorry for the girl. She didn't look much older than Alice, and she'd come face to face with a dead body only that morning.

'It was such a shock, miss, finding her lying there with her head all bloody.' She produced a grubby handkerchief from the pocket of her apron and blew her nose.

'You've spoken to Inspector Greville, I suppose? I hope he was kind to you?' Kitty knew he would have been; his sometimes-abrupt manner masked a gentlemanly, fatherly demeanour.

'Oh yes, miss, he was ever so nice and patient.' Gladys hesitated.

'Is there something troubling you, Gladys?' Kitty asked, the maid's hesitation telling her that the girl had some information she hadn't shared with the inspector.

The maid bit her lip. 'I don't know, miss. I mean, it might be nothing at all and I don't want to get anybody in any trouble or bother the inspector if it isn't anything.'

'Well, why not tell me first, and if it's important I'll tell Inspector Greville.' Kitty attempted to put the girl's mind at ease.

Gladys glanced around as if afraid of being overheard. 'It's her shoes, miss.'

'Whose shoes?' Kitty asked.

'The furrin' lady, Miss Viola. They is nice shoes, you know for evening, patent with a nice little rosette on the front and they was all covered in mud, like she'd been out in the garden in them. Well they aren't them kind of shoes, miss, and they was all nice and clean earlier because I done them myself so she could wear them to dinner last night.'

'I see. Thank you, Gladys. Yes, you've done the right thing to tell me, and I think the inspector would be interested to hear about this.'

The maid's round, plain face brightened. 'I was worried because I hear she said she went to bed after dinner but then why would her shoes be muddy, miss?'

'It is very curious. She must have made a mistake. I'll speak to the inspector and let him know. Now, is Cook available? I hoped to have a quick chat with her.' Kitty wondered where Viola may have been to get her evening shoes dirty.

'I'll go see, miss.' Gladys darted off, back into the depths of the kitchen. After a minute she heard the distant rumble of female voices before Cook emerged, wiping her hands on her long white apron.

Her round cheerful face beamed. 'Miss Kitty, please come through to the housekeeper's room. Mrs Jenkinson is happy to permit me to use it on her afternoon off. I'll get Gladys to bring us a tray of tea and a bite of fruit cake.' She gave the hapless Gladys a meaningful look and the girl darted away.

Kitty took a seat on the slightly shabby but clean chintz armchair in the small room. Cook sat opposite her and they waited while Gladys carefully carried in a scrubbed wooden tea tray set with delicate, old-fashioned cream china cups patterned with flowers, milk jug, sugar bowl and teapot. A large homemade fruit cake sat on a china platter.

'Thank you, Glad, go on back to stringing them beans.' Cook dismissed her. 'She's a good girl. Not the brightest mind, but willing. It was terrible what happened this morning. It's fair upset her, upset all of us. What with the master's papers being took as well, Mrs Jenkinson is all of a lather.' Cook ignored the tea strainer and poured the tea straight from the pot into the cups.

'I know, it's really quite dreadful.'

'I don't know what the world is coming to.' Cook shook her head.

'I wanted to speak to you about something else, though. Alice said you remembered my mother visiting here some years ago?' Kitty eyed the inky dark brew emanating from the teapot with trepidation.

'As soon as I clapped eyes on you, I thought, I've seen that lass before.' Cook set the teapot down on the tray. 'It was out the ordinary you see, when your mum came here. Then when I saw you, it all came back. I were a kitchen maid then, like young Gladys.

There were a lot more staff in the house, although we'd lost a lot of the young men to the war of course, and some of the girls had gone to factory work.'

'No sugar for me, thank you,' Kitty interjected hastily as Cook picked up a teaspoon. Cook raised her eyebrows but proffered the milk jug instead. 'Yes, milk would be lovely.'

Cook added a generous amount of milk to the tea, turning the turgid dark brown liquid a slightly more palatable colour. 'It were the talk of the house when your ma came. Lovely pink costume she had on, like a fashion plate. Missus didn't realise that Mr Edgar had a wife and a little one. At least that were what she said but your pa used to write her, every now and again. She always hid they letters from the master as he…' Cook paused and took a draught of her tea. 'Begging your pardon, miss, but he didn't hold with your pa. On account of him not enlisting and him asking Missus for money all the time.'

'My father is quite disreputable,' Kitty remarked drily and risked a tentative sip of tea, hoping she wouldn't swallow any of the leaves.

'I were in the kitchens but the gossip was that your ma came to ask Missus for help finding your pa. She were concerned he hadn't wrote her for some time and she thought something had happened. She brung photographs and letters with her to prove who she was. Missus wanted to get rid of her before the master come home from London as he would be angry. She give your ma an address to try I think but your ma had to stay overnight at the house before she could get a ride to the station to get the next train.'

'I don't suppose… Did anyone know where she was going when she left?' Kitty asked.

Cook took another drink, draining her cup. 'No, not for certain. We thought she might go to Plymouth or maybe on to London. She said something to the driver about stopping off in Exeter, I think. Of course, with the war, everything was so difficult.'

Kitty swallowed her tea, trying to suppress a shudder at the strength of the brew. It wasn't much, but it was new information, and she would at least have something concrete to tell her grandmother. 'Thank you for talking to me. We never knew where my mother went on the day she left. All the information was that she'd bought a ticket for London but was thought to have left the train at Exeter. My grandmother employed detectives but they could only find dead ends and I know my grandmother believes she is dead. The detectives she employed never mentioned her coming here and my father was unaware of everything until recently.'

Cook nodded sagely. 'I wish I knew more, miss. Missus doesn't like to talk of it. Nanny Thoms might have remembered a bit more, but sadly...' She looked at Kitty's empty cup. 'Shall I read they leaves for you, miss?' Without waiting for a reply, she upturned Kitty's cup on the saucer and rotated it before turning it back upright again.

'I always reads the leaves. Got a gift I have, my mother was the same way. Predicted Mrs Glover's twins in the village and Golightly's gout, I did. Oh, dear me, maid! Be very careful. There is the death symbol in your cup.' Cook's previously florid face had paled. She indicated a group of leaves.

'I can't see anything,' Kitty said.

''Tis a special skill you need. There's a coffin there, my maid. A warning of danger to you.'

'Perhaps it is Nanny Thoms's demise you are seeing.' Kitty didn't wish to believe in such a load of superstitious tosh but even so a cold chill danced along her spine.

'Maybe,' Cook agreed. 'Just have a care, miss.' Her pleasant face still looked troubled.

Kitty forced a smile. 'I will. Thank you for the tea and for telling me about my mother.'

'My pleasure, miss.'

Kitty called a farewell to Gladys as she made her way back through the kitchen and scullery. The tea leaves had made her uncomfortable and she was anxious to escape from the servants' quarters and return to the main part of the house.

Kitty made her way outside, thinking about what Gladys had told her. It appeared that Viola may not have been entirely truthful about her movements last night if she had mud on her shoes. She wondered what Viola had said during her interview. The ground was fairly dry as there hadn't been any rain for a few days, so how could Viola's shoes have become muddy? Where had she been?

As she rounded the corner of the manor, she spied Matt smoking a cigarette out on the terrace. In the short time she'd known him, she'd come to realise that he only ever smoked when something was wrong. Usually it meant that something had triggered some memory from his time during the Great War.

'Is everything okay, Matt? Has Inspector Greville completed the interviews?' she asked as she drew near.

Matt nodded and put out his cigarette, dropping it onto the floor and grinding it underfoot. He appeared pale in the late afternoon sunlight.

'Fancy a stroll?' she asked.

He offered her his arm and they set off down the steps leading into the rose garden. She told him about Viola's shoes as they walked.

'So, she must have stepped outside after dinner, either before Nanny Thoms went to her room to offer her the hot drink or after Nanny Thoms had left her.' He stroked his chin thoughtfully with his free hand. Kitty was relieved to see some colour had returned to his cheeks.

'I think it most likely that it may have been before Nanny Thoms caught up with her in her room. Otherwise she would have had time to change her shoes before going outside.' The delicate perfume of the roses was soothing to her senses and it was disturbingly pleasant to be holding Matt's arm listening to the fat, melodious droning of the bumble bees in the flowers.

Matt seemed to consider her response. 'Unless something caught her attention after Nanny Thoms left and she didn't have time to change. Do you know which is Viola's room?'

They paused and turned to look back up at the house looming above them. Sunlight glinted on the leaded panes and Kitty tried to work out where the bedrooms were. 'At the side of the house. It must be – her room is near Lucy's.'

They continued along the gravel paths until they had a view of the side of the manor. 'That window there, third along, I think that one must be Viola's room,' Kitty said as she worked out the layout of the upper wing.

'Now then, what could she see from there?' Matt asked. 'Something that would make her pause and come out of her room in her evening shoes and cause them to become muddy?'

'If she is the thief then she could have been awaiting an accomplice to pass the documents over,' Kitty suggested. 'Or an assignation, perhaps, someone signalling?'

'Possibly, although Sir Horace has the place under surveillance. Let's walk out of the garden across to the other part of the grounds.'

'I think that area leads to the lake,' Kitty said. 'I walked that way with Lucy and Daisy the other day.'

'Isn't the gardener's hut that Mr Henderson is using for some of his kit out this way?'

'There's a small building in a copse over there.' Kitty pointed to a small grove of trees surrounding a stone-built hut with a red tiled roof.

Matt's gaze linked with hers and moving together, they left the gravel path to walk across the springy grass towards the shed. The building appeared to be deserted, and the green painted wooden door was fastened with a small brass padlock. Matt rubbed a peephole in the grimy glass and peered inside through the small lead-paned window.

'Wheelbarrows, spades, usual paraphernalia.' He stepped back and dusted his hands together.

'Is it worth getting Sir Horace to search it?' Kitty asked.

'It needs to be done, if it hasn't been searched already, even if the whole thing is a needle in a haystack without some kind of lead.'

Kitty paced around the hut, experimentally stamping on the grass with the toes of her shoes. 'Ground feels fairly dry, no sign of mud.' She frowned at the small puffs of dry dirt spurting upwards as she stamped.

'Then let's go towards the lake; if anywhere is likely to be muddy then that would be our spot.' He proffered his arm to her once more and they walked further on towards the open stretch of water twinkling at them through the trees.

A few minutes more brought them to the edge of the lake. Out on the water, a few ducks bobbed on the surface and a disinterested swan glided by. A large wooden diving pontoon was secured in the centre of the lake and a small red-painted rowboat was dragged up on the shoreline. The mud near the boat was marked by webbed feet and also the ridged soles of heavy shoes. Kitty guessed either the gardeners or Mr Henderson must be responsible for those. There also appeared to be fainter, more feminine footprints.

'Viola,' Kitty said.

'But what was she doing here? Surely no one would be using a boat in the middle of the night?'

CHAPTER THIRTEEN

Matt parted company with Kitty back at the manor and went to find Sir Horace. After informing him about the hut and suggesting a search, he telephoned Inspector Greville, who had already left for his temporary headquarters at the Railway Engine public house at Newton St Cyres.

'Good work, Captain Bryant. I suggest we talk to Frau Fiser in the morning about her shoes and what she may have been doing at the lake. In the meantime, see what emerges during dinner. Tension appears to be rising and our man may make a mistake. We'll arrange a wider search of the grounds tomorrow when I can get the manpower organised.'

'Very good, Inspector.'

After changing for dinner, he joined Sir Horace and Lord Medford for pre-dinner drinks in Lord Medford's study where they compared notes.

'Cook said as you had a nice cup of tea together this afternoon. Said it fair took her mind off everything being so horrid this morning.' Alice fastened up the tiny buttons at the back of Kitty's favourite dark green satin evening gown.

'Yes, she told me a little more about my mother's visit here. I really must try and speak to my aunt about it again when she's a little recovered from the loss of Nanny Thoms.' Kitty twitched the skirt of her dress a touch straighter and sat back in front of her dressing table mirror in order to fasten her earrings in place.

'Gladys told me an interesting story about Viola's shoes.' Kitty's eyes met Alice's in the mirror.

'She mentioned it to me, miss, in confidence, like. Proper worried she was, and I said to her to tell you as you would understand.'

Kitty smiled. 'Well done, Alice. Is there any more news from below stairs?'

'Well, miss, there is a tale that Mr Rupert was up in the night an' all. One of the other girls had a toothache and couldn't sleep so she fetched some aspirin from the kitchen. She didn't see Nanny Thoms but she did think she saw Mr Rupert a creepin' about on the landing near Miss Lucy's room when she come back up.'

'Really… Hmm. A few weeks ago, Viola said she thought she saw a man at one of the windows. She is sure she is being watched. There may be a tramp or poacher in the grounds.'

Alice's eyes brightened. 'Want me to find out, miss?'

'Be careful, Alice, this isn't the pictures, I don't want you to be hurt.'

'Cook told me what she seen in your cup, miss.' Alice shuddered. 'I'll be careful.'

Kitty hurried downstairs to the sitting room. Her cousin, Daisy and Aubrey were already there.

'Drink, Kitty, darling?' Lucy waved a cocktail glass at her.

'That would be super, thank you.' She was relieved to see that Lucy appeared to be at least somewhat recovered from the distress of the morning. Aubrey and Daisy were deep in conversation by the fireplace. Aubrey also appeared to have recovered some of his composure.

'No Rupert? Or Mr Henderson?' Kitty asked as she accepted a cocktail from Lucy.

'Playing billiards again. Mother should be joining us for dinner. She managed a little nap this afternoon and I think she's feeling better.'

'Viola is running late.' Kitty glanced at her wristwatch.

'Oh, she was in a dreadful flap after she talked to your inspector. She went in ranting and raving to Mother. Poor Mummy wasn't up to dealing with her histrionics so sent her away with a flea in her ear. You've seen what Viola's like; she's probably upstairs sulking.'

The gong sounded in the hall for dinner and the gentlemen appeared at the sitting room, accompanied by Lady Medford.

Kitty fell into step next to Matt as the party made their way to the dining room. 'Viola is late,' she murmured as they took their places at the table.

'Where is darling Viola?' Rupert drawled as he took his seat. 'For all she pecks at her food like a sparrow, she's usually very punctual. It's a national trait, I believe.'

'It's terribly tiresome,' Lady Medford snapped. 'I really can't bear unpunctuality.' Her gaze automatically fell on Nanny Thoms's empty seat as if she were about to dispatch her to fetch Viola before remembering the events of the morning.

Mr Harmon stepped forward discreetly and murmured in her ear before withdrawing from the room, leaving one of the maids to continue serving. The girl had barely finished serving the soup when the butler arrived back in the dining room.

He spoke urgently in a low tone to Lord Medford, who dropped his napkin back on the table and stomped out of the room, accompanied by the butler. Kitty pushed her soup away, untouched. She had a nasty sick feeling in the pit of her stomach that all was not well.

A few minutes later, Mr Harmon was back, his complexion ashen as he approached Sir Horace. 'His Lordship requires you and Captain Bryant urgently, sir.' He looked at Matt as he spoke.

The two men got up from the table and followed him from the room.

'What on earth is going on?' Rupert asked.

'Perhaps they've found the papers? Do you think it was Viola after all?' Daisy suggested in a hopeful tone.

Mr Henderson scraped the bowl of his spoon on the bottom of his dish and smacked his lips as he finished the last drop of soup. 'Delicious soup, Lady Medford.'

The maid hovered uncertainly at the edge of the room, clearly unsure if she should clear the table with three of the gentlemen absent.

Time ticked by and the men failed to return. Lady Medford heaved an exasperated sigh and signalled the girl to take the dishes. 'The roast is growing cold. Where have they all gone?'

'Maybe Viola has been taken ill?' suggested Lucy.

'And why would that require your father, Sir Horace and Captain Bryant?' Lady Medford demanded.

Rupert raised an eyebrow. Kitty could see that he too appeared perturbed by the continued absence of the others. Mr Harmon re-entered the room and approached her aunt.

'His Lordship requests that you all carry on with dinner, my lady.'

Henderson heaved an audible sigh of relief as Lucy gave him a disproving look. Kitty didn't think she could manage a bite to eat. Something was afoot and it irritated her that she wasn't privy to it. She just hoped that it wasn't anything bad.

The remainder of dinner and dessert was passed swiftly, in virtual silence. Apart from Mr Henderson no one ate very much, and Cook's magnificent apple pie was sadly unappreciated. Kitty was quick to rise from her seat and follow her aunt and the other ladies to the sitting room. Rupert, Aubrey and Mr Henderson went to take port in the billiards room.

Mrs Jenkinson wheeled in the tray and Lady Medford started to dispense after dinner coffee. Lucy stood by the French windows looking out across the terrace. Daisy took her cup and went to join Lucy.

'Kitty?' Her aunt was poised with the coffee pot.

'No, thank you, not this evening.' She forced a smile. Where was Matt? What was happening? She was twitchy with curiosity.

The door opened and her uncle entered, his face grave. 'Ladies, I'm terribly sorry to have to tell you that Viola has been found dead in her room.'

There was a crash behind her as Daisy dropped her coffee cup and saucer. The delicate china cup shattered into pieces as it landed.

'Dead? I don't understand?' Lady Medford stared at her husband. 'What's happened to Viola?'

Lucy assisted Daisy to a chair and perched on the arm. 'Papa?'

Her uncle's usually florid face had a greyish tinge as he placed a hand on his wife's shoulder. 'Viola has been murdered, strangled with her own necklace. There is no way to sugar-coat this or keep it from you all.'

'Murdered? By whom?' her aunt demanded.

Kitty would have laughed out loud at the manner of her aunt's query if the news wasn't so shockingly awful.

'Inspector Greville is here now, my dear. He will want to talk to all of us in turn.'

'Viola, murdered? But who would want to kill Viola?' Lucy repeated her mother's question, apparently dumbfounded.

'There is a maniac on the loose. First poor dear Nanny Thoms, and now Viola. She said she'd seen someone watching the house and watching her. This proves it. Has the inspector sent for more men? They must search the grounds to find this madman or we might all be murdered in our beds,' Lady Medford said.

'I must return to my office, my dear. The inspector has matters in hand.' Lord Medford patted his wife awkwardly on the shoulder once more before leaving.

'I'll call a maid to clear up this china.' Lucy went to the fireplace to tug on the embroidered satin bell pull. Kitty noticed her cousin's hand shaking.

'I'm sorry, it was such a shock. Poor Viola.' Daisy appeared to be on the brink of tears.

A maid entered, followed by Rupert, Aubrey and Mr Henderson. It seemed Lord Medford had been to the billiards room to break the news about Viola there. Aubrey, unsurprisingly, went straight to Daisy. Rupert, Kitty noted, appeared pale and concerned, his usual cocky demeanour no longer in place. He went to join Lucy and they moved to a sofa in the corner of the room. Thomas Henderson helped himself to a brandy and took up a stance near the fireplace while Lady Medford continued to complain and insist that a vagrant must be responsible.

Matt stood outside in the shadows of the terrace and took a long pull at his cigarette. The image of Viola Fiser, her eyes covered with her lavender sleep mask, sprawled strangled with her own necklace across her bed was imprinted on his mind. The blue lips, the scattered glass beads and her pale limbs loose like a marionette with the strings cut. He blew out a plume of smoke. He had seen too much of death in the Great War. Death had a smell, a scent that clung afterwards to the living, tainting them. Nicotine helped to cleanse the ghosts and send them away.

Footsteps sounded close by with a brief flare of a light illuminating Sir Horace Blunt's sombre face as he too lit a cigarette. 'This is a bad show, Bryant.'

'Sir.'

'We should have gone to see that bloody woman sooner. Dash it all.'

'What next, sir?' Matt asked. He understood his superior's frustration.

'Greville will question everyone again to establish where they were before dinner. The woman had clearly gone to take a nap, she'd said she was a poor sleeper. Our man obviously spied his chance.'

'Why, though, sir? She'd already spoken to Inspector Greville. What made him think that there was information she held that we didn't?'

Sir Horace exhaled a long stream of smoke as he considered Matt's question. 'I see what you mean. Doctor Carter is on his way. He'll narrow down the time of death if he can, but I understand your meaning. What if Frau Fiser stomped off after her interview with the inspector and hinted to various people that there was more information?'

Matt caught the glimmer in his eyes in the shadowy light. 'Precisely, sir.'

'Hmm, Henderson followed after her, and I understand she went to see Lady Medford and her daughter,' Sir Horace speculated in a quiet tone.

'She may also have exchanged words with Rupert Banks; the two of them disagreed over a number of matters.'

'Hang it all, man. That's practically everyone.' Sir Horace extinguished his cigarette.

Matt stayed outside a moment longer after Sir Horace had gone. He needed the quiet stillness of the terrace with the faint scent of roses to blow his mind clean again. The recurring nightmares that had followed him back from the trenches, although less frequent as the years passed, still lurked. He knew the best way of avoiding them was to carve out these moments of calm for himself. To allow the images to fade and dissipate like the smoke from his cigarette into the night air.

Seeing the woman's body so soon after Nanny Thoms's death had dragged those buried memories dangerously close to the surface. Memories of his dead wife and baby daughter, killed in a raid on London. Other men must have looked on Edith's body like he had looked on Viola's, with that ghoulish mix of horror and pity. He pulled out a second cigarette to try to chase the older ghosts away.

His equanimity somewhat restored after his second cigarette, Matt met Doctor Carter and Inspector Greville at the foot of the main staircase. He shook hands with the genial doctor.

'I've just told Greville here, I reckon you're looking at about two hours before dinner for time of death. Garrotted by her own necklace; one of those bead strings was on a kind of fishing line stuff. Reckon they had broken in the past and she'd restrung them herself.' Carter, as always, sounded cheerful and unperturbed despite the horror of Viola's death.

'Force required?' Greville asked. His moustache appeared even more defeated than usual against the other man's cheeriness.

'Not a massive amount of force needed to do something like that, so it could have been a man or a woman. Took her by surprise. She was lying with her back to the door, her eyes covered with that shade thing. Whoever did it crept in behind her and Bob's your uncle.'

'Thank you, Doctor Carter,' Greville said drily.

The doctor beamed good-naturedly at them all. 'Right, I'll be off then. By the way, super motorcycle outside, a Sunbeam, very nice.'

'That's mine,' Matt said. He recalled the doctor's love of speed from the brief journeys he'd taken with him during the Dartmouth investigation.

'Nice machine, perhaps you'll let me take a turn someday?'

'Of course,' Matt agreed, and privately vowed not to let Doctor Carter anywhere near his machine.

'Right then, we'd better start the process all over again.' Greville sighed as he reached for his notebook. 'Lord Medford has agreed to allow us the use of his library once more.'

'You give no credence to this being the work of an outsider, as Lady Medford and Frau Fiser suggested?' Matt asked.

The inspector shook his head. 'No, this is tied to the theft of those papers and one of those people in the house is both a thief and a murderer.'

CHAPTER FOURTEEN

When they arrived at the library, Matt was surprised to see Alice, Kitty's maid, assisting the house staff in placing a large silver tray of roast beef sandwiches and a pot of coffee on the library table. Alice gave him a cheeky wink as she slipped away, and his stomach grumbled, reminding him of his missed dinner.

Inspector Greville's eyes lit up as he surveyed the supper platter.

'Who would you like to talk to first, sir?' Matt asked as the policeman filled his plate.

'I think we should start with Lady Medford. She was too upset earlier over Nanny Thoms's death to give us much information, but I understand she had a visit from Frau Fiser this afternoon.'

'Yes, she may have said something to her ladyship that gives us a clue to why she was killed.' Sir Horace had joined them. 'Lord Medford is in his study; he is quite distressed over the lady's death. He feels responsible that he didn't take her concerns about being watched more seriously.'

'Shall I fetch her, sir?' Matt asked as yet another sandwich disappeared inside the inspector. At this rate there would be none left by the time he returned.

'Yes, please.'

Matt wanted to see Kitty – not that he would have the opportunity to speak to her, but at least he could check that she was safe and not too distressed by this latest murder. She was seated near Lady Medford who was still propounding her theory about a homicidal vagrant. Henderson appeared bullish, legs apart and balloon glass of brandy in his hand as he glared at the room. Rupert and Lucy had their heads together and Aubrey was comforting Daisy who seemed to be sobbing quietly into a lace handkerchief.

'Lady Medford, could you spare us a moment in the library please?' His gaze met Kitty's as he spoke, and she gave him the tiniest of smiles to show she was all right. Relief washed through him that she seemed unaffected. Her aunt rose to accompany him, and he knew Kitty would have loved to be in on the interviews.

Luckily there were a couple of sandwiches left when Matt returned to the library. Once Lady Medford was seated, he took advantage of Greville's momentary inattention to seize a plate and acquire them. Then he took a seat discreetly out of Lady Medford's eyeline and ignored the police inspector's baleful look.

'Why are we wasting time, Inspector? The perpetrator will be miles away. Was there anything missing? Had she been robbed?' Lady Medford shook out her skirts as she sat and fired questions at Inspector Greville.

'Nothing has been taken as far as we can see. You seem very certain that some stranger has stolen your husband's papers and committed two murders?' the inspector asked mildly.

'What other answer can there be? You've searched the house and found nothing, and you can't seriously suggest that a member of the household or one of my guests has committed these awful crimes? Impossible.' She folded her arms, raised her chin and glared at the inspector.

'Is that what Viola Fiser thought, Lady Medford, when she came to see you this afternoon?'

Lady Medford's spine stiffened and she sat up a fraction straighter. 'Yes. Viola, as usual, was quite hysterical. She was insistent that she leave the manor as soon as possible. She said she was being followed, that there were strange men watching the house and that she was in danger. She said her husband had been murdered and she would be next. Naturally I assumed it was her usual persecution complex, so I tried to reassure her.' Her ladyship's voice trembled, and her shoulders drooped once more. 'I should have listened to her, perhaps if I had she would still be alive. I was so upset over Nanny though, I couldn't deal with Viola's histrionics, so I sent her away.'

'Viola mentioned seeing a face at the window I believe shortly after she arrived at Enderley?'

Lady Medford nodded. 'Oh yes, she screamed the house down. Harmon took the under footman, Mr Henderson and one of the gardeners, but they could find no trace of anyone. We chalked it up to her paranoia. There are things happening abroad in her own country which had affected Viola deeply. I believe she had lost her husband in strange circumstances, so she was very suspicious of everyone.' She produced a small white handkerchief and dabbed at the corners of her eyes.

'Did she say anything else?' Inspector Greville asked.

Matt finished the last bite of his sandwich and waited.

'She said she knew things. She said she had discovered proof that there were strangers prowling in the grounds.'

'Did she say what this proof was?' Sir Horace interjected, speaking for the first time.

'I'm afraid not, she was hysterical, pointing her finger, shaking, being Viola.' Lady Medford heaved a sigh.

'Did you see her later?'

'No. She went for a lie down. I was exhausted myself so I took some aspirin. Lucy was with me until I dozed off.'

'Your daughter was present while Viola was telling you about her concerns?'

Lady Medford bridled. 'Lucy has spent much of the day with me. She knew how distressed I was over poor Nanny. The only times she left me were to exercise that wretched dog of hers.'

'I see, thank you, Lady Medford.'

She bestowed a gracious nod of her head at the inspector and took her leave.

Greville stared mournfully at the now empty sandwich platter. Matt couldn't help wishing there had been a few more too. His stomach was still rumbling. As if on cue, Alice reappeared, her lace cap slightly askew on her auburn curls. She was accompanied by another maid. They bore apple pie, dishes and a large jug of custard. They cleared away the sandwich plates and departed.

By mutual consent the men made short work of the pie before sending for Lucy Medford.

Lucy was pink-eyed but composed when she joined them, Muffy trotted at her heels. She took her place in the seat her mother had recently vacated. The dog lay under her chair, her tail beating a slow, hopeful welcome on the parquet flooring.

'Thank you for seeing me, Miss Medford. I'm aware the hour is growing late so we'll try to get through things as swiftly as possible.' The inspector smiled at her.

'I'm not sure what I can add.' Lucy waved her hand. 'I was with Mother almost all day except when I took Muffy here out or had a sanity break.' She glanced at Sir Horace and at Matt. 'You've met my mother,' she added in a wry tone.

'You were with Lady Medford when Viola came to see her?'

'Oh yes, she'd had her interview with you, and she'd worked herself up into a rare old state. She said that there were people spying on her and on the house and we should take her seriously. She said she couldn't possibly stay here and that she knew things, she had proof. She kept waving her notebook and pointing her finger.' Lucy made a small fluttering movement with her hands. 'It was typical Viola. She was prone to making these big, dramatic statements without a shred of proof of anything. And now she's dead.' Her voice quivered.

Inspector Greville's moustache appeared to take on a more distinctive droop. 'You never had any reason to believe Viola about there being someone following her or spying on the house?'

Lucy shook her head, her dark curls dancing against her cheek. 'No, no one else saw anything. Mr Harmon, Rupert, Mr Henderson, Mr Golightly and the undergardeners searched the grounds.' She fidgeted on her seat as if awaiting permission to leave.

'You didn't see Viola again after she left your mother's room?'

'No, I stayed until Mother fell asleep. Muffy had gone out and I knew she would be up to no good. I finally found her eating some purloined sausages she must have stolen from the kitchen, then I walked her around the gardens before meeting Rupert for a quick game of tennis before getting changed for dinner.'

'I see, thank you, Miss Medford, that's been most helpful.'

'Better have Rupert Banks next,' Sir Horace said as soon as Lucy left.

'Kitty says that Viola and Rupert were often sparring at one another. I've seen this for myself.' Matt leaned back in his chair.

'Not to mention that tale from the servants about him being out on the landing the night Nanny Thoms died.' Greville looked at Sir Horace. 'Send him in.'

Matt stifled a yawn as Rupert entered the library. The early start had begun to tell on him, and the hour was growing late. There was a visible change in Rupert's demeanour from the cocksure young man they had met earlier, as he entered and took his seat. A certain wariness in his expression made him seem less sure of himself.

'I apologise for the late hour, Mr Banks, but I felt it was important to speak to as many people as possible whilst their memories of the evening were still fresh. Can I ask, when did you last see Viola?' the inspector asked.

Rupert folded his arms across his chest. 'I met her shortly after she'd left Lady Medford's room this afternoon. I'd gone to find Lucy as she'd promised me a game of tennis later in the day and I met Viola on the stairs.'

Greville scribbled some notes in his book. 'And how was she when you met her?'

'Furious. She said her life, all our lives, were in danger and no one was taking any notice of her. She said her husband had been murdered in Austria and now they were coming for her.'

'What did you say to that?'

Rupert sighed. 'Stupidly, I said, "Who would bother wanting to kill you?"'

Sir Horace looked up at that statement.

'Reassuring, I'm sure. What did Viola say to that?' Greville asked.

'She said she knew things. She had proof. I ribbed her a bit and said it was a load of tosh. If she knew something about the missing papers or Nanny T then she should go to the police.'

'And what was her response?' Sir Horace asked.

'She said she didn't trust the police. Said they were part of the establishment. Knowledge was power, she would make her own arrangements.' Rupert fixed his gaze on Inspector Greville's face. 'I didn't take her seriously. I just thought it was Viola trying to make herself important. I keep thinking now that I should have come to you and told you what she was saying. Maybe she would still be alive.' His shoulders hunched and he scrubbed at his face with his hands as if trying to erase the idea from his mind. 'Viola and I didn't get on. She was full of her art history and her long list of connections in the art world. She dismissed my work which annoyed me considerably.'

'I understand you are an artist yourself?' Greville asked.

'Yes, still a bit of an amateur but I've been told my work has promise. Viola disagreed.'

'You didn't see Viola again after this encounter?'

Rupert shook his head. 'No, I popped my head in to give Lucy a time for tennis then went to read some papers my solicitor had sent from London a few days ago. Complex financial stuff that I needed time to think about. After that I met Lucy, we played a game and then we both went to dress for dinner. I came downstairs with Aubrey and Henderson.'

Greville flicked back through his notebook. 'I have a statement from someone, that last night when Nanny Thoms died, you were seen on the landing. Care to tell us what you were doing?'

Rupert threw his head back and stared at the ceiling for a few seconds before returning his gaze to the inspector. 'Yes, I went to push a note under Lucy's door. You can ask her if you like. We'd had a bit of a tiff earlier in the day and I wanted to square things with her.'

'May we ask what the tiff was about?'

'I asked her to marry me and she refused.' A spot of high colour tinged Rupert's cheeks at this confession.

Matt bit back a whistle of surprise. He hadn't thought Lucy and Rupert were involved in that kind of relationship. He'd witnessed a little flirtation, but Rupert flirted with all young women, including Kitty. For some reason that had irked him a little.

'Is Lord Medford aware of the nature of your interest in his daughter?' Greville too looked a little astonished by this latest revelation.

Rupert laughed, a short bitter sound. 'No, Lucy didn't want her father to know anything. Her idea was that I should get to know him during my stay here. Things haven't really gone to plan, and Lucy has been rather chilly towards me on the romantic front lately. Please, don't mention anything to Lord Medford.'

'So, when you were delivering your note to Miss Medford – and we will ask her to corroborate this – did you see or hear anything?' Matt asked.

'I thought I heard Viola's door close, but I couldn't swear to it. It might have been my imagination. That's all I can tell you, I'm afraid.'

'What did you make of that?' Sir Horace asked after Rupert had departed.

'Interesting. We can ask Miss Medford to corroborate his tale in the morning.' Greville frowned as he studied his notes. 'Who have we left to see?'

'Daisy, Aubrey and Henderson.' Matt stood and paced about the room. If he never set foot in another library after this case was solved it would be too soon. With the lamps lit, the faded gilt lettering on the spines of the books took on a different appearance, the shelves like bars caging him in. He hoped the remaining interviews would be swift.

'Better have the girl next, then,' Sir Horace said.

Greville inclined his head in agreement and Matt offered to fetch her. Aubrey was seated next to Daisy in the drawing room while Henderson studied a horticultural catalogue. Kitty was missing and he wondered if she'd retired for the night. At least she had Alice with her to keep her safe.

'I'm sorry this is so late, Miss Banks.' Greville glanced at the marble clock on the mantelpiece as the girl took her seat.

Daisy looked tired, her make-up was smudged and there were dark circles under her eyes. 'That's all right, I don't expect I shall sleep very well tonight anyway.' A shudder ran through her and she twisted her handkerchief on her lap. 'Poor Viola. We all poked fun at her you know, none of us took her seriously.'

'When did you last see her?' Inspector Greville had adopted his fatherly tone again.

'I don't know. Before lunch, I think.' Daisy screwed her face up in thought. 'She was working on the mural. Aubrey was with Lord Medford. Lucy was with her mother and Rupert had some dreary papers to read. I was bored so I wandered upstairs to the long gallery. Of course, Viola was annoyed to see me. She hated anyone disturbing her. I told her she could keep her precious mural and I went out into the garden and strolled around the roses.'

'Did you meet anyone else?' Greville enquired.

'No, I think Mr Henderson was busy digging one of his test bed things. I thought I caught a glimpse of that dreadful old jacket he wears. He was walking towards the lake.'

'And before dinner?' Sir Horace asked.

'I was with Aubrey, of course.'

Daisy was dismissed and Aubrey called in. He confirmed that he had been with Daisy until they had gone to change for dinner.

'And of course, any of them might have slipped into Viola's room whilst dressing for dinner,' Sir Horace said gloomily. 'Right, let's have Mr Henderson and see what he has to say for himself.'

The grandfather clock in the hall chimed midnight as Thomas Henderson entered the library.

'Right, let's get this over with. Some of us have to get up early in the morning.' He took his place and glowered around at them all. Matt wondered how much of Lord Medford's brandy he had consumed.

'Very well, when did you last see Frau Fiser?' Greville reopened his notebook.

'She was at breakfast, pecking at a bit of toast as usual. I went out to finish pegging out some layouts for new beds. I don't think I saw her after that. She was usually busy on her painting thing and didn't come for lunch.'

'Did you see anyone else during the day?' Sir Horace intervened.

Henderson sniffed. 'Couple of the gardeners. That girl, Daisy, was drooping around the rose garden.'

Greville asked a few more questions and finally allowed Henderson to leave.

'I think we need to call it a night, gentlemen, and reconvene after breakfast tomorrow.' Sir Horace rose.

'I agree. We can look at this afresh in the morning.' Inspector Greville walked with them into the hall to receive his coat and hat from Mr Harmon.

Kitty slept badly despite having told herself she wasn't frightened of staying in a house where two murders had occurred. She was glad of Alice's company next door; knowing the girl was so close gave her some reassurance. She was strongly aware though of missing her grandmother and the comforting, familiar creaks of the Dolphin.

Alice had assisted the household staff the previous evening on Kitty's instructions. She had fetched and carried and kept her ears and eyes open, reporting back to Kitty when they had shared a late night cup of cocoa in the safety of Kitty's bedroom.

From Alice, she had learned that Mr Henderson was not liked by the staff as he was not a gentleman and that her cousin and Rupert were more closely involved than she had suspected.

This morning, Kitty was eager to speak to Matt to learn what he had discovered during the inspector's interviews.

'There's a lot of policemen outside in the grounds, miss,' Alice informed her when she brought up a tea tray. 'They's looking around the lake and in the gardener's hut. Old Golightly the gardener's not very happy about it, nor is Mr Henderson. He says as they is holding him up from his work.'

Kitty guessed they must be checking out the lead she and Matt had uncovered yesterday. 'Do you know if anyone has gone down for breakfast yet?'

'Mr Henderson had his early. Cook wasn't best pleased at having to make his porridge separate from everybody else on account of him wanting to be outside so early. Lady Medford has asked for breakfast in her room, so has Miss Daisy. Mrs Jenkinson is quite put out as it's disrupting her routine making up trays, but these are funny times, says she. His Lordship and Mr Aubrey has gone down with Sir Horace.' Alice bustled around the room as she spoke.

'Captain Bryant?' Kitty asked.

Alice gave her a knowing look. 'Not yet, miss.'

Kitty dressed swiftly with Alice's assistance and hurried downstairs. To her surprise, she realised she was actually quite hungry, perhaps because she'd eaten so little at dinner.

Rupert was the only person at the table when she entered the room.

'Good morning, how are you today? Did you sleep?' She slipped into a seat and helped herself to a cup of tea.

'I've had better nights. You?'

'Not well,' she admitted and smiled her thanks to the maid who served her with a steaming bowl of porridge. 'Has anyone else come down?'

'Sir Horace, Aubrey and your uncle went out a few minutes ago. I believe they are expecting the inspector again shortly.' Rupert looked tired.

'My maid said the police were searching the grounds.' Kitty tucked into her breakfast.

Mrs Jenkinson carried in fresh cups and started to check the breakfast dishes.

Rupert looked up from his coffee cup. 'Wonder what they're looking for?'

Kitty shrugged. 'Maybe they're hunting for Viola's mystery man at the window.'

Mrs Jenkinson dropped the lid of the silver kidney dish with a clang. She collected the used crockery and left.

'Do you think it could be true? No one else ever saw anyone.' Rupert frowned. 'Do you think she really was being followed or watched?'

'I don't know. I hope the police may have the answers later.' She wondered if the police would find anything during their search. Was there some vagrant living in the woods, perhaps?

Rupert excused himself and Kitty continued her breakfast alone until Matt entered the room. She noticed that the sharp angular bones of his cheeks appeared more starkly defined and the lines deeper at the corners of his eyes.

'I take it that you too had a bad night?' she asked as she poured him some coffee.

His head inclined briefly. She knew that Matt suffered terrible nightmares when stressed. Yet another legacy of all he'd seen and suffered during the war. Once he'd asked her to lock him in his room and return the key the next day as he could be destructive or sleepwalk when sleeping badly.

'Inspector Greville's men are being most industrious.'

She smiled. 'Alice told me. Do you think they will find anything?'

'Clearly, Viola went to the lakeside for something. Maybe whatever she thought she saw has gone or maybe she met someone there.' He frowned as he added sugar to his cup.

A shiver of dread danced its way along her spine, casting a shadow over a previously sunny morning. 'You think you know what they're going to find?'

A glance at his face told her she was correct. 'I would like to be wrong, but Viola and Nanny Thoms are both dead and I'm afraid there will be more deaths to come.'

'More?' Fear clutched at her. 'You think someone in the house is at risk?'

'I don't know. I think the police may find something at the lake. I suggested to Inspector Greville that the men take out the boat to the pontoon and check below the waterline.' He sipped his coffee as if the large quantity of sugar he'd added to the cup would imbue him with strength for what lay ahead.

*

Matt had little appetite for breakfast, but he could see that his comments had worried Kitty, so he forced himself to eat a little toast to appease her.

'I called Grams this morning. I told her what I'd learned from Cook about my mother's disappearance. I didn't mention the murders.' Kitty set her napkin down on the table.

'Probably wise.' A wry smile lifted the corner of his mouth as he pictured Kitty's grandmother's face if she knew what was happening at the manor. She would probably have been straight in Mr Potter's taxi cab to Enderley ready to insist Kitty return to the Dolphin.

A scampering Muffy preceded Lucy into the room at that moment, dancing around her feet with obvious glee.

'Morning, have either of you seen Rupert?' she asked as she took her place at the table and helped herself to coffee.

'He left a few minutes ago. He said he had some paperwork to attend to.' Kitty eyed her cousin's pale face.

'There are policemen everywhere. Do you think they'll catch Viola's murderer? It's a horrid feeling, so unsafe in one's own home. I feel as if I can't trust anyone any more. I'm so glad you're here, Kitty. I know this must be beastly for you and not at all the lovely holiday we had planned but I do feel safer having you around.' Lucy stared gloomily into her cup while Muffy sat hopefully at her feet waiting for titbits. 'Surely it has to be a vagrant or someone, doesn't it, who's done this? Viola said she was being watched.'

Matt saw Kitty slip Muffy a bit of toast. 'I have every faith in Inspector Greville. You can see he's being very thorough.'

'Absolutely. He and Sir Horace are good men,' Matt agreed. He couldn't go along with the vagrant theory; it simply didn't make sense and there had been no evidence for it beyond Viola's testimony, but he wanted to give Lucy some crumb of comfort.

They left Lucy to share the rest of her breakfast with Muffy and stepped out together onto the terrace. The elevated position at the back of the house afforded them glimpses across the rose gardens to the meadows and the lake beyond.

Daisy was tucked around a corner finishing a cigarette. She relaxed when she saw them, dropping the stub onto the flags and extinguishing it with the toe of her shoe. 'Aubrey hates me smoking, but I feel so on edge. What are they all looking for?' She waved a hand at the police who were collecting by the lake shore.

'I'm not sure.' Matt had an idea of what he expected them to find but he hoped he would be proven wrong.

'It's all too ghastly.' Daisy flipped out the ends of her blonde curls and disappeared back inside the house. Kitty exchanged a speaking look with him and shrugged her shoulders.

CHAPTER FIFTEEN

In the distance there came a faint cacophony of whistles.

Matt stiffened. 'They've found something.'

Kitty placed a hand on his arm as if to brace herself against whatever was about to come their way. He covered her hand with his, the warmth of his touch reassuring. 'I expect we will learn very quickly what has been recovered.'

There seemed to be a lot of movement on the edge of the lake, and the sound of shouting. 'There's something in the lake.'

He had barely finished speaking when a young police constable emerged from the garden, running up the steps and onto the terrace. Despite his exertions there was a faint greenish pallor to his complexion, and he was obviously disturbed.

'Begging your pardon, miss, sir, could you direct me to the telephone?'

'Of course, come, it's in the hall. I'll show you. Do you need to contact Inspector Greville?' Matt asked as he led the way to the hall.

'No, sir, the inspector is already at the lake. It's Doctor Carter I'm to get.' The lad followed Matt and Kitty tagged along behind, eager to discover what was afoot.

'Is someone hurt?' Matt asked, showing the constable the telephone.

'No, sir, the man we found is well beyond any mortal man's aid,' the man replied as he lifted the receiver and started to dial.

Matt left him to his call and rejoined Kitty.

'You heard?' he asked in a low tone.

She nodded. 'It is I think as you feared? Another body? Viola's vagrant, perhaps.'

Matt's mouth was compressed in a grim line. 'I expect it to be the case.'

The constable completed his call. 'I must find Lord Medford and Sir Horace.'

'Of course.' Matt directed him.

Lucy emerged from the dining room with Muffy at her heels. 'I thought I heard whistles and voices? Have the police apprehended the murderer?'

'I fear the police have found another body, by the lake,' Matt said.

Lucy paled. 'Not an arrest?'

Kitty took her cousin's arm, concerned she was about to faint. 'No, my dear, not yet. Another victim, it seems.'

'Oh God. That's just awful, so awful. Is it… is it someone we know?'

Matt shook his head. 'I doubt it. We don't know any details, but it seems unlikely.'

Lucy's knees buckled and Kitty had to hold her cousin upright. 'How can you be so calm?' Lucy asked.

'I suppose after everything that occurred a few weeks ago, I have become a little inured to situations that otherwise would have been shocking.' Kitty's own recent near-death experience at the hands of a lunatic had indeed left its mark. Although she hadn't seen the bodies on those occasions, she had known two of the victims well, unlike this case where she had barely begun to know Nanny Thoms or Viola.

She wondered if anyone would know this third victim. She longed to go to the lakeside however horrifying it might be, to see the evidence for herself. Perhaps the servants might know the mystery man. They were probably aware that he had been present in the grounds at some point. He must have requested work or food from the back door if he were a vagrant. Yet surely the staff would have spoken out when the papers were stolen and Nanny T and Viola killed if he had still been near the manor.

The constable returned to the hall, accompanied by Sir Horace and her uncle.

'Captain Bryant, I would be glad if you would come with us to the lake.' Sir Horace's voice matched the severity of his expression.

Lucy swayed on her heels once more and Kitty was forced to steady her.

'Kitty, take great care.' Matt's tone and eyes spoke a warning as he moved to follow the other men.

She steered her cousin from the hall into the sitting room and installed her on the sofa next to Daisy, who was flicking listlessly through a fashion magazine. Daisy discarded it as soon as she saw the expression on Lucy's face.

'What is it? Are you okay, Lucy?' Daisy placed her arm around Lucy and looked to Kitty for an explanation.

Kitty rang for a tray of tea, hoping that a cup of the hot beverage liberally laced with sugar and perhaps a splash of brandy, might aid her cousin.

Daisy looked as if she too needed some comfort when Lucy told her what they had just learned. Kitty only paid half an ear to their speculations. She hoped Matt would be all right. It would be an ordeal for him if he were forced to see yet another body in so short a time. She could see how each viewing so closely together had been haunting him and she hated the idea that he was being forced into such a situation.

Once a maid had scurried in and deposited a tray of tea, Kitty assisted her cousin and her friend to take some drinks. She continued to think about what she might learn if she could make good her escape from the others. It was all very well Matt warning her to be careful, but she couldn't simply sit around sipping tea if there was something she could be doing to assist the investigation.

She determined to make her way to the kitchen and try Gladys, to see if she could shed some light on the possible identity of the mystery man. She knew from Alice that news travelled swiftly in the servants' quarters. If anyone knew anything then the staff had to be the first port of call.

A little later Kitty spied her opportunity to escape the sitting room and made her way round the side of the house towards the back door. Thomas Henderson was skulking about near the rhododendrons, his attention seemingly fixed on the activities of Greville's men, who could just be seen through the trees in the distance.

Instinct made her wary of alerting him to her presence and she slipped quietly past and through the open rear door leading to the scullery. Once inside she heard raised female voices and loud sobbing. Kitty paused for a moment before creeping quietly forward, her back against the cool white painted brick wall of the passage, to listen into whatever was going on.

'You should have come to me right away, my girl. You'd no business keeping something like that to yourself. What if he's the one they been looking after?'

She recognised Cook's voice and stationed herself behind the door to listen.

'I didn't mean no harm. I only give him a few scraps. An old soldier he was, he had trouble getting work he said, 'cos of his arm not working right. Mrs J-Jenkinson knew all about it.' The other voice was punctuated with sobs and sounded like the hapless Gladys.

'You didn't ought to have done it. What if he was the one who murdered the foreign lady? You never said nothing when she was a shrieking and hollering about there being a face watching her at the window and Mr Harmon outside with Mr Golightly risking their lives looking for strangers,' Cook said hotly.

'I thought as he'd gone. Mrs Jenkinson said as he'd left the area. He was headed to the village he said, to try his luck there. How was I to know he'd been d-done in?'

'You'd best stop your blarting, young Gladys. You'll have to tell that policeman what you know. Lord knows what Mr Harmon will have to say to you, I dread to think, and I'm surprised as Mrs Jenkinson hasn't said nothing.'

Kitty decided she'd heard enough and edged her way quietly back outside without letting Cook or Gladys know she'd been there. She walked back towards the rose garden, this time without seeing any sign of Mr Henderson.

The perfume of the roses and gentle hum of the bees proved a balm once more to her senses as she made her way along the gravel walk towards the arbour. She intended to sit for a while and ponder the information she'd just heard when she realised the arbour already had an occupant.

Aubrey was seated on the wooden bench, his head buried in his hands as if he wished to shut the world away. He lifted his head and stared dully at her as she entered.

'I'm so sorry. I didn't realise anyone was here.' She went to retreat as he appeared to be in no mood for company.

'No, it's all right, Miss Underhay.'

Kitty hesitated for a second then took a seat on the narrow bench next to him.

'Forgive me, but you seem very troubled. Perhaps I can help in some way?' She waited for a response, wondering if it were the missing papers, his relationship with Daisy or this latest find that had laid the heaviest burden upon him.

'It is all too much, Miss Underhay.' He groaned and sat upright, tilting his head back to rest against the wooden wall of the arbour. 'I feel such responsibility.'

'But why, Aubrey?' She wasn't sure what he meant.

'It was my duty to ensure Lord Medford's papers were secure. I should have taken them to the laboratory safe after the meeting.'

'I think the blame for the missing documents lies with whoever took them. Do you not think that this villain must be truly desperate to have killed twice, and now possibly a third time? He may have attacked you and slit your throat to gain those documents.' Kitty's tone was gentle.

'A third victim?' Aubrey asked.

'You have not heard the commotion? There has been a discovery at the lake and Doctor Carter has been sent for, but the constable indicated there was no hope.'

Aubrey was ashen. 'Is it… is it one of the party? I was unaware. I came here straight after breakfast.'

'I believe it is a stranger to us. Sir Horace has gone with my uncle and Captain Bryant to meet with the inspector.'

Aubrey groaned.

'I think there is something more troubling you?' she probed.

She sensed he was struggling with his conscience.

'I'm sure you are aware, Miss Underhay, that there is an attachment between myself and Miss Banks. My mother has been a widow for a number of years and though my father was an excellent man, unfortunately he did not leave us in very prosperous circumstances. I am her only means of support and I have not yet broached the subject of my engagement to Miss Banks.' He paused as if to gather his thoughts before continuing. 'Daisy is from a good family, but she has little money. I cannot afford to support two households and I fear that Daisy and my mother…' He broke off.

'I understand,' Kitty said. Daisy, with her bleached hair and rouged cheeks would perhaps not sit well as a suitable choice of bride to present to his mother.

'Then there is the issue of Daisy's brother. You know he has certain political beliefs? He is an activist and an agitator. If all of this reaches the papers, my mother would be distraught. The scandal. She would never accept Daisy, and with Rupert...'

'You have concerns about Rupert?'

Aubrey blew out a sigh. 'I don't wish to think ill of him. He is Daisy's brother, but I know he was up during the night when Nanny Thoms was killed. He and Viola argued constantly. She ridiculed his art and his ideals. Then one evening he told me that for two pins he would like to wring her blasted neck.' His voice trembled as he spoke, and misery was writ large on his face.

'People often say things they don't mean in the heat of the moment, but if it is troubling you, perhaps it would help your conscience to mention this to the inspector,' Kitty soothed. If he refused to speak up then perhaps she should mention it to Matt.

'I wish it was only that. Rupert has asked a lot of questions about your uncle's work. At first I thought it only to back up his ideology about the oppressed masses or to try and win favour from Lord Medford. Rupert is wooing your cousin, although I confess I don't know the depth of feeling between them. Daisy believed that Lucy might become her sister-in-law at some point in the future. I was circumspect with my answers of course but now with recent events, well it makes one question everything.'

'These documents are clearly very valuable. But can they really contain information that can drive someone to murder?' Kitty asked.

'Your uncle has discovered a potential new material which, if mass produced, could lower costs and weights for various military applications. The formula requires some work and more testing, and the proposition was for Sir Horace to secure government funding in order to develop it further. But if it falls or has fallen into the wrong hands, then it gives any enemy of our country a huge advantage. Imagine the implications for any future conflict.'

'That is serious indeed, Aubrey. I feel you must discuss these concerns about Rupert with Inspector Greville,' she said.

He shook his head and kicked a small stone out of the arbour, sending it bouncing out onto the gravel walk. 'I have a loyalty to Daisy and when I voice these concerns out loud they are purely speculation. You must see my dilemma.'

'And yet they worry you deeply. There is no conflict of interest that I can see. I think you must speak to the inspector and discuss these worries with him. If these concerns are baseless then it will put your mind at ease and can only assist Rupert and Daisy. It may even help prove Rupert's innocence somehow.'

Aubrey blinked and scrubbed at his face with his hands. 'You are right, Miss Underhay. Thank you. My duty is clear; I will speak to Inspector Greville.'

'I'm glad to have helped, and please, call me Kitty.' She smiled at him, pleased to see some colour had returned to his cheeks.

CHAPTER SIXTEEN

Matt hoped Kitty would heed the warning he'd given her. He knew she was chafing at the bit to be involved more deeply in the investigation. Looking at the bloated and disfigured face of the vagrant who had been pulled from beneath the pontoon on the lake that morning, he was glad she was not party to the scene.

He gave the corpse only the briefest of glances, noting the worn, shabby clothing. He had seen too many bodies in this state, abandoned on the battlefield, unable to be retrieved safely by their comrades, their flesh bloated and rotting in the mud. He had no desire to revisit those memories. Sir Horace and Inspector Greville, themselves both former military men, appeared to share his disinclination, turning away from the scene as soon as decently possible.

'Nothing on the fellow to identify him, I suppose?' Lord Medford held a handkerchief over his nose and mouth, muffling his words.

Matt accepted a cigarette and a light from Sir Horace. His hand trembled slightly as he lit his cigarette and he despised the involuntary betrayal of his feelings. The cool rush of nicotine and resulting smoke helped mask the odour starting to arise from the corpse which lay just a few feet away.

'No, sir. His pockets are empty, and he has no watch or wallet.' Inspector Greville looked across the meadow to where the cheery, rotund figure of Doctor Carter was making his way towards them.

'Another one, eh, Greville? You're giving my motor plenty of outings I must say,' the doctor remarked as he drew closer. He tipped his hat to Lord Medford and Sir Horace before opening his bag and approaching the corpse.

As of one accord, Matt and the others moved a little further away whilst the doctor completed a brief examination. He joined them as they were finishing their cigarettes.

'I'd say he was knocked over the head before hitting the water. Probably been in there for at least a couple of weeks, judging by the state of him. I'll be able to tell you more later.'

'Then he may have been Frau Fiser's face at the window?' Sir Horace said.

'Possibly, sir. At least the first one she saw,' Greville agreed.

Matt was relieved to see that a sheet had now been placed over the poor, deceased soul and arrangements were being made to remove him from the scene.

'A case of being in the wrong place at the wrong time perhaps?' Matt asked.

Greville met his gaze. 'Perhaps.'

'But if that chap was killed a couple of weeks ago, well, that was before the documents were taken. What the blazes is going on in my own damn house?' Lord Medford said.

'If we consider the wax Captain Bryant discovered, indicating the planning involved in the theft of the papers, then it seems likely that this chap stumbled upon something he was not meant to see or hear. Though he may not have been aware that he'd witnessed anything out of the ordinary. Our murderer is intent on ensuring there are no witnesses to his or her actions.' The inspector's tone was grave.

'You still feel the documents are here at the house somewhere?' Sir Horace asked.

'Yes, I do, or I think our villain would have made an attempt to flee.'

'There's no hope of avoiding the press on this now I suppose?' Lord Medford asked.

Sir Horace grimaced. 'We've kept a lid on things so far but three deaths in such a short space of time, even with pressure from the high-ups, cannot be suppressed for much longer.' He looked at Greville. 'I'm afraid the onus is on you, Inspector. We need a speedy resolution and the return of those blasted papers.'

The inspector's expression was impassive. 'I'm awaiting some more information, sir, which may prove helpful.'

Matt wondered what he hoped to learn. There was concern over Thomas Henderson's previous employment, and Rupert Banks's links to various socialist and communist groups and activities. Perhaps there was more to be learned from Viola Fiser's background. What exactly had happened to Herr Fiser, for instance?

Once the body had been moved and he could get away, he located Kitty in the rose garden and quickly updated her on what had happened down by the lake.

'How awful. That poor man.' A delicate shudder ran through her. She peeked up at him. 'Are you all right?'

He was touched, if a little embarrassed, by her concern. Her friendship meant a great deal to him. Something he'd realised even more since he had come to Enderley. 'It was unpleasant, but Doctor Carter was soon at the scene.' He fell into step beside her as they dawdled along the path, the peaceful sunlit scene incongruous after the harrowing events of the morning. He listened carefully to what she'd discovered in his absence.

'Gladys saw this man a couple of weeks ago?'

'He probably went begging at the back door for food, or enquiring after work. She said Mrs Jenkinson knew he had come calling.' She left out the part about the man's claim to be a veteran judging that it might upset Matt, coming so soon after he had viewed the body. 'It seems Gladys found him some scraps and gave him directions to the village. She was convinced he had left the area.'

Matt turned to face Kitty, placing his hands on her shoulders. 'I meant what I said earlier, old girl. Whoever is responsible for these deaths is highly dangerous. Please ensure that neither you nor Alice are placed in harm's way.'

She opened her mouth as if to protest.

'No, Kitty, don't deny that you have had Alice playing spy for you.'

She plucked a petal from a rose as she passed. 'Very well, I shall not deny it, but I have warned her to be cautious. I am well aware of the dangers and I would not want her harmed.'

'Try to stay in company, do not be alone with anyone if you can avoid it.' He could see from her face that his words were scaring her, but he would never forgive himself if he didn't try to protect her.

'I will try to be good.' She smiled and slipped her hand into the crook of his arm. He wasn't fooled by the smile. Her gaze met his for a moment and he wondered how she would react if he were to kiss her now.

'Kitty!' The peremptory tone could only belong to Lady Medford. Kitty released his arm and they turned to see her aunt hurrying towards them. She was dressed in a tweed skirt and a silk blouse with a gardening trug over her arm.

'Captain Bryant.' She inclined her head towards him. Her face was flushed, and she appeared breathless after her rapid approach.

'Are you all right, Aunt Hortense?' Kitty asked.

'My dear, I was quite concerned. Lucy said you were out in the garden alone. After this horrid news this morning, my dear, it is not at all safe. I have insisted Golightly accompany me today.' Kitty's aunt compressed her lips together.

'I am quite safe. Captain Bryant was escorting me.'

Matt murmured his agreement. He could tell that Kitty didn't wish to alarm her aunt.

'I am relieved to see you are accompanied. One can't be too careful. I have instructed Lucy and Daisy to remain indoors and I wish you would join them until this maniac is caught. You are my guest and I feel responsible for your welfare.'

'I agree, Lady Medford. I was just impressing upon your niece the need for caution.' Matt earned himself a steely glare from Kitty.

Lady Medford smiled with relief.

'Allow me to escort both of you ladies into the house.' Matt proffered his other arm to Kitty's aunt. Fortunately, the path was wide enough to admit all three and they strolled back to the stone steps leading to the terrace.

'I saw Mr Henderson out earlier. Surely he should not still be working?' Kitty asked, clearly a little irked at being forced indoors.

'The redesign is almost complete. The new plans will be most labour-saving. Such a shortage of manpower since the war. We are too rural here and of course one needs to be physically fit.'

'Mr Henderson was highly recommended to you, I believe?' Matt asked as they ascended the steps.

'Oh yes, he has worked on several of the finest gardens in England. He trained at Kew, you know. The Earl of Dunhaven is most pleased with the changes he made at Craigmurray House.' Lady Medford beamed at Matt, her concerns for Kitty's safety swept away by thoughts of her beloved garden. 'He is not, of course, a gentleman, although he has aspirations. You must have noticed his table manners. He actually eats his peas with a knife.' She gave a small shudder.

They reached the French doors and Lady Medford relinquished Matt's arm. 'I must check with Cook about how much tea and how many biscuits she is supplying to those policemen. So inconvenient having them trampling about the estate. And they all seem to have such large feet and appetites to match. I expect luncheon will be ready soon. We're late today what with the commotion at the lake, and Mrs Jenkinson is behaving most oddly.'

She excused herself as he and Kitty joined Lucy and Daisy. Lucy was trying to teach Muffy to beg using titbits of sausage as a reward. Daisy was admiring her manicure. Both girls appeared to have recovered their composure.

'Any news?' Daisy asked, setting aside her nail file.

'Not yet.' Matt took a seat next to Lucy and was immediately investigated by Muffy. He wondered if the inspector would join them for lunch. If so, it should make for an interesting meal.

CHAPTER SEVENTEEN

Lunch was a dreary affair. The inspector made it clear he would not discuss the case nor indulge in speculation and so conversation was stilted and desultory. The only people at the table with any appetite were Mr Henderson and Inspector Greville.

Lord Medford, who had chosen to be present, contented himself with scowling ferociously at each guest in turn after every morsel of food. Lucy moved the contents of her plate from one place to another, Aubrey kept glancing at Daisy when he thought himself unobserved, and Rupert for once abstained from making facetious or provocative comments.

Toward the end of lunch, Mr Harmon informed the inspector that the documents he had been expecting had arrived and had been placed in Lord Medford's study. Kitty noticed that everyone made a great show of pretending not to be interested in this piece of information.

Inspector Greville, Sir Horace and Matt repaired to the study as soon as lunch was concluded. Lady Medford collared Thomas Henderson and went to the library while Lord Medford and Aubrey returned to work at the laboratory. Rupert excused himself with the plea of not having completed his paperwork, leaving Kitty with Daisy and Lucy.

'What do you suppose the papers are that the inspector was expecting?' Lucy asked as the girls made their way back along the hall towards the sitting room.

'I've no idea,' Kitty said. Privately though, she suspected it might be background information on her fellow guests and possibly Viola Fiser and her late husband.

'I'm so bored,' Daisy announced. 'All this staying indoors and thinking of nothing but what's happening is making me jumpy.'

'I don't see why we shouldn't go out for a walk and get some air if we're together and stay near the house,' Kitty said.

'Oh yes, I really need to get out. It feels so oppressive in here,' Lucy agreed.

Kitty squinted out of the French doors. 'The sky looks as if it's clouded over again. I'll just fetch a cardigan. Shall we meet here in five minutes?'

The others agreed and Kitty and Daisy both hurried upstairs. Like Kitty, Daisy was also wearing a light, cotton summer frock. Lucy had opted to collect Muffy's lead from the hall cupboard so the little dog couldn't run away on their walk.

Kitty was relieved to be outdoors once again in the fresh air. The atmosphere inside the house was suffocating, with everyone eying each other with suspicion. She wondered how Matt was faring in the study with Sir Horace and Inspector Greville.

'When do you think this will all be over?' Daisy asked as they walked alongside the tennis court.

'I suppose as soon as they either recover Papa's papers or catch the killer. Hopefully both, assuming it's the same person.' Lucy frowned and waited for Muffy to investigate a dandelion protruding through the asphalt path.

'What if they don't, though?' Daisy halted next to Lucy. 'I mean, suppose they don't find the killer or get the papers back? What then?'

Kitty found both girls looking at her as if expecting her to have the answer. 'I don't know. I'm sure they will catch whoever it is. They cannot keep us all here forever. Inspector Greville is very well thought of though, and Sir Horace is no fool, so I'm sure they will solve the case.'

They resumed their stroll, Muffy running on ahead of them on her lead.

'Does your boyfriend tell you anything about the case, Kitty?' Daisy asked.

'Daisy!' Lucy glared at her friend.

'Matt is not my boyfriend. We aren't walking out together, and I only really know what you know.' She was aware that her cheeks had pinked slightly. Partly because she wasn't being strictly truthful but also because she never liked to think too hard about her relationship with Matt. Just lately she had wondered what it would be like if their friendship were to change into something closer. Sometimes she thought that there might be a spark between them, like earlier, before her aunt had interrupted them.

Daisy sniffed as if she found Kitty's statement hard to believe.

'What about you and Aubrey?' Kitty asked.

Daisy frowned as they turned the corner to continue past the vehicles parked on the gravel. 'I wish he would tell his mother about us. I really ought to meet her soon. Perhaps when this is over we can think about announcing our engagement publicly, and planning our wedding.'

The scent of woodsmoke filled the air as they rounded the front of the black police car and Matt's new motorcycle. A pile of ancient leaves and a few branches was heaped untidily on the scrubby grass. A thin spiral of smoke coiled lazily into an increasingly grey sky. An empty wheelbarrow and a rake were placed nearby. Muffy's attention was caught by a movement on the far side of the ground and she bolted towards the bonfire, tearing the lead from Lucy's hand.

'Muffy!' Her cousin set off in pursuit with the others following after her.

As they drew nearer the fire, the other two continued after the little dog who clearly thought it was a great game. Kitty paused as something struck her as odd about the fire. The pyre seemed badly constructed and unlike the usual neat piles she'd seen previously that her uncle's gardeners made when they were clearing rubbish.

Kitty looked more closely; surely there was something else in the pile of garden detritus that didn't belong there? She picked up a long stick lying on the ground and gave the smouldering heap a poke. To her astonishment, hidden under the garden rubbish were garments. Men's clothes. Moving swiftly, she hooked out the remains of the items before they could be consumed by the flames.

Daisy and Lucy came panting back up to her, Muffy once more secured.

'Kitty, whatever are you doing?' Lucy asked.

'Oh, what on earth?' Daisy asked as she saw what Kitty had rescued from the bonfire. Her face paled beneath her make-up as she saw the clothes.

'I think we need to fetch Inspector Greville,' Kitty said.

'I'll go.' Daisy set off at once towards the front door of the manor, her heels clicking rapidly across the ground.

'What is all this?' Lucy stared at the garments as Kitty pulled them out straight with the end of her stick.

'I don't know but whatever it is, someone wanted these things destroyed.'

The sounds of footsteps approaching behind them caused them to turn. The inspector was hastening towards them, accompanied by Sir Horace, Matt and Daisy.

'I noticed these hidden in the bonfire.' Kitty waved her hand at the pile of clothes spread in front of her. 'I couldn't see a reason why someone would be trying to destroy good clothes in this way.'

'Well spotted,' Sir Horace said. 'I agree, it's very strange.' He and the inspector bent to examine the finds. A dark twill pair of trousers, dark shirt and cap. 'No labels.'

Muffy sniffed curiously at the cap and Lucy tugged the lead to move the dog away before she could make off with her prize.

'Thank you, ladies.' The inspector waved over one of his constables and gave some instructions.

'Do they belong to the man from the lake?' Lucy asked.

'Unlikely,' Matt said.

'Then who?' Lucy began, stopping when she saw Daisy's expression.

'There is little point in speculating. We will check these items against measurements of all the men in the house, including the staff.'

Daisy's brow cleared when the inspector mentioned the staff and Kitty suddenly realised that Daisy was concerned that either her brother or Aubrey could be the owner of the clothes.

The party turned and started back towards the house. Lucy and Daisy were in front with Sir Horace and Muffy, while Matt walked on one side of Kitty with the inspector on the other.

'Inspector Greville, I wondered if it might be worth Kitty taking a look at Frau Fiser's room? I know you and your men have already searched it, but it struck me just that maybe a woman's eye might see something we may have missed.'

The inspector glanced at Kitty, then at Matt. 'Well, I can't see as it would do any harm if you would oblige us, Miss Underhay?'

'Certainly, I'd be happy to try and help.' Kitty blinked in astonishment. She had been wondering if they had discovered anything in Viola's room that might provide a clue to her killer. However, she hadn't envisaged that Inspector Greville might allow her to assist in any way.

The inspector delved in the pocket of his jacket and handed a Matt an old-fashioned iron key. 'Please ensure you relock it when you've finished in there, Captain Bryant.'

'Certainly, Inspector.'

'And report anything at all that you may find that could shed light on these murders or the missing papers.' He looked directly at Kitty.

'Of course,' she agreed. She thought she detected his moustache lifting slightly, as if faintly amused by her ready acquiescence, before he strode forward to catch up with the others, leaving herself and Matt to dawdle along behind them.

'Who do you think those clothes belong to?' Kitty asked as soon as the others were out of earshot.

'You saw Daisy's reaction, then?'

'I'm guessing she recognised them. Aubrey or Rupert?'

A mischievous glint was in his eyes. 'Are we making a bet?'

'Rupert,' Kitty replied, smiling in response.

'Not Aubrey? Interesting.' Matt openly grinned at her.

'No. I can't see Aubrey sneaking around at night dressed in dark clothing. Besides, assuming whoever these clothes belong to is connected to the theft and the murders, then it couldn't be him. He can go where he wants and see what he wants without impediment. If he was a traitor, he could have made copies at any point of those missing documents. Plus, he already had ready access to the keys, he wouldn't need to make copies. My money is on Rupert; his manner seems to have changed lately.'

'No rank outsiders in the running?' he asked.

They strolled along the terrace away from the sitting room. 'No, I don't think Mr Henderson would fit in those clothes and they looked good quality. Too expensive for our most recent corpse or for one of the servants.'

'I agree. I don't think Mr Harmon would go sneaking around like a burglar, and he too has access to keys.'

The hall was deserted as they entered the front of the house, their footsteps sounding on the black and white marble tiled hallway. Kitty gave an involuntary shiver and Matt gave her a concerned look. 'Are you all right, Kitty? You don't have to do this, you know.'

'I'm fine about it, really. It just struck me how easy it is for anyone to wander in and around the house. I think someone was stepping on my grave, as Aunt Livvy would say.'

She knew the other house guests were in the sitting room, that the servants were behind the green baize door and that her uncle and aunt were in other rooms nearby. Still, the eerie silence and the sudden awareness of everything that had happened had struck a chill deep inside her and she was glad that Matt was next to her as they ascended the stairs.

The wide landing was equally empty as they passed the various bedroom doors until they reached the room Viola had occupied.

'Still sure about this?' Matt asked as he drew the key from his pocket ready to insert it in the lock.

'Of course.' She did her best to sound blasé and confident.

Matt unlocked Viola's door and they stepped inside the room. It was a pleasant room, smaller than her own with no dressing room but nicely decorated in shades of pink. The air still smelled faintly of the oriental rose scent Viola had favoured. Kitty automatically glanced at the bed, relieved to see it had been remade without even a crumple on the satin quilted eiderdown to show where Viola had been killed. She tried not to think of how the scene must have appeared to Matt.

Viola's earrings were in a small china dish on the bedside cabinet next to a carafe of water and a glass. A pale lavender silk eye mask lay discarded next to them with a small travelling alarm clock in a leather case.

Matt had strolled over to the window and pulled the part-drawn curtains back, allowing more light into the room. 'There is a good view from here over the meadow path to the lake. You can even see the gardener's hut through the trees and the corner of the games pavilion next to the tennis court. We were right when we calculated the position of her room.'

Kitty joined him to look out. 'You think she saw something and went out to investigate?'

'I don't think we can rule it out.'

Kitty turned away and opened Viola's wardrobe. 'There are several pairs of shoes in here, including a pair of walking shoes. If she had planned to go out, she would have changed her shoes for something more suitable.' She bent to examine Viola's evening shoes. She recognised them as the ones she regularly wore. 'These aren't the kind of shoe one would choose to wear to go along a rough path towards a lake at night.'

'Fair point. She saw someone or something out there then, and dashed out in a hurry. Or else she didn't come up to her room before heading up to the lake.'

'You said Doctor Carter indicated the mystery man's body had been in the water for some time, so it can't have been the murder or the killer moving the body that she saw, so what was it?' she mused.

'Our man in black?' Matt suggested. 'She may have thought it was the person she believed was watching her. She could have been eager to apprehend him since no one appeared to be taking her concerns seriously.'

Kitty closed the wardrobe door and moved to take a seat before the dressing table. A small pile of art history books were stacked at one end, next to a vase containing some almost dead roses in a crystal vase. More colourful bead necklaces lay in a long china tray with some glittering coloured stone brooches. A bottle of perfume, a hairbrush and comb lay where Viola had left them, and to the side stood a small black-and-white photograph of a man and woman in a leather case.

Kitty picked it up to examine more closely. 'A wedding photograph. I assume of Viola and her husband. The woman looks like a happier, younger version of Viola.'

'Greville said he was killed in an automobile accident crossing the street. Viola believed it was deliberate because of his religion and beliefs. She left Austria for Paris and was working there when your uncle offered her this position restoring the mural.'

'That's so sad. Poor Viola.' Kitty set the frame down gently. She opened the drawers of the dressing table and peered inside. 'More jewellery, some cosmetics.' She closed them again and swivelled around on the stool to survey the room.

'What is it?' Matt asked.

Kitty stood and went to the chest of drawers, opening and closing each drawer in turn as she checked the contents. 'It's not here.'

'What's not here?'

Kitty looked around the room once more, then spotted Viola's cream leather handbag. She pounced and upended the contents onto the bed. A powder compact, handkerchief, pencil and small purse tumbled out onto the counterpane.

'Where is Viola's notebook?'

Matt stared at her.

'Viola had a small notebook, she took it everywhere. She made notes in it from her reference books and Lucy said when she went to see Aunt Hortense after seeing Inspector Greville she waved the notebook around saying she had proof her life was in danger.' Excitement built in her stomach. If Inspector Greville had Viola's notebook, then surely he would have said so.

'What are you doing?'

Kitty had dropped to her knees and was peering under the bed. 'Checking to see if she hid it somewhere or if the killer took it.' There was nothing visible under the ornate wooden bed frame. Undeterred, she jumped up and started to feel between the mattress and the frame. 'Help me look.'

Matt shook his head and began to feel under the mattress on the other side of the bed. 'Nothing.'

'Then it's gone. We need to tell the inspector.' She started towards the door.

'Kitty, wait.'

Something in his voice made her stop. Turning back, she saw that his face was sombre, and she could see the concern in his eyes. Her pulse kicked up a notch. 'What is it?'

He took hold of her hands. 'Let's not talk about this to anyone except the inspector.'

His fingers warmed her flesh where she had suddenly chilled at the note in his voice.

'Matt?'

'Whoever has that book may have killed for it. Listen, I think perhaps you should leave here, go back to the Dolphin until this man is caught.'

She slid her hands free from his grasp and tore her gaze from his. 'No, I couldn't abandon Lucy. She's my cousin, she needs me. I won't be sent away.' She couldn't believe he'd suggested that she leave. Just when she had thought they were working together as partners to solve the case.

Matt escorted Kitty back down the main stairs and went to find the inspector. If he wasn't in possession of Viola's notebook, then Kitty was right. Whoever had murdered Viola had probably taken the book.

The creeping sense of unease that had filled him ever since Nanny Thoms's murder was now running at full pelt. One of the house party was clearly the murderer. His hunch that Kitty might spot something that the police had missed seemed to have paid off.

Kitty was clearly angry at his suggestion that she leave the manor, but his concern was purely for her safety. He toyed with the idea of suggesting to the inspector that Kitty should leave since she wasn't involved in the murders. Only the knowledge that she would murder him herself if she found out he'd even considered such a thing prevented him.

Greville was in the study with Lord Medford and Sir Horace. He appraised the three men of Kitty's discovery.

'Is this true? Viola kept a notebook?' Greville demanded. He pulled his own notebook from his pocket and began to leaf through the notes he'd made.

Lord Medford sighed. 'She had a small book she used to scribble in. It was always either in her hands or in her bag.'

'And neither of you thought to mention this before?' Greville muttered, glaring at Lord Medford and Sir Horace. His fingers stilled. 'How did we overlook this? Lucy mentioned it in her interview.' He scowled at his companions.

Kitty's uncle looked shamefaced. 'She used to make notes from her reference books, and I believe Nanny Thoms gave her some recipes for jam. It didn't occur to me that there might be anything of significance written in there. I thought you knew about it.'

Greville scowled. 'This man is making fools of us. Frau Fiser's notebook is missing, the woman was murdered under our noses and still no sign of the papers.' He summoned a constable and immediately ordered a discreet search for the missing book.

'Now look here, Greville,' Lord Medford spluttered a protest.

'Arguing won't help at this point. We know about the notebook now, and until we find it, don't forget that we have another lead with those clothes. We need to find out who they belong to,' Sir Horace said as he drew a cigarette from his case and tapped it on the lid before striking a match and lighting up.

'The odds are either Banks or Henderson,' the inspector said.

'You think one of them is our man?' Sir Horace asked and blew out a thin stream of smoke.

'I told you about Banks right from the start. A bounder if ever there was one, with his communist tendencies,' Lord Medford muttered.

'I fancy young Banks is somewhat on the horns of a dilemma at present.'

The attention of everyone present fastened on the inspector at this pronouncement, Matt included.

'What do you mean?' Lord Medford demanded.

'Our youthful friend is very vocal about his causes. His political beliefs about the rights of the working man, etcetera.'

'Undermining society and stirring up disquiet. Load of rot. Never done a stroke of work in his life,' Lord Medford interjected.

Matt exchanged a glance with Sir Horace. 'What kind of dilemma?'

'Young Banks is the great nephew of the recently deceased Lord Woodcomb.'

'Ha.' Sir Horace's expression cleared. 'Bertie Woodcomb was a bachelor, used to rattle around in that great house of his, Thurscomb, like a dried-up old pea.'

Inspector Greville cleared his throat. 'Precisely. Mr Banks is now the new Lord Woodcomb and owner of Thurscomb house.'

Lord Medford's mouth gaped open and he stared at the inspector. 'That wastrel has inherited Woodcomb's title and Thurscomb House?'

'Apparently, Rupert and Daisy's father fell out with Lord Woodcomb before Daisy was born. Rupert was under the impression that although he would eventually inherit the title, his great uncle had disinherited him from the property and the estate. It appears this wasn't the case. He has the house, land, title and now a considerable bank balance.'

Matt let out a low whistle as he contemplated what the inheritance would mean for Rupert and Daisy. 'I see what you mean about a dilemma. With Rupert carrying on about the rights of the impoverished working man and all, now he's been left substantial assets.'

'Quite,' the inspector remarked drily.

'Is Daisy aware of their change in fortune?' Matt asked. He wondered if she too had inherited anything from her great uncle. Even if she hadn't, surely Rupert would settle some money on his sister? The dynamics of the household had suddenly changed considerably.

'I don't believe she has received any bequest in her own right, and as far as we're aware, Mr Banks hasn't shared his good fortune with his sister as yet. The estate is still going through probate. Certainly her fiancé is unaware of this turn of events.' The inspector looked at Lord Medford.

'Good Lord, yes, Aubrey would have said something, I'm sure. I shan't mention anything to him of course.'

Greville turned his attention to Matt. 'Now, back to the notebook. I hope you impressed on Miss Underhay the need to stay silent on the subject?'

Matt dug his hands deep in his trouser pockets and sighed uncomfortably. 'Kitty won't say anything, sir, but do you think it safe for her and the other ladies to remain here?' The question popped out despite his intention not to voice it aloud. He noticed Lord Medford's brow crease in alarm as if the consideration of his wife and daughter's safety had not occurred to him.

Greville stroked his moustache thoughtfully. 'I see no immediate danger for Lady Medford or your daughter.' He looked at Lord Medford. 'And I have found Miss Underhay to be both clever and resourceful. She will take care not to place herself in danger. Miss Banks, I think, is also unlikely to come to harm.'

Lord Medford's brow cleared. 'Hortense has warned the young ladies to stay together and to keep to the house until this villain is caught. Any news from the foreign office?' His attention turned to Sir Horace.

'If you mean, "is there any indication that an enemy of the country has received those papers?" then there is no news. This is a good thing. By now, if there had been a leak then one of our people would have heard a whisper.' Sir Horace extinguished the remains of his cigarette in the large crystal ashtray on Lord Medford's desk.

The long case clock in the hall struck the hour.

'I'll leave you to prepare for dinner. I'll talk to Banks and Henderson tomorrow about the contents of the bonfire. I don't think it will do any harm to leave them to worry for the evening.' Inspector Greville collected his hat from the hook on the back of the oak study door. 'If there are any urgent developments, call me immediately.'

CHAPTER EIGHTEEN

Alice was in the bedroom laying out Kitty's dress ready for the evening.

'I thought the dark red one might make you feel a bit more cheery tonight, miss.' Alice smoothed the chiffon fabric with a loving hand.

'Thank you, Alice.' Kitty flopped down on the fireside chair and slipped off her shoes and wriggled her stocking-clad toes, relishing the freedom of the cool air on her flesh.

'Shall I go and run you a bath, miss? Put some of them smelly bath salt things in?' Alice offered.

'I am so glad you came with me.' Kitty smiled at her maid.

Dimples flashed in Alice's thin face. 'It in't half been exciting.'

'That's one way of looking at it.' She found the girl's bubbly enthusiasm for life infectious.

'The gardeners told Gladys you found a man's clothes in a bonfire by the tennis courts. They didn't set that fire either, miss.'

'Oh?' Kitty asked.

'No, miss.' Alice straightened the dressing table set. 'They had raked all the rubbish up in a heap and put it in the barrow as Missus doesn't like smoke getting into the house, so they was going to wheel it further away and burn it. Mr Golightly was fair put out. He'd had to leave his barrow to go with your aunt round the rose garden.'

'So, whoever wanted to get rid of the clothes must have seen the debris and spied an opportunity.' Kitty frowned. She wondered if

Inspector Greville was in possession of that information yet, and whether she would get a lecture from Matt about interfering if she mentioned it.

'I'll go draw your bath, miss, or else you'll be late for dinner.' Alice slipped out of the room, closing the door behind her. Kitty closed her eyes and leaned her head back against the chair, weariness washing over her.

She shouldn't have been so angry when Matt had suggested she return to Dartmouth. She knew he had merely wanted to protect her. If she were honest with herself, she was a little frightened by recent events, but at the same time she had never felt more alive. Being at the hotel doing the same work, day in, day out, made her feel trapped. Since Matt had arrived and they had become embroiled in their joint adventures she had felt as if she had a purpose, as if her wits were finally being properly utilised. She had also been enjoying the closer relationship with Matt, and if she was being honest with herself, hadn't hated it every time Daisy referred to him as her boyfriend.

Alice bustled back into the room holding a thick white towel over her arm. 'Take your wrapper with you, Miss Kitty.' She scooped up Kitty's dressing gown and handed it to her.

'Thank you.' Kitty took the bundle and, yawning, walked across the landing to the bathroom. The steamy air held the faint scent of perfume from the salts added to the water.

She locked the door and undressed, placing her clothes on the wooden chair next to the bath. The water was deliciously warm and soothing against her skin. She closed her eyes and slid down into the water. It would be all too easy to allow herself to drift off to sleep for a few minutes.

She must in fact have nodded off for a short time. The water was cooling when she heard someone trying the door of the bathroom. Kitty went to call out that the room was occupied but something about the almost furtive testing of the handle gave her pause.

Carefully, Kitty eased forward and stood up, being careful not to splash. She picked up her towel and wrapped it securely about her person, shivering a little as the cool air met her damp skin. Despite her care, she caught the chair and it scraped on the wooden boards of the bathroom floor. Immediately the fumbling of the lock stopped. Cursing under her breath she rushed to the door, turned the key and cracked the door open to peek out.

The corridor was empty. 'Drat.' She closed the door and scrambled into her dressing gown. Gathering her things together, she returned to her room.

'I was about to knock the door for you, miss; you're cutting it a bit fine.' Alice clicked her tongue as she helped Kitty to finish drying off.

'Alice, did you see or hear anyone in the corridor just now?'

The girl paused from where she was drying Kitty's foot. 'No, miss.' Her bright eyes held a perplexed expression. 'Why?'

'Someone tried the door to the bathroom, and there was something about the way they did it that wasn't right.'

'They din't get in, miss?' Alice was horrified at the thought.

'No, annoyingly I caught the chair and made a noise so they moved off before I could see who it was.' The incident had left Kitty feeling uncomfortable.

'You must tell Captain Bryant, miss, and be careful. I din't like what Cook saw in the leaves. A coffin, remember. The other staff say she's really good at telling the future from the leaves. She saw a medical problem for Mrs Jenkinson, the housekeeper, and blow me if her lumbago didn't start up the very next day.' Alice had continued assisting her to dress while she'd been talking.

She rolled on her stockings and secured the suspenders before shimmying into her dress with help from Alice. 'Sit down, miss, as I can do your hair.'

Kitty perched on the stool in front of the dressing table mirror. 'I wonder what they hoped to achieve by entering the bathroom?'

Alice's reflection in the mirror revealed a troubled expression. 'I don't know, but I don't like it. Seems to me that whoever killed Miss Viola and Nanny Thoms is proper off his nut. He must think as you know something if he was trying to get in the bathroom. He could have held you under the water and drowned you. That might be what become of that poor soul they found in the lake. I seen a picture about that the other week.' Her forehead creased in concentration as she finished styling Kitty's hair. 'There, just your earrings now, miss, and I think you're ready.'

Kitty obediently took the elegant gold earrings that Alice was holding out and fastened them on her earlobes.

'The dinner gong will be going in a minute.' Alice stepped back as Kitty stood and slipped on her evening shoes.

'Alice, I want you to be careful. Make sure that you lock the door if you leave the room to go downstairs, and if you're in here later, lock yourself in. Only open it when you hear my voice.' Kitty picked up her wrap.

'I will, miss.' Alice nodded earnestly.

Kitty was relieved to see her cousin walking along the corridor towards the stairs when she left her room. She didn't want to be alone just at the moment.

'You look smashing, Kitty, so calm and unruffled. I wish I was more like you,' Lucy said. She smiled and linked arms with her. Her cousin was dressed in a dark grey chiffon dress in a sleeveless style, not dissimilar to her own, with a silver diamanté ornament sparkling in her dark hair.

'Thank you, so do you, and I assure you these events have unnerved me quite as much as you.' They made their way downstairs together and headed for the sitting room.

'Might just about have time for a quick drink before dinner.' Lucy winked at her as they entered and released her arm. 'I have a feeling we may need one.'

Everyone was already assembled and most of the party had a glass in their hands so Lucy quickly made her way to the drinks trolley. Matt stood near the French doors, now closed for the evening. For a second, Kitty forgot she was still a little cross with him as his gaze met hers.

Some men suit evening wear and she had always thought it suited Matt. His lean frame appeared to advantage in a dinner jacket, and he lost the slightly rakish look he favoured in his everyday clothes, looking more polished and elegant.

She moved to join him at the window, and he bent his head to lightly kiss her cheek in greeting, sending a frisson of electricity through her body.

'You look very nice,' he murmured in her ear and heat rose in her cheeks at the compliment.

'Thank you, Alice suggested I wear something a little cheery this evening.' She caught Lucy grinning at her from near the fireplace and hastily turned her face away from her cousin.

The dinner gong sounded from the hallway and there was a rustling of satin and clinking of glasses as everyone moved towards the dining room. Kitty caught hold of Matt's sleeve as he prepared to follow the others.

'Now don't lecture me, Matt, but someone tried to get into the bathroom just now while I was in there.' She kept her voice low so the rest of the party wouldn't overhear her as they trailed at the back of the group.

'I take it this wasn't simply someone hoping to bag the bath?' he asked.

'No, it was odd, quite surreptitious, as if they knew I was in there and… I don't know, I can't explain it. It sounds silly now saying it out loud.'

He placed a comforting hand on hers. 'I understand. You aren't the kind of girl given to paranoid imaginings. I don't like it, though.

I meant what I said earlier about you returning to Dartmouth. I want you to be safe.'

They lingered in the hall for a moment as the others all went to take their places at the table.

'Why would I be in any particular danger though, Matt? You should be more at risk than me. I got you into this mess and I'm not going to leave you in it. Besides, Lucy really does need me here.'

He heaved an audible sigh. 'All right, old thing, but I'm not happy about it. Please stay on your guard.'

Her spirits rose at the familiar endearment. 'I will.' She risked a quick kiss on his cheek and darted into the dining room, leaving him to follow her.

Like lunch, dinner passed in a sombre fashion. Lady Medford appeared determined that they should avoid all mention of the murders or her husband's missing documents. Rupert was still uncharacteristically silent, Sir Horace and her uncle were discussing politics in Europe, Lucy and Daisy were planning a trip to a party at the home of a mutual friend in a few weeks' time. Her aunt was talking about the best time of year to move rhododendrons, while Mr Henderson shovelled overloaded forkfuls of food into his mouth and nodded in agreement. Aubrey seemed lost in his own thoughts, merely jumping or wincing every time Henderson's knife scraped the china dinner plate.

There appeared to be a consensual air of relief when the last of the dessert dishes were collected and they were free to leave the room. Her aunt, as usual, summoned the ladies of the party to the drawing room for coffee, while her uncle proposed port in the library to the gentlemen.

Kitty dutifully accompanied her cousin and Daisy as her aunt led the way. Matt gave a quick farewell squeeze of her fingers before departing with the rest of the gentlemen. Muffy appeared and curled up next to Lucy as Lady Medford dispensed coffee in dainty china cups and saucers along with a mini lecture on sticking together until the maniac was caught.

'It's pretty horrific, isn't it?' Daisy said as she sipped her drink. 'One of us could be the murderer.'

Lady Medford snorted. 'Don't be ridiculous, Daisy dear. This latest corpse shows it must be the work of an outsider.'

'How so?' Lucy asked.

'The theft of your father's papers may be coincidental. If Nanny got up in the night to prevent an intruder, then he could have attacked her.'

'But what about Viola? And this vagrant?' Lucy frowned.

'The vagrant was apparently killed before all this began. This maniac could have seen the miscreant up to no good.'

'And Viola?' Lucy continued.

'He obviously tried to break into the house once more. He could have thought Viola had jewels or money in her room. She may have awoken as he was robbing her.' Lady Medford leaned back, a pleased expression on her face.

Lucy exchanged a speaking glance with Kitty.

'Oh, stop, just stop. I can't bear it.' Daisy jumped up from her seat and slammed her cup and saucer down on the tray, making the crockery jangle.

'Daisy, dear.' Lucy tipped Muffy from her lap and went to comfort her friend.

Daisy's body trembled as Lucy embraced her. 'It's so awful, everyone looking at everyone else and I know that beastly police-man thinks Rupert did it and that is just too awful for words.' A sob burst from Daisy's lips.

'Oh, Daisy, I'm sure he doesn't.' Lucy steered her to a seat.

Lady Medford snorted. 'Of course he does. If by some chance it's not a vagrant then he'd be a fool if he didn't suspect him.'

'Mother!'

'Well, if it isn't a maniac, though I strongly believe it must be, then Rupert must be a suspect. I'm sorry, Daisy dear, but you must face facts.'

Daisy fled from the room, her handkerchief pressed to her mouth and tears streaming down her cheeks.

'Now look what you've done.' Lucy hurried after her, Muffy at her heels.

'Well, really,' Lady Medford huffed.

Kitty swallowed the last of her coffee. She could well understand Daisy's distress on her brother's behalf.

'And you, my dear niece? Do you think Rupert is the man or do you agree with me that it must be an outsider?' her aunt asked. 'You seem to be privy to the inspector's thoughts, unlike the rest of us.'

'I don't know Inspector Greville's thoughts. I'm sure he is taking all possibilities into account.' For a wild moment Kitty considered whether her aunt might be capable of murder. She had opportunity, possibly motive and she was certainly tall and strong enough to be capable of the act.

'Humph, I'm not seeing much sign of progress in the case. Really, with all of us terrified for our lives, it's a wonder Sir Horace has not put his foot down.'

'I'm certain the inspector is doing all he can. We are not party to all the discoveries he may have made so cannot see any progress, but Sir Horace of course is better placed,' Kitty said.

Her aunt appeared to ponder her reply. Kitty decided to seize the moment and try to tackle her aunt once more about her mother's visit.

'Now we are alone, Aunt Hortense, will you not share with me what happened when my mother visited you? I realise it was a long time ago now, but surely you can see how important this is to me.'

Her aunt pursed her lips, a dull flush creeping along her jawline. 'I do not wish to offend you, Kitty, but you must understand that the relationship between myself and your father has been strained for many years.'

'My father's behaviour is reprehensible on many counts.' Kitty's pulse quickened, it seemed as if she might finally hear directly from her aunt's lips the purpose of her mother's visit.

The admission appeared to mollify her aunt somewhat. 'Your father had told me he was married on one of his infrequent visits. You know your uncle disapproves of Edgar. His decision to return to America at the start of the war to avoid enlisting was appalling and your uncle's situation could have been badly compromised by his perfidy.'

Kitty gave a nod of understanding.

Her aunt continued, 'Your uncle refused to acknowledge the relationship and insisted that there be no contact. I received infrequent letters due to the war but naturally I could not let anyone know, as your uncle's position had to be considered and his wishes as head of the household respected. The last message came at Christmas in nineteen-fifteen. I was aware that Edgar had a child, but I was unsure if you and your mother had accompanied him to America.'

'My mother and I were in America before the war when I was a baby, then we lived in London up until the outbreak of hostilities. My mother and I returned to live at the Dolphin when my father went to America.'

'I was unaware of this until your mother visited in the June of nineteen-sixteen. She had, she said, sent messages, but these did not reach me. Hence her arrival at Enderley was a source of great consternation, especially given your uncle's express wishes regarding contact.' Her aunt sighed. 'I was placed in a very difficult position. It was fortunate that your uncle was away from home when she arrived.'

Kitty could understand what her aunt meant. It must have been very awkward at the height of hostilities to have her mother suddenly arrive on her doorstep.

'Any way,' her aunt continued, 'I do heartily regret that I wasn't more welcoming towards her and that I didn't take more notice of you.' To her credit, she did look shamefaced at her admission. 'I instructed the servants not to mention her visit to your uncle and I got rid of her as soon as I could because I expected your uncle's return from London at any time. He had contracts with the war office, and we were about to move back there within a few days.'

Kitty swallowed the lump that had appeared in her throat as she thought of her mother making the difficult, war time journey to a hostile house. She fumbled in her small silver evening purse for her handkerchief.

'I appreciate this is distressing for you, and I confess, I am ashamed of my part in the affair, but I did not know your mother had gone missing until I heard from your father asking that I reconcile myself with you, for your sake, if not for his.' Her aunt reached across and gave her free hand an awkward pat.

Kitty blew her nose. 'I do understand.'

'Your mother had letters from your father with her, photographs of you as a family. She had left her marriage lines and your birth certificate at the hotel.'

'That would be why we couldn't find any letters or photographs from my father when she disappeared. We thought it was strange but of course she had them with her.' Kitty realised she now had the answer to something that had puzzled her for years.

'She had regular contact with Edgar, as regular as it could be at that time. Sometimes several letters would arrive altogether if there had been delays due to shipping and bombing.' Her aunt shook her head. 'You were very young then, and Lucy was only an infant, but it was a terrible time with the zeppelins and the war losses.'

Kitty thought of Matt. He had suffered terribly at the Front, the effects still haunted him. It rankled that he told her so little of what had happened to him or how he had lost his wife.

'The letters had stopped but Elowed had heard a rumour that he'd been seen in England. She didn't see how this could be, as the last letter she'd received had said he intended to remain in America, and it would have been both difficult and unwise to return then unless he planned to enlist.'

Now it was Kitty's turn to snort. 'An unlikely occurrence.'

Her aunt smiled. 'Exactly, but your mother was worried. She wanted to know if I had heard from him. I'm sorry to say we had an argument. I had no desire to become embroiled in Edgar's problems when I had enough of my own at the time. Your mother stayed the night. I could hardly throw her out, it would have been the talk of the village. Next morning, she left to take the early train.'

'Did she say where she was going?' This was the big question. It might give the next clue to her mother's intentions.

Lady Medford's brow creased in concentration. 'I've thought about this a great deal since you arrived and poor, dear Nanny slipped up and called you by your mother's name. I rather think she wanted to try to discover if your father had chanced his arm and gone to the family house in Ireland, but I could be mistaken. I suggested she might contact a rather disreputable former connection of your father's in Exeter. I wish I could recall his exact address, but it's been so long. Dawkins, I think his name was.'

'Despite everything, you decided to agree to my father's request to reconnect with me?' Kitty asked. She had wondered what might have prompted her aunt's invitation.

'Lucy saw the telegram. Your father knew I would not ignore a telegram. I was curious and Lucy so eager to at least meet you, she persuaded your uncle that we should invite you.' Her aunt smiled and reached out to touch Kitty's hand. 'I hope you know that I'm very glad we did, my dear, despite all the awful events of this week.'

CHAPTER NINETEEN

Matt was seated in the billiard room watching Thomas Henderson and Rupert Banks play when the door cracked open and Kitty entered. The two players barely paid her any attention as she walked over to join him.

She placed a cut-glass tumbler of whisky in front of him and one for herself on the small rosewood side table before taking a seat in one of the dark green leather tub chairs next to him. He wondered what had happened in the drawing room to drive Kitty to whisky.

'Your match, Henderson. I can't seem to concentrate tonight.' Rupert stepped back from the billiards table and replaced his cue on the rack. He collected his jacket from one of the chairs and slipped it on. 'Dash it all, a confounded button has come off, wonder when that went missing.' He examined the cuff.

Henderson grunted an assent and pocketed the money which lay on the side of the table, a smirk of satisfaction on his face. He glanced around the floor, 'Bad luck, old boy. I think I'll call it a night, then.' He inclined his head towards Matt and Kitty, shook hands with Rupert, and left.

Rupert flung himself down on one of the remaining free chairs.

'He's quite the player, isn't he?' Matt commented.

'Yes, he's got his own cue; the fellow's a bit of a shark,' Rupert said. His countenance was downcast, and he appeared deeply affected by the events of the day.

Matt took a sip of whisky. 'It's been a rum kind of day all round.' He looked at Kitty. Her face was pale in the soft mellow light of the green glass-shaded side lamp.

'Very queer. It's so horrid, isn't it? Everyone suspecting everyone else is just beastly.' She picked up her glass and swished the liquid around as if watching the light glinting on the sides of the glass.

Rupert stared gloomily at the pattern on the Turkish rug. 'Do you think there'll be an arrest soon?' He directed the enquiry to Matt.

'I don't know. I believe the inspector has more lines of enquiry to follow.' He picked his words carefully. Rupert had to be aware that he was one of the prime suspects.

'Who do you think is responsible?'

Rupert's question took Matt by surprise. Not that he had asked, but that he had asked in so direct a manner.

'There are a number of suspects, I believe. The inspector does not share all his thoughts with either Sir Horace or myself.'

'I expect I'm one of the suspects. It has to be one of us, doesn't it? No use of course saying that it wasn't me. I expect everyone says that,' Rupert groaned.

'Well, was it you?' Kitty asked. 'Your sister seems very distressed.'

It had occurred to Matt, and no doubt to Inspector Greville and Sir Horace, that Daisy and Rupert could be working together.

'Daisy has always been a sensitive soul. She feels things more deeply than people give her credit for,' Rupert said.

Silence hung heavily in the air between them. Matt noticed that Rupert had made no further protestations of his innocence. He took another sip of whisky and waited.

'Can you tell Greville I'll see him tomorrow? There are things I need to get off my chest.' Rupert rose from his seat as if he had suddenly come to a decision.

'I expect the inspector will be here first thing.' Matt wondered what Rupert had to say. A confession, perhaps? Was he the document thief? Or the murderer? Or both?

'Good.' Rupert nodded good night to Kitty and left the billiards room.

'What do you suppose that was about?' she asked, her tone thoughtful.

'Clearly, there is something he feels the inspector should know.' Matt watched Kitty as she stared into her glass, apparently deep in thought.

'What's the matter, old girl? Something has happened tonight, I take it? Or is it the incident in the bathroom that is playing on your mind?' He watched for her reaction. Kitty had the kind of features that displayed her thoughts and emotions.

'I finally had the opportunity tonight to talk to Aunt Hortense about my mother's visit to Enderley the summer she vanished.' She took another swallow of whisky, shuddering a little at the taste.

'What did she have to say? Did you learn any more?' His interest was piqued by the turn in conversation. The mystery of Kitty's mother's disappearance was an ongoing puzzle with few clues to what had happened to her.

'I feel as if I finally have the answer to why there were no letters or photographs of my father in my mother's possessions. That, I suppose, is a relief.' Kitty met his gaze.

'Do you know where she was headed when she left from here?' He knew that neither the private detectives Kitty's grandmother had employed at the time nor the police had been able to find any clue to her intended destination. There had been several so-called sightings and a few hints but they had all come to nothing.

'Aunt Hortense wasn't sure. There was a rumour my father had been seen in England but neither my aunt nor my mother gave it much credence. My mother apparently thought that if he were anywhere other than England, then he might be at the family estate in Ireland. This too seems unlikely. Aunt Hortense suggested Mother may have gone back to Exeter to try to find someone my father knew back then, Dawkins, but she couldn't recall an address. She appears genuinely upset over what happened. But that isn't much help now.'

He watched helplessly as a tear trickled slowly down Kitty's cheek. 'Steady on, old thing, don't get upset.' He fumbled in his jacket pocket for a handkerchief. He pulled out a clean white linen square and passed it to her.

'Thank you.' She dabbed carefully at the corners of her eyes and gave him a watery smile. 'I don't know why I'm getting upset. It all happened so long ago. It must have been an awful time for everyone with the war…' Her voice trailed away.

His thoughts immediately went back to that summer. He had been in Belgium. It had been a dull, cold, wet month. Edith had written complaining of the difficulties in drying the washing and that she had needed to keep the fire burning all day in order to drive the chill from the house to keep baby Betty warm. Only a few months later, in September, she and Betty were dead, killed in a zeppelin raid.

His grip instinctively tightened around the whisky glass in his hand.

'Matt.' Kitty's voice recalled him to himself, her hand covering his with the tender warmth of her touch returning him to the present.

'I'm sorry.'

'You have no need to apologise to me,' she said.

He wondered how much of his story she knew. He was aware that she knew he had been married and that something had happened during the war to end this. He still struggled to talk of Edith and Betty even with Kitty, who he instinctively knew would understand. Unlike his father, who frequently stated his opinion that Matt should be over that business by now. He finished the whisky. His father, a retired military man himself, with many connections in government and the foreign office, was of the school that a stiff upper lip should be maintained, and one should never look back over personal tragedy.

'Makes a fellow maudlin and can't change anything,' were his parent's oft repeated words.

'I suppose we must wait now for morning to learn what Rupert wishes to impart or confess to Inspector Greville,' Kitty mused and drained her own glass.

'Do you feel he is our man?' Matt asked.

'I hope not, for Daisy's sake and for Lucy's. It is too awful to contemplate, but I suppose he could be. He has motivation politically, and opportunity.'

'And Daisy could be involved too,' Matt said.

Kitty shivered. 'Yes, I suppose so. It's quite frightening. I shall be so glad when this is over. I'm tired of suspecting everyone. I even began to wonder if Aunt Hortense could be involved earlier this evening.'

'Hmm, I think that is very unlikely. Come, I'll walk you to your room.' He stood and offered her his arm.

She accepted it and together they started for the hallway.

'Is Alice waiting up for you?' he asked.

'Yes, I instructed her to keep the door locked for her safety,' Kitty said as they walked slowly up the stairs.

'Lock the door behind you and place a chair before the door when you go to bed. Take no chances, Kitty,' he instructed quietly as they reached her room and she knocked gently to alert Alice.

'I will take care,' she said as the maid cracked the door open and peeped out at them, her face lighting into a smile when she saw them.

He gave the small of Kitty's back a gentle rub of reassurance as she turned to enter her room. He could only trust that she would heed his request.

Alice secured the door behind her and dragged a chair in front as Matt had instructed. 'I been thinking, Miss Kitty. I reckon it'll be nice to go home soon, back to the Dolphin away from this. It's frightening watching everybody and wondering if they want to do you in.'

'I suppose they don't really show you that side of things at the cinema,' Kitty mused as she unclipped her earrings and dropped them into the small china tray on her dressing table.

'No, but the police always get their man. Unless there's a big gun fight or something,' Alice said thoughtfully as she assisted Kitty with her dress.

'Goodness, let us hope there will be no guns and certainly no more deaths.' Kitty stepped into her nightgown as Alice hung her evening gown back in the wardrobe.

'Well, they are usually the pictures with those American mobsters in them.'

Kitty's thoughts immediately flew to her father and his entanglements with various unsavoury characters on the other side of the Atlantic. Alice's comment had reignited her anxiety for his safety and she appreciated fully for the first time her mother's concerns. No wonder she had returned to the safety of the Dolphin with Kitty when Kitty was a child.

It took her a long time to fall asleep and she lay awake in the darkness for quite a while listening to Alice's gentle snores from behind the curtain. It felt a long way from Dartmouth and the people she knew and loved in these small, still hours of darkness. She finally fell asleep shortly before dawn.

Alice woke her with a cup of tea an hour after her usual time. 'You looked so peaceful, miss, as I didn't think it would hurt if you was to be a bit later today. Shall I ask Cook for a breakfast tray?'

Kitty pushed herself into a sitting position and gratefully accepted the proffered cup of tea. 'No, I'll take breakfast downstairs, I don't wish to inconvenience Cook or Mrs Jenkinson. Has Inspector Greville arrived yet?'

'No, Miss Kitty, his motor car isn't on the drive. Do you think he'll arrest someone soon?' Alice lifted a lightweight cotton dress in a blue floral print from the wardrobe and held it up for Kitty to approve.

'I hope so. It's very hard on everyone at the moment and the longer it continues, the worse it will be.'

The dining room was deserted when she arrived downstairs. She helped herself to the last of the bacon and a slightly cold egg before the plates were cleared away. As she left the room, she heard masculine voices from the far end of the hall. Sir Horace and Matt were meeting the inspector near the front door.

Inspector Greville was divesting himself of his hat and outdoor coat when Matt spotted Kitty and greeted her.

'Good morning, Miss Underhay,' the inspector turned and added his own welcome as he passed his garments to Mr Harmon.

'Good morning, Inspector, Sir Horace, Matt,' she smiled at all three men.

'Inspector Greville, I must speak to you.' Rupert came hurrying towards them, a determined expression on his face. Sir Horace raised his eyebrows at the intensity of his approach.

'Would Lord Medford grant us the use of his library once more do you think?' the inspector asked.

'His Lordship is working at the laboratory with Mr Aubrey, sir. He has said you may avail yourself of any room you require,' Mr Harmon replied and disappeared with the inspector's hat and coat.

Kitty hovered around the edge of the group as they started towards the library.

'Come on,' Matt murmured in her ear.

She tagged along after them and slipped into the back of the room next to Matt as the inspector took a seat opposite Rupert and waited to hear what he had to say. Her heart thudded in her chest as Sir Horace perched on the corner of the library table. Surely Rupert was not about to confess to being the killer?

'Right then, Mr Banks, what is it you need to tell me?' Inspector Greville was poised with his notepad and pencil.

Rupert hunched forward in his chair; his brow set in a determined crease. 'The clothes you recovered from the bonfire in the garden, those were mine.'

Inspector Greville squiggled some hieroglyphics on the page, his face impassive. 'I see, sir.'

'It was a stupid thing to do, but I panicked. I knew that you had to regard me as one of your prime suspects and that if the clothes were discovered in my wardrobe, your men would attach the worst kind of significance to their presence.'

'Why would that be, Mr Banks?' The inspector eyed Rupert, a hard glint in his gaze and a deceptively mild tone to his voice.

'I wore those clothes a few weeks ago at a rally in Hyde Park to protest for the rights of the unemployed. I was present as one of the organisers and activists. The men had marched for some distance and there were agitators amongst the crowd.'

'I remember that rally. Dashed nuisance in terms of security. Didn't they have some left-wing keynote speakers? Damage done to property too. Communists,' Sir Horace huffed, his complexion taking on a puce tinge.

Rupert groaned. 'Whitewash on a government car and a statue. I knew there were splashes of paint on the clothes and I suppose I feared you would think they might be from Viola and the materials she was using for the mural.'

'Why not come forward straight away and explain yourself?' the inspector asked as he scribbled away in his book.

'Like I said, I panicked.' Rupert shifted on the chair.

'Several arrests were made that day. Still looking for some of the miscreants, I believe. As you said, a ministerial car and several statues were damaged, paint thrown, boughs pulled from trees.' Sir Horace scowled at Rupert.

'You realise this confession places you in a very poor light, Mr Banks? Is there anything further you feel I should know?' The way the inspector asked the question sent a shiver along Kitty's spine. There was something else in play here, but she wasn't sure what.

Before Rupert could say anything further, the library door banged open and Daisy appeared. Her face was chalk-white as she glared at the inspector and her brother.

'What's happening? Rupert, what are you doing?' She flew to Rupert's side, dropping to her knees at the side of his chair as she clung on to his arm.

'It's all right, Daisy. I was telling the inspector about the clothes.' He patted his sister's hand.

'Please, take a chair and join us, Miss Banks.' Inspector Greville stood and pulled another seat forward, placing it next to Rupert's.

Daisy took the seat, still clinging fast to her brother.

'Did you recognise the clothes as your brother's, Miss Banks, when Miss Underhay pulled them from the bonfire?' the inspector asked.

Daisy lowered her gaze before turning to Rupert in mute appeal.

'You had better tell the inspector the truth,' Rupert said, his tone gentle.

Daisy gave a small hiccupping sob. 'Yes, I knew, as soon as Kitty hooked them from the embers, that they belonged to Rupert. I didn't know what to do. I couldn't think why they would be there.' She produced a small lace-edged handkerchief and dabbed at her eyes.

'And yet you didn't think to say anything to us? You must be aware that this paints a concerning picture.' Sir Horace eyed Daisy sternly and she shrank back in her seat.

'I didn't know what to do. I wanted to speak to Rupert. I was so frightened. I couldn't understand how his clothes could have got there or why they would be burning.' Tears flowed freely down her cheeks.

'There is another matter which I would like to discuss.' Greville fixed them both with a hard stare.

Rupert looked confused and Daisy continued to cry quietly into her handkerchief.

'I had nothing to do with Lord Medford's missing documents or the murders, Inspector,' Rupert said.

'When my men conducted a thorough search of the gardener's shed near the lake, they made a very interesting discovery.' Greville leaned forward slightly in his chair with the air of a dog on the scent.

'I don't understand, Inspector. I've never been inside this hut. It's the domain of the gardeners and, I believe, Mr Henderson. Gardening is not my thing.' Rupert continued to look blank. 'Sorry, old chap, I haven't the foggiest.'

'Hidden inside an adapted can behind the garden equipment under a pile of hessian sacking we found something. More than one thing in fact. It was only due to the vigilance of my men that it was uncovered.' Greville continued to look keenly at the brother and sister.

Kitty's ears perked up. This was new information; no one had mentioned that Greville and his men had discovered anything interesting inside the hut.

'A crystal wireless receiving set. Ring any bells? No doubt to communicate with your commie friends,' Sir Horace interjected, the trace of puce on his cheeks now flooding further along his jaw in an angry tide.

Kitty felt Matt's stance stiffen beside her. This was clearly new information for him too.

Rupert drew himself up, anger sparking in his eyes, and Daisy gasped in astonishment.

'I can assure you, sir, I know nothing about a wireless set. I have never set foot inside the gardener's hut. Henderson is the most likely man to question about that. He's in and out of there all the time.' Rupert's eyes blazed.

'It's true. Why would Rupert have such a thing?' Daisy raised a tear-streaked face towards Sir Horace.

'To sneak around at the dead of night, dressed in black, to send secret messages or to receive instructions, spreading civil unrest? Perhaps to organise handing over the formula?' Greville mused.

'No, Rupert wouldn't. You can't possibly think such a thing,' Daisy protested. 'Rupert, tell them. Tell them!'

CHAPTER TWENTY

'What did you make of that? Is he our man?' Kitty asked once they were out of earshot in the garden. Rupert had been taken away from the house under escort to Inspector Greville's temporary police station at the public house in Newton St Cyres.

Daisy had collapsed weeping and Aubrey had been summoned from his work to sit with her until she was calm again.

'I'm not sure. He does have motivation and opportunity and Greville has to fully explore the line of questioning, I suppose.' Matt strolled alongside her.

She tugged her cardigan more closely around her. The weather had changed to become duller and more overcast and it felt as if rain was likely to be coming in.

'I take it that you were unaware of the discovery of the wireless receiver set?' she asked.

'Greville doesn't take Sir Horace or me fully into his confidence. Although it sounded as if Sir Horace had been in on that discovery.' Matt smiled at her.

'No, I suppose he doesn't have to tell us, really. I'm just nosey. I like to know everything that's going on.'

'Daisy seems frightfully upset,' he mused.

'Well, he is her brother. They both appeared genuinely shocked about the wireless, though.'

Matt paused in their stroll and they looked out across the vista of roses towards the lake in the distance, grey and menacing on such a dull day. 'Either that or they are good actors. She could be his accomplice.'

'I suppose the inspector will wish to speak to Mr Henderson and Mr Golightly. They are the ones who have used the hut and the garden more than anyone.' She couldn't see that the elderly, very grumpy gardener would be the type to send messages to an enemy.

'Yes, that is why we are none of us to mention the wireless set. Aubrey is not sitting with Daisy simply to ease her mind. He is also there to ensure that no one learns of the inspector's discovery until he is ready to share it.'

They started to walk once more. Fine specks of rain pattered onto her cheeks and left dark marks on the pale blue knit of her cardigan.

'We had better return to the house.' Kitty speeded her steps to match Matt's longer stride.

They reached the front door at the same time as Thomas Henderson. He was dressed for his gardening work in heavy boots and dark twill trousers and jacket.

'I say, is it true? Young Banks has been arrested?' Henderson accosted them as soon as he saw them. The shoulders of his jacket were damp from the rain and there was a faint whiff of manure that Kitty suspected came from his boots.

'I'm not sure that he has been charged. I believe the inspector had some questions he wanted him to answer.'

Kitty knew Matt had chosen his reply carefully.

'Hmm, not a bad billiards player, young Banks, but all this political nonsense, rights of the unemployed and all that stuff. Wouldn't put it past him to have stolen those papers,' Henderson said as he scraped the mud from his boots on the iron attachment at the side of the stone doorstep.

'You believe he may have attacked Nanny Thoms and Viola?' Kitty asked, as he bent to unlace his boots. 'Or killed the man found in the lake?'

'Now I didn't say that. Though if he was the one that stole your uncle's papers then he could well have killed them. He didn't like Viola and he's a fit, strong young man. Agile, too – got all the fire of youth and with his communist leanings, well I reckon an arrest will happen soon enough. Wouldn't be surprised if his sister wasn't involved too.' Mr Henderson drew off his boot and began to undo the other one.

'I suppose so,' Kitty said. 'It's so awful though, isn't it, to think that someone one has come to know could be capable of such dreadful things.'

Henderson finished unlacing his boot and drew it off, leaving him standing on the step in his stockinged feet. 'I suppose so. Good job he paid his billiard debts last night.' He smirked and collected his boots, ready to place them inside the hall cupboard where her uncle had said he could keep his things. 'I wonder which little bird tipped the inspector off?' He cast a sly glance at Kitty. 'I suppose we can sleep safely in our beds though tonight.'

Kitty and Matt watched as he stomped away down the hall. Kitty shuddered. 'Such a charming man. I thought he and Rupert were quite good pals with their billiard games. Henderson certainly spent more time with him than with the rest of us.'

Matt frowned. 'He knows he is under suspicion himself, so I expect this is an opportunity to throw more aspersions at Rupert to deflect attention from his own activities. He is not yet out of the woods, but he is right to assume that things do look bad for Rupert…'

Lucy was in the drawing room with her mother and Muffy. 'Oh, Kitty, is it true? Have they really arrested Rupert?' she asked.

'I do not believe he has been arrested. But he has been taken to assist the police with their enquiries. He has admitted that the clothing we found in the bonfire was his,' Kitty said as she took a seat on the sofa beside Lucy.

Matt crossed over to the French doors to stare out at the rain which had started to beat more heavily against the glass.

'I was afraid that might be the case. Poor Daisy is distraught. She became quite hysterical. Aubrey had to be called to sit with her.' Lucy stroked Muffy's ears as she spoke.

'That girl lives for drama.' Kitty's aunt gave a dismissive sniff. 'I hope you are not pining for that young man's company?' She gave Lucy a sharp glance.

Lucy looked unhappily at Kitty. 'I can't believe Rupert would steal Father's papers or that he would ever harm anyone. He certainly would never betray his country.'

'Darling, you've seen those dreadful political pamphlets he kept trying to show your father,' Lady Medford said.

'Just because Rupert cares about the working class and the fate of the unemployed doesn't make him a thief or a murderer,' Lucy protested.

'True.' Matt turned to face Lucy.

'Oh please, that boy and his sister!' Lady Medford shook her head as if despairing of her daughter's taste in friends.

Matt strolled over to one of the wing-backed armchairs near the fireplace and took a seat near Lucy. 'He asked you to marry him, didn't he?'

She blushed deep crimson as her mother pounced. 'He did what? Oh, Lucy, really, please tell me you refused him.'

'Mother!' Muffy barked at the sharp note in her mistress's voice and Lucy moved her hands to soothe her pet.

'Well, darling, really, what chance of happiness would you have with that boy?' Lady Medford tutted. 'No money or prospects. Probably already a criminal record. I daresay that's what put the inspector onto him.'

'You were not aware then, Lady Medford, of Rupert's inheritance?' Matt asked.

This information immediately caught her attention. 'What inheritance?'

'Rupert is the new Lord Woodcomb and has inherited the Thurscomb estate.' Matt flicked a piece of lint from the knee of his trousers.

'Lucy, is this true?' Kitty's aunt turned on her poor cousin.

'Oh, Mother! Yes, it's true. It's a terrible dilemma for Rupert, he did not expect to get the estate. He doesn't really want it but has to think of the men and women working there. We had an argument about a few things, and I turned him down. We were never that serious, you know.'

'This business gets worse and worse.' Lady Medford glared at her daughter.

Mrs Jenkinson had entered the room whilst they had been talking and was clearing the remains of the morning tea tray from the side table.

'I wish we knew more of the identity of the man in the lake,' Matt mused. 'It must be the man who was here begging a few weeks ago.'

There was a crash of china as Mrs Jenkinson staggered with the laden tray. Her pleasant middle-aged face had paled.

'Mrs Jenkinson?' Lady Medford looked at her housekeeper.

Matt leapt to his feet to take the tray from the woman's shaking hands. 'Are you feeling all right?' He placed the tray back on the table and steadied the trembling woman, guiding her to the seat he had just vacated.

'I'm so sorry, sir, my lady.' The woman pressed her hand to her lower lip. She appeared to be on the brink of tears.

Kitty's gaze met Matt's and she recalled how jumpy the housekeeper had been ever since there had been any mention of the vagrant. She slid from her place and knelt at the woman's feet.

'My dear Mrs Jenkinson, whatever is the matter?'

Lady Medford looked as if she were about to interrupt, but a fierce stare from Lucy silenced her, at least temporarily.

'Forgive me, sir, I should have spoken sooner, but I really hoped and believed it could not be true.' Mrs Jenkinson's lips trembled.

'Is this about the man in the lake?' Matt asked.

The woman startled. 'Oh, sir, I had so hoped it wasn't him but then the police constables described his clothes and I didn't know what to do.'

'You knew that person the police found in the lake?' Lady Medford asked, unable to restrain herself any longer.

'I'm afraid I think I do, my lady.'

Kitty took hold of the woman's hand and ignored her aunt's gasp of astonishment. 'Who was he?'

'He was my younger brother, Edward. I hadn't seen or heard of him for months. I thought he might be dead. He lost his job and then couldn't afford his rent. He was injured you see, in the Great War. His arm didn't work right so he couldn't do heavy manual work and those younger and fitter than him would get picked for the jobs.' The woman sighed and drew a small square of plain white cotton from the narrow belt about her waist. She dabbed at the corners of her eyes before continuing. 'He showed up here out of the blue. I gave him what money I could spare and Gladys, the girl, I told her to give him some scraps. He wouldn't take the money, only a few coppers and a pair of old boots from Mr Golightly, said he didn't want charity, even from me.'

'Oh, you poor thing,' Lucy said.

'He said he was going to go into the village and see if he could get work there. He had slept a couple of nights in the gardener's hut. It's been so cold early on for all it's June. Golightly didn't mind. There was a spirit lamp and a few biscuits in there. He didn't do any harm.' The woman turned tear-filled eyes upon her employer.

'Of course not, he was your brother,' Lucy interjected before her mother could speak.

'I thought he'd moved on. I didn't think that it was Edward they'd found. I had convinced myself it must be some other unfortunate soul.' A sob broke from Mrs Jenkinson's lips.

'We must let Inspector Greville know about this,' Matt said.

Mrs Jenkinson nodded and hurried from the room, leaving both the tea tray and a stunned silence behind her.

'I'll go and telephone.' Matt went out into the hall.

'Oh goodness, what a thing. Do you think Edward was Viola's face at the window?' Lucy asked. 'But if he was, then surely Golightly would have said something when he and Mr Harmon went out to look for intruders.'

'Unless, like Mrs Jenkinson, they believed he had already moved on to the village or were engaged in conspiring to keep his stay in the hut a secret, knowing that he was harmless,' Kitty said.

A shiver ran along Kitty's spine and the fine hairs at the nape of her neck stood on end. Everything appeared to be leading back to the gardener's hut and the lake.

When the drawing room door reopened, she looked up, expecting to see Matt. Instead, Thomas Henderson sauntered into the room.

'I just passed the housekeeper woman crying in the hall. Extraordinary behaviour and no gong for luncheon yet. What's happened?'

Kitty eased herself back into her seat. 'Mrs Jenkinson has just learned that the man the police found in the water was her younger brother.' She watched Henderson closely to study his reaction.

'By Jove, how extraordinary.' His face gave away only surprise.

Lady Medford glowered at him. 'Quite. I really do not know what this house is coming too.'

The gong sounded from the hall summoning them for luncheon. Mr Henderson barely had the patience to wait for his hostess to rise and lead them into the dining room. Kitty followed behind with Lucy, Muffy danced along at Mr Henderson's heels.

'Muffy adores that man. I really don't know why because I don't think he's at all an animal lover,' Lucy confided.

'He probably smells of food,' Kitty whispered, making her cousin giggle and lightening the atmosphere left by the latest revelations.

The telephone call to Inspector Greville took Matt longer than he had anticipated. It took the constable at the inn some time to find the inspector.

'The housekeeper's brother, eh? Well, well,' Greville remarked.

'She appears genuinely distressed. I believe she had convinced herself that our body must be that of someone else and that her brother had already moved on.'

'I'll send a constable to collect her. It would be better if she came here and could make certain of the identification from the couple of personal possessions he had about his person, a handkerchief and a ring. I would wish to spare her the sight of her brother in such a poor state.'

Matt swallowed the bile which rose suddenly in his throat as he recalled the bloated, disfigured expression on the dead man's face. 'Yes, that would be best, I think. She is in her room and I believe the cook is with her.'

'Poor woman, I'll send a car straight away. The sooner the identification is settled the better for all concerned.' Greville sounded thoughtful.

'Has there been any breakthrough with Rupert Banks?' He wasn't sure if Greville would tell him anything, but he couldn't resist asking the question. Kitty's curiosity must be rubbing off on him, as normally he would be more circumspect in his enquiries.

'We expect to return Mr Banks to Enderley in the next few hours.'

The reply took Matt by surprise. 'Is he not our man, then?'

There was a short pause and Matt guessed the inspector was calculating how much he should reveal.

'Let's say, he still could very well be our man, but I don't have enough to make it stick and I still don't have those papers of Lord Medford's yet. He's our best fit at the moment and you know what they say about giving a man enough rope. When we discovered the crystal set we also discovered a button which matched with one missing from a jacket belonging to Mr Banks.'

'I see. You hope he may convict himself if he returns to the house?' Matt asked. He recalled Rupert mentioning his missing button. Could he have been covering his tracks or had Henderson taken it and planted it in the hut?

'I think we may help matters along a little. I have some ideas. And if our man should be innocent, perhaps the real culprit may be lured into the open.'

'That sounds dangerous, Inspector.'

There was a deep sigh at the other end of the line. 'These are dangerous times; three innocent people are already dead. If those papers are not recovered soon with events in Europe moving as they are then more lives could be lost.'

Matt knew only too well the implications behind the loss of those documents if they were to fall into the wrong hands. The inspector too remembered all too well the horrors of the last conflict.

'Do you feel that Banks is our man?'

There was another pause.

'There is a lot of evidence, but it is mainly circumstantial. There is opportunity and there could be considered a motive given his ideologies. And yet—' Inspector Greville broke off.

'It could have all been planted to set him up as our man, and as you say, we have nothing to absolutely convince a jury that he should hang for the murders.' Matt peered around over his shoulder at the empty hall to ensure his conversation was not being overheard. He was fairly certain that the others were all at lunch, but there was still the matter of the servants.

'I would appreciate you keeping the information about Mr Banks's return to yourself at present. If it transpires that he is not our man, then there is still a murderer on the loose.'

'Of course.' Matt ended the call.

The hall had remained empty throughout his conversation with the inspector. From the dining room he heard the chinking of crockery and a few faint snatches of conversation. He couldn't face joining the rest of the party just yet. The implications of his conversation with the inspector weighed heavily on his mind and he headed outside. A smoke in the fresh air should calm his nerves and clear his head.

Matt stepped outside into the cool damp air. The rain had stopped, although the sky remained a dull, gunmetal grey. He lit a cigarette and inhaled deeply. Was Rupert Banks the killer? Or was it someone else in the party? If it was Rupert, then did he act alone? Was Daisy or even Aubrey involved? He leaned his shoulder against the brickwork under the lea of the stone canopy above the front entrance and watched the trail of smoke drift languidly skyward.

As he stood there, he became aware of the distant sound of female voices arguing. He put out his cigarette and went to investigate. As he rounded the corner of the house, he saw the young housemaid, Gladys, embroiled in a debate with a plump, older woman.

'Gladys Best, as I live and breathe, I swear you go looking for trouble. Ideas above your station, that's what you got. First poor Nanny Thoms, then you goes and gets involved with that brother

of Mrs Jenkinson. And that foreign woman's shoes. Now this book.'
The older woman paused for breath and Matt stepped forward.

'I'm sorry, I don't mean to intrude, ladies, but did I hear you
mention a book?' His pulse quickened when he saw what Gladys
held in her hand. A small black leather-bound notebook.

Gladys flushed a fiery red and the other woman pinked.

'It's the furrin' woman's notebook, sir. Glad found it this morning
when she went to light the drawing room fire.' She glared at the
hapless Gladys.

'Where did you find it, Gladys?' Matt held out his hand to
take the book.

'It was in the coal scuttle, sir. The big copper one in the drawing
room. I'd filled it a day or so ago. 'Tis heavy when it's full and I
don't like the coal place, 'tis full of spiders, so I fill the scuttles to
the top, so I don't have to go so much.' Gladys sucked in a breath
and carried on, her words tumbling over themselves. 'Well, I
knowed it would be running low by now, so I hauls it out and in
the bottom was this book. 'Tis all black with coal dust.' She offered
it to Matt by the corner.

'I told her she should bring it right to you or give it to that
policeman.' The older woman continued to glare at Gladys.

'I was going to, but then they said as Mr Rupert had been
arrested so I thought as it probably wasn't very important. Nobody
hadn't said anything about it being missing, but it seemed a funny
thing to be in the scuttle. And there was a constable a hunting at
summat the other day,' Gladys rattled to a halt.

'Mmm, well, thank you, ladies, I'll get this to Inspector Greville.
It could be important.'

Gladys preened and the other woman pursed her lips in disapproval.

Once they had returned to the kitchen, Matt pulled out his
handkerchief and wrapped it around the notebook to try and

remove the last of the coal dust. He flicked the small black leather-bound book open to look at the last entries. Unsurprisingly, the last couple of pages were gone, clearly torn out, leaving only the ragged edges behind.

He muttered an oath under his breath and tucked the book inside his jacket pocket. Why place the book in the coal scuttle? Surely after removing any incriminating pages the book could have been left anywhere within the house. The pages had probably been burnt on the same fire, but the book would have been difficult to get rid of unless it was supposed to be a temporary hiding place.

Or, if Rupert had taken the book, then he could have burned it on the same fire in the garden where he'd tried to destroy his clothes. The rain started up again as he headed back, deep in thought, towards the front door.

CHAPTER TWENTY-ONE

Kitty went in search of Matt as soon as luncheon was over. She had expected him to come to the dining room once his call to the inspector had ended. His absence bothered her, and she wondered where he had gone.

'Matt?' She eventually discovered him in the billiards room, moodily practising shots. A cigarette smouldered on the edge of the crystal ashtray on the side table. 'You've missed lunch, aren't you hungry?'

He leaned across the table, lined up his shot and struck the ball with his cue. The balls plinked against each other before disappearing neatly into the various pockets.

'I had things on my mind.'

Kitty closed the door to the billiards room behind her and took a seat in one of the leather tub chairs. 'What did the inspector have to say?' She crossed her stocking-clad ankles neatly in front of her and waited for his reply.

'He's sending a constable with a car for Mrs Jenkinson to make a formal identification of her brother.' Matt walked around the table retrieving the balls from the pockets before setting them up ready for another shot.

'And what else?' Kitty asked.

She watched through narrowed eyes as he continued to focus on his trick shot.

'Gladys found Viola's notebook this morning at the bottom of the drawing room coal scuttle.' He took aim once more, scattering the balls across the baize.

'In the coal scuttle? How extraordinary. Are the pages all there?'

Matt straightened; his gaze still fixed on the table. 'Naturally, the ones we are interested in are missing.'

She wafted a hand in front of her face to disperse the smoke drifting her way from the forgotten cigarette in the ashtray. 'What's wrong?'

'I'm trying to get things straight in my mind.'

Kitty stood and crossed over to the rack of billiard cues fixed to the wall. 'And what is it you are struggling with?' She surveyed the cues before selecting one.

'What are you doing?'

'I'll give you a game. It might help you think.'

The corner of his mouth quirked upwards. 'You can play billiards?'

'I was brought up in a hotel, remember. Rack them up.'

He moved to follow her instructions. 'I don't remember the Dolphin having a billiards room?'

Kitty laughed. 'Grams had the table removed when she renovated a few years ago. She felt it was lowering the tone and encouraging a lower class of guest.'

Matt grinned. 'Does she know you can play?'

'Don't be fooled by my grandmother or my great aunt Livvy. Mickey, the maintenance man, taught me but Aunt Livvy and Grams can both play too.'

'Let's see what you're made of then.' He stood aside to allow her to break.

They each played some shots, focusing on the game.

'Hmm, looks like I'm playing a billiards professional, Miss Underhay. Maybe you should take on Mr Henderson. You could relieve him of some of Rupert's money,' Matt suggested.

Kitty straightened up after taking her shot and looked at the rack of cues. 'He certainly has a very nice cue.'

Henderson's cue was placed at the end of the rack; his monogrammed black case stood beneath it on top of a small polished rosewood trophy cabinet.

Matt took his turn and potted a ball. 'He told Rupert he could have turned professional. He learned while he was in the army.'

'Oh?' Kitty was confused. She couldn't see how Henderson could have had time to hone his billiards skills during a conflict.

'Apparently, he has some sort of medical condition that ruled him out of active service. He spent the war in supplies, organising supply chains and counting tins of corned beef.'

Kitty couldn't fail to hear the note of cold derision in Matt's voice.

'I suppose someone has to do it. An army marches on its stomach after all, at least that's what I'm told. It seems odd now though that he has quite a physical job. Although, of course, there is a fair amount of desk work too, drawing up the designs, I suppose.' She studied Henderson's cue. 'This is an expensive piece, top maker. Beautifully made.' She stretched out her hand to touch the handle.

'Admiring my cue?'

She almost dropped her own cue at the unexpected stentorian sound of Henderson's voice. She hoped he'd only heard the latter part of the conversation as he'd entered the room.

'Yes, it's a beauty.'

'I'd appreciate it if you didn't touch it. I'm very fussy about my cue. Idiosyncratic of me I know, but it means a lot to me.'

'Oh, of course.' Kitty exchanged a glance with Matt.

'Forgive me for interrupting you both. I heard the sound of the balls and wondered who was playing. I didn't realise you played, Miss Underhay.'

'Oh, only a little. Matt was showing me a few tips.'

Matt's eyebrows raised at this untruth.

'Then I take it I shan't have the pleasure of besting you in a game?' Henderson asked.

Something in his tone caused a cold tickle of fear to tease at the edge of her mind. Matt had continued to play, and she wondered if he had picked up on the change in the room's atmosphere.

'I'm afraid not, Mr Henderson. Perhaps Matt may give you a game now that your regular playing partner is no longer here.' She strove to keep her tone light and carefree.

'Yes, perhaps after dinner this evening, if you're free.' Matt came to stand next to Kitty. 'Although I would rather not place any money on the table. I've seen your skills in action.'

Henderson gave a thin-lipped smile. 'I shall look forward to it. I fancy it may prove interesting enough even without a wager.'

The door to the billiards room opened once more as he finished speaking and Mr Harmon appeared. 'Her ladyship is asking for you, Mr Henderson. She is his in his lordship's study and requests that you bring the planting schemes.'

'I'll be right there,' Henderson replied, and the butler withdrew.

'My aunt is indefatigable where her garden is concerned,' Kitty said.

'So it seems.' He gave a funny little nod of his head to them both and left.

Kitty replaced her cue in the rack. 'My appetite for billiards appears to have diminished.'

'Yes.' Matt placed his cue next to hers and started to collect the balls from the pockets of the table. 'Of course, if it should transpire that Rupert is not the murderer, then Henderson has to be the next suspect.'

Kitty shuddered. 'Ugh, it wouldn't surprise me if he were up to no good. There is something unpleasant about him, but surely Inspector Greville is quite certain?'

True, she had difficulty in reconciling Rupert's character as that of a thief and a murderer, but the evidence had been stacked against him. She realised Matt hadn't answered her.

'Matthew Bryant, are you withholding information from me?'

'There are things in this case that don't add up. I wish I could sort it out better in my mind but it's not straight yet.' He placed the last ball in the frame.

She knew it would do no good to continue asking questions. 'Very well, I shall leave you to think. I promised Lucy I would take a turn sitting with poor Daisy so that Aubrey might go back to work.'

'Very well, but be careful, Kitty. I have a feeling this business may have more twists and turns to come. We do not yet know if Daisy is involved in some way.' His tone was grave.

'Of course. Alice is going to accompany me.' She wished the cold chill that teased her senses would leave her. If Rupert was the culprit then surely she wouldn't still feel afraid, unless of course he hadn't acted alone.

Daisy was asleep when Alice and Kitty slipped into her bedroom. Lucy leapt to her feet, casting her book aside when they entered.

'Kitty, darling, thank you so much for offering to sit with Daisy. Mother was creating the most dreadful fuss. Poor Daisy, it must be awful for her. I simply can't believe Rupert killed anyone, I really can't.' Lucy kept her voice low as she spoke.

Alice took a seat in the far corner and began upon the basket of mending she had brought with her.

'How has she been?' Kitty asked, glancing at Daisy.

'Doctor Carter, the police doctor, gave her a sedative. She was completely inconsolable.' Lucy followed Kitty's gaze. 'She seems more settled now. I sent Aubrey away to take a break. He's exhausted.'

Kitty thought her cousin looked equally tired. 'Poor Daisy, and poor you too. To have this happen in your house to your friends must be awful.' Lucy sank back down onto the chaise longue.

Kitty moved her cousin's book and sat next to her. 'Did you know them well, in London?'

Her cousin shrugged. 'Yes, at least I thought I did. It was so nice to have a girl friend to go shopping with, to talk to. Rupert was fun and attentive. He was so passionate about his concerns for the ordinary working man and his art…' Lucy trailed off; her expression downcast.

'Did you know about his involvement with the rally in Hyde Park?'

Guilty crimson colour flared in her cousin's cheeks. 'Please don't tell Mother or Father, but I was there. Rupert didn't want me to go, but I wanted to see for myself all those people who had walked such a long way to protest against how harshly they were being treated. I borrowed some clothes from one of the maids and went along to watch.'

Kitty couldn't help but admire her cousin. She certainly couldn't reprimand her, as it was exactly the sort of thing she would do herself.

'Lucy, are you in love with Rupert?' Kitty asked.

Lucy's blush deepened and she smiled. 'I think Rupert took our friendship more seriously than I did. I wasn't anticipating a proposal of marriage. For me it was harmless flirtation. You've seen that he often flirts with other women. Half the girls are in love with him. I didn't think he was in love with me.'

'And now?' Kitty felt for her cousin. Lucy was obviously deeply affected by Rupert being taken away by Inspector Greville.

'I don't know what to think or feel. At the rally he was so compassionate, trying to help those men. I just feel certain that the man I know would not and could not be capable of such terrible things.'

Daisy stirred in her sleep.

'I should go, Muffy will want her walk.' She kissed Kitty's cheek. 'Thank you for trying to help us. I'm so happy Uncle Edgar persuaded Mother to invite you here, despite everything that's happened.'

Daisy shuffled and resettled as Lucy left the room.

'What do you think, Alice?' Kitty asked.

'I'd say as Miss Lucy is much more in love with Mr Banks than she is letting on, miss.' The maid held her needle up to the light and began to poke thread through the eye.

'Yes, I thought the same thing.'

Daisy moaned and turned on her side. She looked younger and more vulnerable without her usual layer of make-up. Her dyed blonde hair was fluffed up and vivid against the white pillowcase.

'And Daisy and Aubrey?' Kitty asked.

'He's proper smitten with her, miss, and I think her with him. He rescued her when her heel broke on her shoe, that's proper romantic, like a film, in't it?'

'I hope so, Alice. In the films they always catch the bad guys,' Kitty said.

Alice's auburn curls bobbed beneath her frilled cap in agreement. 'Well, the police has Mr Banks, don't they?'

'But is he the bad guy, Alice?' Kitty asked.

The maid appeared to consider her answer, her busy fingers stilling as she thought. 'I don't know, miss. It was his clothes that was on the bonfire and he's one of them communist activists. He kept arguing with Miss Viola.'

Kitty sensed a 'but' was coming. It was the same issue she had and probably what was troubling Matt.

'I don't see him pushing Nanny Thoms down them stairs or killing Mrs Jenkinson's brother. Maybe strangling Miss Viola in temper if they had a row but Mr Rupert never seemed to have a temper like that. I heard as he had a sharp tongue, but nobody ever seen him in temper. Still, they do say as most murderers seem like nice people.'

They were silent for a moment. Kitty adjusted the covers on Daisy's bed and resumed her seat on the chaise longue.

'Suppose you're right, Alice, and our misgivings are correct. If not Rupert, then who?'

Alice frowned, scrutinising the stocking she was darning. 'Mr Henderson, I suppose would be a suspect. He is outside a lot and goes in that hut by the water, so he could've done it. He has a temper too, miss. He proper shouted at Gladys the other day. Said as she'd moved something of his, went all red in the face and the veins in his neck stood up and his eyes popped out. Lucky for Glad as Mr Harmon heard the commotion and came along to sort it out. I can't see as Mr Aubrey would do anything like that or Miss Daisy. But, I can't think as why he would do it all?'

'My uncle and aunt would have no cause, or my cousin. Certainly, none of the servants have any motive. Everyone appears to have loved Nanny Thoms and had no cause to attack Frau Fiser or Mrs Jenkinson's brother.'

Alice continued to sew. 'It comes back around to Mr Rupert then, don't it, miss?' She glanced at Daisy. 'Poor love, it's going to be hard for her if it's true.'

CHAPTER TWENTY-TWO

Kitty had been sitting with Daisy for some time when there was a knock on the bedroom door. To her surprise, Mr Harmon was outside.

'Excuse me, Miss Underhay, Sir Horace and Inspector Greville would like you to attend on them in the library.'

'Oh, certainly, I'll be right down.' The request confused her. What could Sir Horace and Inspector Greville want of her?

'Very good, miss.' The butler left.

She turned to her maid. 'Alice, would you be able to stay with Daisy while I find out what the inspector wants? Pull the bell if she should wake.'

'Of course, miss.'

Kitty checked her appearance quickly in Daisy's dressing table mirror, smoothing down her hair and straightening the collar on her dress. She hurried down the main staircase to the library. Perhaps they wished to ask her something about Daisy?

Sir Horace, Inspector Greville and Matt were present, and a constable was stationed outside the door. She saw that all three men had cigarettes and grave expressions. All conversation stopped as she entered, and Kitty felt the weight of their attention upon her.

'Thank you for joining us, Miss Underhay. Please, take a seat.' Sir Horace offered her a chair. Once she was seated the men resumed their own seats.

'We have asked your uncle to join us also.' Inspector Greville indicated a vacant chair.

'This sounds very serious.' Kitty looked towards Matt for a clue.

What she read on his face did little to reassure her. His mouth was set in a grim line and his dark blue eyes held a spark of anger.

Her uncle bustled into the library and took his place in the group.

Inspector Greville spoke first. 'Thank you for agreeing to this meeting. I had hoped that I would be able at this juncture to return the missing papers and confirm that we had arrested and charged the murderer of Nanny Thoms, Frau Fiser and Edward Allsop. Alas, that is not the case.' He cleared his throat and continued. 'We have two main suspects. Mr Rupert Banks has motive, opportunity and a certain amount of circumstantial evidence against him. However, we have not been able to confidently determine his guilt, nor have we come any closer to recovering the documents.'

Kitty noticed that her uncle's complexion had taken on a distinctly claret tinge at this statement.

'Our other suspect is Thomas Henderson. He had opportunity and easy access to the gardener's hut and its environs. But he has a good job here and no apparent motive for committing the crimes. However, the background information we have dug up on him suggests that he could be into some shifty dealings.'

'In what way, Inspector?' Kitty asked.

'One of his past jobs was for a marquis. There were also a series of robberies at that estate shortly after his departure. The family silver and the lady of the house's jewellery were targeted. And the thief seemed to know exactly where to go.'

Her uncle looked increasingly perturbed at this new information. 'If you know all this, then why can't something be done? Haul him in for questioning or something. See what you can shake out of the bounder.'

Sir Horace patted him on the shoulder. 'You know it's not as easy as that, old chap. Wish that it was, would save us all a lot of work.

Again, it is quite circumstantial and unlike Banks, Henderson's motivations are less clear-cut.'

'So, what happens now? I presume you have a plan and that's why we're here?' Kitty asked.

She could see the dilemma before them. Something had to be done and soon. They couldn't hold Rupert forever without charging him and they couldn't keep the story from the press for much longer. If they allowed everyone to leave Enderley, then the papers might never be recovered or the killer caught.

'We need to force our man out into the open. We have to assume that the theft of the papers and the murders are connected. Our man wants those papers desperately and will stop at nothing to keep hold of them until he has delivered them to his paymaster. If anyone threatens him in any way, then those people have been removed.' Sir Horace paced about the room as he spoke.

'If this man is as dangerous as you say then what if someone else gets hurt, or worse?' Kitty asked.

Her heartbeat had accelerated as Sir Horace had been speaking. Matt had turned his head to stare out of the window, his jawline rigid. She knew that whatever Sir Horace's plan might be, Matt did not approve of it.

'My niece is right. I cannot risk my wife or daughter's safety in this, or any other member of my household,' her uncle declared.

'I'm afraid we have little choice if we are to catch this man. Three people have died. If that formula falls into the wrong hands, then the prospect of more unrest and perhaps even another war could be on our heads. We have at least to try.' Sir Horace's tone was firm.

'What do you propose, sir? What is your plan?' Kitty asked.

Sir Horace paused in his pacing. 'This is where you all come in. All of you will need to play a part and play it convincingly if we are to pull this thing off.' He looked around the group.

She could feel the tension emanating from Matt's direction even though he stayed silent. She wondered where the inspector could possibly hide his men without causing suspicion. The idea of a constable lurking in her wardrobe behind her evening gowns almost made her giggle out loud despite the seriousness of the matter.

'Rupert Banks will return to the house this evening. We will let it be known that we have new information which will lead to an arrest very shortly. It is important that both he and the rest of the house believes that he has been cleared of all suspicion. If he is our man, this should force his hand.'

Lord Medford snorted, but was ignored by Sir Horace as he continued to outline his scheme.

'Aubrey will discover new and updated test results. Without this, the formula is useless.'

'There will of course, be an increased police presence around the house and grounds.' Inspector Greville spoke quickly.

'Bait.' Lord Medford nodded approval.

'But surely the killer won't fall for that?' Kitty could see the theory behind the scheme, but surely the killer would see through the subterfuge? It seemed infantile.

'Can he afford to take the chance? He has risked all for those papers. If the formula is flawed and unusable then it has been for nothing. This is a chance to take the missing page and get out before he can be arrested.' Inspector Greville leaned back in his seat.

'How will you make it plausible? And to both men?' Kitty asked. It appeared an impossible task to her.

Sir Horace looked at the inspector.

'This is where you come in, Miss Underhay.'

'Me?' She swallowed hard. 'I am no actress.'

Matt stood and walked away from the group, keeping his back to them. She could see his fists were clenched and his spine rigid.

'Mr Banks appears to find you plausible and sympathetic as a source of information. He, like Mr Henderson, believes you to have inside knowledge about the progress of the case.' Inspector Greville looked at her. 'We know from the events at the Dolphin that you have courage and a cool head. Captain Bryant has noticed that Henderson has been hinting that you may know things about the murders or the theft. Banks seems to confide in you.'

Matt remained motionless, his shoulders held back. She could tell that he was deeply opposed to her becoming involved.

'I don't understand, what do you think I could do?' she asked.

'Aubrey will let it be known that the formula is useless without the extra paper.' Sir Horace stroked his chin thoughtfully. 'You will hint to both men that the inspector intends to make an arrest very soon. He has a witness that could transform the case. Our man has eliminated all other witnesses, he cannot afford to be identified at this point when he is so close to escape.'

'But won't Aubrey or my uncle be in danger then? Surely the formula will be in the laboratory safe and they are the only ones who can gain access.'

'We have considered that. The timing for this is important. Banks will return any time soon. Aubrey will be working late in the laboratory tonight. He will not be alone. It should be easy to introduce the idea of an imminent arrest either before or during dinner. As a trusted source of information, backed up if needed by Lord Medford, they will have no call to doubt your veracity. Our man should be tempted to take the bait and try the laboratory to secure the missing document.' The inspector met her gaze.

'Is that all you need me to do?'

Kitty didn't underestimate the risk. It sounded a small task, but no one knew how the killer would react.

'I still think it would be better for me to undertake the task instead of Kitty.' Matt spoke at last.

'Henderson is suspicious of you and would probably realise this is a set-up. The same goes for Banks. You are recognised as official in the minds of the house party. Miss Underhay is not.' Sir Horace was firm.

Kitty rose and went over to Matt. 'I understand your concern but I'm willing to take the risk. The inspector and Sir Horace seem to have considered all the dangers and planned accordingly. You will be here too.' She touched his arm, willing him to soften.

'I won't be here. The inspector feels it will be better if I stay out of the house while the game is afoot.' His eyes blazed.

Bewildered, Kitty turned to Inspector Greville. 'Who else will be present? Sir Horace, will you be there?'

The older man shook his head. 'Part of the story is that both I and Captain Bryant have been called to Newton St Cyres to review the new information and interview the witness.'

Kitty's heart began to race once more. 'I see. Then who will be present? Uncle?'

Lord Medford rose and took her hands in his, his grip gentle but firm on her fingers. 'Yes, I shall be present, my dear. You shall not be unprotected. Captain Bryant and Sir Horace shall not be far away either, just not in the house.'

The genuine concern in his expression as he clasped her hands in his gave her a degree of reassurance.

'I still cannot approve of this venture.' Matt turned to her uncle. 'I appreciate your vigilance, sir, but I'm sure you can see the risks.'

Her uncle sighed. 'I wish there were another way, but this is the safest route at hand to capture a killer and recover the formula.'

'I am prepared to take the risk, Matt. I understand the dangers, but my role is very small, and I have good company to protect me.' She wished he would understand. He knew that capturing this man was important.

Yes, she was scared, but at the same time she felt more alive than she had for a long time. Fear and excitement tangled together in her stomach.

Matt's jaw was set, and a fine pulse ticked in his cheek. 'Are you determined on this, Kitty?'

'Never more so.'

Matt could tell from the determined tilt of her chin and resolution in her gaze that he would not be able to deter Kitty from her course.

'Then there's nothing more to say.' He clasped his hands behind his back and turned away.

He couldn't fully explain why he felt so strongly about Kitty placing herself in jeopardy in this way. In principle her role was small, but if the murderer thought she was trying to trick him or thought she knew something then he might try to dispose of Kitty as he had the others. The incident of the bathroom door concerned him. He did know, however, that once she had made up her mind, there would be no chance of changing it.

Sir Horace coughed. 'It is almost five. Rupert Banks will be returning to the house soon and I believe dinner will be at seven thirty. Medford, will you let her ladyship know that Rupert will be rejoining the party? And, perhaps ask your daughter to give Banks's sister the good news of her brother's return. If Banks is the man, then his sister may be involved also.'

Kitty's uncle agreed. 'Very well. I believe Lucy was going to relieve my niece's maid of her duties.'

'I would like to ensure Alice's safety,' Kitty said.

'Of course, my dear. Once you have dressed for dinner, I suggest you send the girl downstairs with the rest of the staff and instruct her to remain there until you are ready to retire. She can then accompany you upstairs.' Sir Horace turned. 'Captain Bryant, will this address some of your concerns for Miss Underhay's safety?'

'Thank you, Sir Horace.'

It was the best he could hope for. At least Kitty would be accompanied. She would protect Alice, and the maid would protect her.

Lord Medford patted Kitty's hand once more. 'Come, my dear, we shall find your aunt and then I shall escort you to your room.'

She gave Matt a glance and left the room, accompanied by her uncle.

'We are chancing a great deal on this plan.' Sir Horace glanced at the inspector and proffered both Matt and Inspector Greville another cigarette from his case.

Matt accepted and took a light. His chest hurt from the amount he had smoked during the day. Normally he would only have one or two cigarettes in the course of a week. It was a clear sign that his stress levels were raised.

'What if it doesn't come off, sir? What if the bait is not taken?' he asked.

The inspector sighed and blew out a thin stream of smoke. 'We cannot keep these people here much longer. Henderson is already packing to leave to commence his next job. Banks wishes to return to London for meetings with his bank and his solicitors. He has to deal with his inheritance. No doubt his sister will accompany him. If we're to catch the culprit, then it's now or never.'

Matt coughed; the cigarette smoke was acrid in the back of his throat. 'Where are the men to be positioned this evening?'

'Sir Horace and two officers will be inside the laboratory. There is an officer upstairs in the house, concealed in an empty guest room. Two other officers will move into position downstairs once the house has retired for the evening. There will be yourself and one other stationed outside in the grounds ready to cut off any attempted escape. Outside the main entrance, by the gatehouse, there is another officer positioned in case our villain gets that far,' Inspector Greville explained.

'That is quite a commitment of manpower.' The inspector and Sir Horace were clearly loading everything onto this last throw of the dice. He could only hope it would be successful.

Alice was busy in the bedroom when Kitty returned.

'Miss Lucy told Miss Daisy as her brother was coming back this evening. Is that right, miss? Have the police let him go?' Alice asked.

Kitty took a seat on the wing-backed armchair in front of the fireplace. 'Yes, Alice. The inspector has some new information that he thinks might finally allow him to make an arrest.'

Alice paused in her bustling to capture her auburn curls and fix them more securely under her cap. 'That's a good thing, then. Be better for Miss Daisy and Miss Lucy if it in't Mr Rupert. It's about time as they caught the villain who murdered Miss Viola and Nanny Thoms and poor Mrs Jenkinson's brother.'

'I agree, it will be good to have the matter settled. However, in the meantime, Alice, we must be careful, this maniac is still at large. My uncle requests that when I go downstairs for dinner this evening you must go to the kitchen and stay with his staff. I shall ring the bell when I'm ready to retire and you can accompany me upstairs. Until this man is safely behind bars, he feels responsible for our welfare as his guests.' She had considered how much she should tell Alice of the plans and had judged it prudent to stick to the official story.

'Oh dear, does that mean it still might be Mr Henderson or Mr Banks, then? Or is it somebody else?' Alice asked.

'I don't know. I think Sir Horace and Captain Bryant have been asked to go to the police station this evening. Something about a new witness.'

The girl's face brightened. 'That might mean as your aunt is right, then. Like she's been saying all along about a stranger. We could go home soon then, once this bloke is caught.'

'I don't know, Alice, but my uncle wants us to continue to be cautious.'

The maid nodded. 'Very well, miss.' She reached into the wardrobe. 'Which dress do you want for dinner tonight?'

Kitty frowned. 'I think the black one.'

Alice's eyebrows rose and her lips pursed. Kitty knew she didn't approve of her choice, but she had very practical reasons for choosing that particular gown. Alice hung it on the outside of the wardrobe and scrutinised it.

'Are you sure you wouldn't rather wear the red or the green, miss? This one is a bit dowdy for what might be your last dinner here.'

'No, that one is fine.' It was the oldest of her gowns and a little dated. There was a small stain on the bodice which had to be hidden by a brooch and it was a little shabby. However, it was also cut more loosely so if necessary she could run and move in it. The colour would allow her to blend into the shadows so she could conceal herself more readily if the need arose. 'And the black low-heeled shoes.'

Alice reluctantly returned the high-heeled patent slippers she had automatically fetched out to match the dress. 'Are you sure, miss?'

'Absolutely, Alice, thank you.'

Her maid sighed and found the lint brush, trying to smarten up Kitty's chosen outfit. Her disapproval radiated from her with every stroke.

Kitty dressed carefully, with minimal jewellery and a simple clip in her blonde hair.

'Oh, Miss Kitty, you look smart but like you'm off to a funeral.' Alice clicked her tongue. 'Won't you at least wear them other shoes?'

'I want to be comfortable tonight, Alice.' She checked her appearance in the mirror. Her maid was right, she did look quite sombre, despite the bold red lipstick she had been persuaded to add at the last minute.

'I suppose if Captain Bryant isn't going to be there then it don't much matter,' Alice murmured.

'Alice!'

The girl blushed. 'Sorry, miss.'

As instructed by her uncle, Alice accompanied Kitty downstairs, leaving her at the door to the drawing room.

'Remember, I'll call for you to accompany me later. Stay with Gladys and Cook until then, please.'

'Yes, miss.'

To her surprise, she discovered Rupert was the only occupant of the drawing room. He stood in front of the French windows nursing a cut-glass tumbler of whisky. Her pulse quickened.

'Rupert, how lovely to see you. I hope they managed to sort everything out?'

He turned at the sound of her voice. 'Yes, the black sheep has returned.' Despite his smart evening dress, Rupert appeared tired, with shadows under his eyes.

'Daisy will be so happy to see you; she's been terribly upset.' Kitty moved over to the drinks cart to pour herself a small sherry to settle her nerves. She hoped the others would come soon.

'Yes, I went straight up to see her. I believe she is intending to join us for dinner. Aubrey has been frightfully good to her, as have you all. She told me that you and your maid had joined Lucy in sitting with her. Thank you for your kindness.' He appeared genuinely grateful for their attention.

'Daisy is a sweet girl. It was the least we could do.'

The door opened as she spoke, and Thomas Henderson entered with Lord Medford.

'Ha, Banks, good to see you back. Off the hook then, eh? Jolly good.' Henderson offered him his hand, while her uncle went to the drinks trolley.

'I hear they may have someone else in the frame.' Her uncle proffered a glass to Henderson.

'Yes, Matt said he had to attend the temporary police station at Newton St Cyres with Sir Horace. Something about the police interviewing a new witness.' She felt, rather than saw, the reactions of Rupert and Henderson to her casual comment.

'There was something going on as I left.' Rupert's brow creased. 'Perhaps that was it. Maybe that was what convinced them to let me go.'

Her aunt entered the room accompanied by Lucy, with Muffy trotting at Lucy's heels. The little dog immediately went to Henderson and sniffed happily at his ankles.

'I see they let you out.' Her aunt looked at Rupert.

'Mother!' Lucy reproved and slipped her hand into the crook of Rupert's arm to steer him away from the group.

Aubrey and Daisy were the last to join the gathering. Daisy looked frail, her complexion pale against the harsh blonde of her hair. The emerald satin of her dress gave her an unhealthy pallor. Aubrey kept a solicitous arm about her waist as he steered her to a seat before bringing her a small glass of sherry. Rupert and Lucy immediately joined them as the gong sounded, summoning everyone to the dinner table.

Thomas Henderson fell into step beside her as they made their way along the hall. 'Allow me to accompany you, Miss Underhay, as you are without your companion this evening.'

'Thank you, Mr Henderson, that is most kind of you.' All of Kitty's senses were on high alert at this sudden attentiveness. Unless he felt the need to protect her in some way.

She found herself seated next to Henderson at dinner, with Aubrey on her other side.

'Something of a celebratory meal then, this evening.' Henderson shook out his napkin.

'I suppose so, as Rupert is back with us and the police seem certain of making an arrest at last. I expect we shall all be allowed to go soon.' Kitty placed her own napkin across her lap.

'Everyone ignored me when I said it had to be some stranger, but it looks as if I was right.' Her aunt signalled the staff to begin serving.

'Quite so, my dear,' Kitty's uncle agreed with his wife.

'I'm simply relieved that they found this witness. I wonder who it could be and what they saw,' Rupert mused as they started the soup course.

'Everyone knew it couldn't be you. The whole idea was horrid, simply horrid.' Daisy shuddered.

'I shan't feel at all safe until they have whoever did this behind bars,' Lucy said.

'It will certainly be a relief,' Kitty agreed. Her nerves felt as tightly strung as piano wire. It was much more difficult than she had imagined trying to keep her voice and expression neutral and all the time watching Rupert and Mr Henderson for any sign that they might be the culprit.

'I hope that Inspector Greville recovers your documents too, my dear.' Lady Medford placed her soup spoon in her empty dish and looked at her husband.

'I remain cautiously optimistic. Still, those papers would not be as useful to the thief as he might have thought.'

'Oh, what do mean, Papa?' Lucy asked, her eyes wide with astonishment.

Her father tapped his finger on the side of his nose. 'Let us just say that when Aubrey and I went back over the test results, we discovered a flaw in our premise. We've solved it now of course but without the readings from the tests those original documents are worthless.'

'Absolutely,' Aubrey agreed. 'The formula is hopelessly unstable without the adjustments and the flaw is tricky to spot. It's taken us a lot of time to unravel it.'

'Sounds as if someone is in for a nasty shock then, eh, if they try and use that formula.' Mr Henderson patted his lips dry with his napkin as the maid removed his empty soup bowl.

CHAPTER TWENTY-THREE

'Of course, it has made a lot of extra work. But it is a relief to think that the papers the crook filched aren't as useful as they would have thought.' Lord Medford beamed approval as a plate of lamb cutlets was placed before him.

'I suppose Sir Horace will be pleased, though?' Kitty asked.

'Yes, indeed. He intends to take the papers back to London tomorrow I believe, once this case is wrapped up and they make the arrest. The proposals for more investment need to be approved by the cabinet. There will need to be more samples made on a larger scale for testing. Sadly, Daisy my dear, you will have to excuse Aubrey for this evening.'

'Oh?' Daisy turned a bewildered gaze towards Aubrey. Her lower lip trembled into a pout.

'I'm very sorry, my dear, but after dinner I need to finish the last part of the transcription and note the final test results ready for Sir Horace's return. Everything must be absolutely in order for him to present to the cabinet.' Aubrey stammered an apology to his fiancée.

Lord Medford added his weight to the discussion. 'It can't be helped, Miss Banks. This is vitally important work, and Sir Horace has had his return to London delayed for long enough by these terrible events.'

Daisy didn't look very happy about Aubrey abandoning her for his work. 'I thought we could have celebrated a little tonight, now Rupert has been cleared.'

'Chin up, Daisy, old girl. Lucy and I can keep you company. Kitty is at a loose end too I suppose, with Captain Bryant called off to assist Inspector Greville.' Rupert reached out and patted his sister's hand.

She gave him a wan smile.

'Oh, of course. I don't know how long this business at Newton St Cyres will take. Matt didn't say much about it but he did seem quite excited. I wonder who the witness might be?' Kitty smiled at Daisy.

'Will you be working late too, dear?' Lady Medford enquired of her husband as she speared a potato with her fork.

'Got to pop over to see Sir Horace and bring him back later on. Still, Aubrey can handle everything. It's just a few details to finish off. A couple of hours should have it all done and in the bag.'

'How very tiresome,' Lady Medford declared.

'It has to be done, my dear. Inspector Greville feels it is important that I verify some information and it will save him sending Blunt and Bryant back in a police car. Dashed if I know what he wants from me, though.'

Kitty's heart speeded in alarm; what had happened to his promise to stay and protect her? Now it seemed she would be alone. Something must have changed. She had to admire her uncle's cool demeanour, however. She wished she could tell who around the table was taking in all this information and if they believed it.

'Did you gain any idea about who they think the murderer might be, Rupert, while you were with the inspector?' Daisy asked.

He shook his head before taking a sip of wine. 'Nothing. There was a telephone call and then there was a lot of excitement. I was in a small room downstairs near the cellar, being watched over by a constable. I didn't hear or see anything, I'm afraid. The pub is next to the railway line and the trains tend to be quite inconvenient for eavesdropping.'

'That dreadful policeman. He should never have arrested you. There was no evidence, he was simply clutching at straws.' Daisy clattered her cutlery down on her plate.

'Steady on, old thing. I wasn't arrested you know, just answering some questions, that's all,' Rupert attempted to soothe his sister.

'I must admit, I'm absolutely alive with curiosity,' Lucy said. 'Didn't Matt give you any clues at all, Kitty?'

Kitty's cheeks pinked under her cousin's bright-eyed gaze. 'No, nothing. He was called away so suddenly he didn't tell me anything. I just got the impression there had been a real breakthrough from a totally unexpected source.'

'How very vexing.' Lucy frowned and slipped Muffy a titbit from her plate. 'I would have thought you would know more than the rest of us.'

'I'm sorry to disappoint you, but as I said, Matt really doesn't tell me everything.' She gave a small dismissive shrug of her shoulders and flashed her cousin a smile.

She noticed a half smile on Rupert's lips at her comment. Had he taken the bait?

'I'd assumed you were in the thick of things. After all, weren't you the one who asked Captain Bryant to assist Sir Horace?' Mr Henderson helped himself to more wine.

'Matt is a friend. My grandmother employed him for a short time when we needed to ensure there was good security at the hotel. When my uncle's papers went missing, it seemed like a simple case of theft and Matt is a private detective, so naturally I suggested he could be helpful. He is very discreet. He recently helped capture an international jewel thief.' Kitty tried to keep her tone light and breezy despite her discomfiture at the turn in the conversation.

'A very good thought of yours too, Kitty, my dear. I believe Inspector Greville and Sir Horace have found Captain Bryant's expertise and discretion most helpful.' Her uncle lowered his brow and fixed Mr Henderson with a steely glare.

'Well thank goodness this witness, whoever they are, has been found. The sooner this is all over with the better. Poor Nanny Thoms, I still don't know how I shall go on without her. To harm a defenceless old lady, shocking, absolutely shocking. And Viola, not safe in her own room,' Lady Medford muttered, setting down her knife and fork.

'Quite agree, Hortense. Don't know what the country is coming to these days,' her uncle agreed.

Kitty was relieved when Lucy changed the subject and dessert passed off without any further references to the murders or the missing papers. She was uncomfortable in both Rupert's company and Thomas Henderson's. Were they wrong? Perhaps neither man was the culprit and her imagination was simply working overtime, making her see shadows of suspicion where there were none.

Her aunt led the ladies back to the drawing room where the usual tray of coffee awaited them. Her uncle had instructed Mr Harmon to bring port to the dining table for the men.

'Lucy, darling, close the curtains tonight. I feel a chill from the glass,' her aunt directed as she took her regular place behind the large silver coffee pot. The grey chiffon of her gown, combined with the black feathers of her hair clip, gave the illusion of a large crumpled bird.

Her cousin obeyed and Muffy seized the opportunity to jump up on the sofa to await her mistress's return.

'Oh, that wretched dog. She shouldn't get on the furniture,' Lady Medford scolded.

Lucy merely laughed and sat down next to her pet. 'Don't fuss so, Mother.'

Kitty wished they had left the curtains open. It was true that the weather had turned chillier with the onset of more rain, but she hated the closed-in sensation that came from excluding the outside. She wondered where Matt was. If he was somewhere in the grounds in the rain or lurking in the gardener's hut perhaps. Although still cross with him, she didn't like the idea that he might be cold and wet somewhere in the dark.

Lady Medford handed a cup of coffee to Kitty and poured a second for Daisy. 'I'm sure Aubrey won't be too long over at the laboratory. It's a good thing they discovered the problem with the formula. I'm sure Sir Horace will be most relieved to take the whole thing back to London, and we can be done with it.'

'I'll be glad when they make the arrest. Rupert and I need to return to London too. He has business with his solicitors over the estate.' Daisy took a sip from her cup.

'What will you and Aubrey do?' Lucy asked.

'Aubrey intends to visit his mother as soon as he can be spared. I shall accompany him, and we shall see what transpires from there. I should like a September wedding.' Daisy's heavily lipsticked mouth twisted in a wry smile.

'Mr Henderson is keen to be off as soon as possible too. He is expected at Cranmore House to sort out their orangery. I have all the plans I require, and the gardeners have their instructions for the coming seasons. The test beds have been most useful in confirming the soil types and the presence of bed rock.' Kitty's aunt settled back in her chair with a smile of satisfaction. 'I shall plant one bed in memory of dear Nanny Thoms.'

'What about you, Kitty? What shall you do? I'm so sorry your stay has been so eventful,' Lucy said.

'My grandmother will be expecting me. I dare say there will be plenty of work demanding my attention when I go back to the Dolphin. My aunt Livvy will be returning to her home in Scotland soon too and I'm anxious to see her before she goes.' Privately, the thought of returning to the confining world of the hotel with her mundane, day-to-day chores was a little depressing. 'You must come and stay with me next time. A little sea air would do you good. You too, Daisy.' She felt obliged to include the other girl.

'Thank you, we should like that, wouldn't we, Muffy?' Her cousin stroked her pet and laughed as the little dog squirmed and attempted to lick her hand.

'That's very kind of you,' Daisy said. She placed her empty cup on the tray and stifled a yawn with her hand. 'Do please excuse me. That powder the doctor gave me has made me so sleepy.'

'An early night is in order then. I shall accompany you upstairs since I intend to retire early myself,' Lady Medford declared.

Daisy put up little resistance before agreeing that she did need to return to bed. They bade Lucy and Kitty good evening and left. Lucy turned on the wireless as they waited for the others to come and join them. The soothing, mellow tones of a piano concerto filled the room, easing Kitty's nerves.

'Did you mean it when you said I could visit you at the hotel?' Lucy asked.

'Of course. It would be such fun to show you around Dartmouth. Plus, we have already had our share of murders so it will be quite safe.' Kitty smiled at her cousin.

'And Muffy?' Lucy's own smile widened.

Kitty laughed. 'Of course with Muffy.'

Rupert and Mr Henderson entered the room as the girls were laughing.

'You two seem to be having a jolly time. Where's Daisy?' Rupert asked.

'She was tired, so Mother has marched her back to bed.' Lucy extended her hand to invite him to take the spare seat beside her.

'Aubrey has gone back to work, like the good soul that he is, and your father has just been driven off to join the group in the village.

Maybe Sir Horace and Matt will have news when they return.'
Rupert took up the seat on the sofa next to Lucy.

'Daddy has been so upset. With the theft of the formula and
then Nanny Thoms and Viola.' Lucy twirled a lock of Muffy's fur
between her fingers.

Thomas Henderson helped himself to another tumbler of whisky
before taking up his usual place in front of the fireplace. 'Dreadful
business, the whole thing.'

'Surprised the police didn't haul you off for questioning too,
old chap. I mean you had the opportunity for bumping off Mrs
J's brother, and you could have shoved Nanny down the stairs,'
Rupert drawled.

Kitty noticed a small pulse ticking on Henderson's jaw.

'I can assure you I was asked plenty of questions, the same as
everyone else. Besides, I have no motive.' He took a sip of whisky.

'Neither did Rupert!' Lucy protested. The increase in her tone
caused Muffy to wriggle and squeak in protest.

'Of course not,' Henderson blustered.

'The authorities do not look with a friendly eye on my political
beliefs,' Rupert said.

'So unfair. I wonder who the murderer really is?' Lucy muttered.

Muffy rolled back onto her stomach, a low growl emitting from
her throat.

'Muffy, darling, what is it?' Lucy asked as the dog stared at the
partly open door to the drawing room.

'Is there someone in the hall?' Rupert jumped up from his place
on the couch. 'Who's there?'

The dog leaped down and dashed out through the door.

'Muffy!' Lucy leapt to her feet.

Kitty's heart bumped in her chest as she followed the others as
they went in pursuit of the dog. She hoped she hadn't heard one

of the policemen secreted within the manor. If so, Lucy's pet could give the whole game away and their scheming could be for nothing.

'Where has she gone? She only usually runs away if she's stolen something.' Lucy peered inside the deserted dining room.

'The door to your father's study is locked.' Rupert tried the handle.

'The billiards room?' Kitty suggested.

Thomas Henderson led the group into the billiards room, flicking the switch on the wall to turn on the light above the table. Immediately the huge brass-trimmed downlighters filled the room with a soft glow.

Muffy came dancing towards them, tail wagging and looking very pleased with herself.

'You naughty little beast. Whatever are you up to?' Lucy scolded her pet.

'What made her come in here?' Rupert asked as he looked around the room. 'Do you think someone else was in here?'

A cold shiver ran down Kitty's spine. Who had Muffy heard or smelled? It clearly wasn't one of the servants.

Thomas Henderson prowled around the table, peering into the shadowy corners of the room as if expecting to find someone crouching in the shadows. Something about his sudden lightness of foot and stealthy manner unnerved her.

Rupert bent to pick something up from the floor. 'I think Muffy may have heard your case falling over, Henderson.' He lifted Henderson's case for the billiard cue back onto the top of the cabinet. 'No damage done, old boy.'

Henderson rushed over to check the case, feeling the corners with his fingers. Kitty couldn't help noticing that while he checked the case, his gaze kept drifting to his cue. A long-forgotten fragment of memory from her childhood tugged at the edge of her mind.

Suddenly she recalled Mickey, the maintenance man at the Dolphin, sneaking her into the billiard room and selecting a cue for her from the rack. She'd had to stand on a stool to take her shot. She remembered stumbling backwards and toppling off the stool. The cue she'd been holding had broken in two pieces and she'd promptly burst into tears, convinced she would be shouted at.

But Mickey had scooped her up and dried her eyes, showing her that the cue was made in two pieces that screwed together and could be parted for travelling. It hadn't broken, it had come undone.

As she noted the quick, darting glances of Henderson's gaze, Kitty recalled holding the two parts of the cue. The outside silky smooth, polished wood and inside the handle, a hollow, dark and mysterious. Mickey had told her many cues were solid wood but that the hollow versions could be used to hide liquor in prohibition America. The brass thread used to join the two halves popped out to reveal a compartment large enough for a small, slim glass flask or something else.

'How fortunate that your cue was in the rack and not in the case, Mr Henderson. It would have been too awful if Muffy had managed to sink her teeth into that,' Kitty observed.

Was it her imagination, or did the wayward muscle in Henderson's jaw twitch?

'Oh, that would have been too dreadful.' Lucy was aghast.

Kitty stretched out her hand as if to lift Henderson's cue from the rack. 'It really is a nice thing.'

His hand snaked out and he seized her wrist before she could lift it down. 'Please don't touch my cue, Miss Underhay. As I said before, I'm quite superstitious about it.' His fingers bit into her wrist.

She gave a pointed look at her hand and he released her. 'It's funny how things come back to one, isn't it? I learned to play billiards when I was a child. My grandmother's maintenance man taught me. I was too small to reach the table, so I stood on a small stool.'

'Really.' Henderson's tone was dry.

'Yes, then one day I fell off the stool backwards, and the cue broke in two.'

'An expensive accident.' Henderson moved slightly as if to block her access to the rack.

'Except, I didn't actually break it. It was a cue that unscrewed to fit into a case, like yours.' Her gaze fell on his case.

'Well, of course, silly, how else would one transport them?' Lucy frowned and hoisted Muffy into her arms.

'Yes, but some cues are not solid. They are hollow so that one could hide things inside them. Small things like a vial of liquor or maybe something that would roll up small.'

Rupert stared at her, understanding dawning, before swivelling to face Henderson. 'You mean things like papers?'

Henderson let out a snarl and grabbed his cue from the rack bringing it down hard on top of Rupert's head. With a loud crack Rupert fell to the floor, a small trickle of blood running from his scalp to form a dark, sticky red pool.

Lucy gave a small scream and dropped Muffy who immediately ran to Rupert and began to lick his face.

'Oh my God, you've killed Rupert.' She fell to her knees to check him for signs of life.

'Shut up.' Henderson reached inside his jacket pocket. Before Kitty could move to warn Lucy, or call out for help, he produced a small handgun.

'You, up!' He waved the gun at Lucy.

'What are you doing?' She scrambled to her feet and clutched Kitty's arm. Kitty looked around for a way of alerting the servants, someone, anyone.

'You two are coming with me.' He pushed Kitty forward towards the door.

Muffy woofed and danced after them, clearly thinking this was a new game.

'But, Rupert…' Lucy protested. She cast a despairing look back at Rupert's prone body on the floor of the billiards room.

'Shut up and hurry up. You're going to persuade your friend, Aubrey, to give me the new formula.' He poked the gun into Lucy's back as he hustled them both along the hall and out of the front door.

The damp, drizzly night air hit them. The chill stung the bare flesh of her arms and she was thankful that her gown was old-fashioned and didn't have the low back that was so popular at the moment.

Kitty was also glad of her low-heeled shoes as they stumbled along the wet path with the wind tugging at their hair. Muffy ran off over the rain-drenched field, enjoying the unexpected night-time excursion. Kitty wondered where Inspector Greville and the rest of the police were. Surely they must have seen them and realised something was wrong by now. Henderson was one of their main suspects.

Lucy staggered and tripped, almost bringing Kitty down.

'Watch where you're going,' Henderson barked at her.

Her cousin whimpered and Kitty did her best to steady her. They were almost at the laboratory. A thin glimmer of light shone out of a crack in the shuttered window, revealing that Aubrey was still inside.

CHAPTER TWENTY-FOUR

'You, stand to the side.' Henderson pulled Kitty away from Lucy, so her cousin was left standing in front of the door. His fingertips bit into the flesh of her upper arm and she was forced to stand still beside him.

'This is crazy.' Lucy's teeth chattered as she spoke. The thin gauzy fabric of her evening gown was soaked and the hem spattered with mud.

'Ring the bell.' Henderson waved the gun and the barrel glinted in the faint light from the window.

Lucy moved to obey. Deep inside the building they heard the metallic ting of the bell. After what seemed like an eternity, a small hatch slid upwards in the door and Aubrey peered out from behind a metal grill.

'Lucy? What on earth are you doing out here?' His gaze was perplexed behind his glasses.

'Aubrey, it's Mr Henderson. He's killed Rupert and he's got a gun.' There was a note of hysteria in Lucy's voice.

'Get me that formula or Miss Medford and her cousin will suffer the consequences.' Henderson pushed his face close to Aubrey's and allowed him to catch a glimpse of the gun.

'I— shall I open the door and you can come inside?' Aubrey's eyes widened and he stammered a response. 'It's wet and the ladies…'

'I'm not that stupid. Go and get the documents now and pass them to me. I'll stay right here with Miss Medford and Miss

Underhay. Any tricks, any movement from that police guard that I'm sure you have in there with you, and these ladies die.'

'Aubrey, please, do as he says,' Lucy begged. 'Hurry.'

The hatch closed, cutting off the light source. Henderson motioned with the gun for Lucy to stand to the side. Kitty's heart banged against her ribs as they waited. Surely Aubrey could telephone and summon help? Or maybe there was another exit so they could be rescued?

A minute later, they heard the scraping of the bolts being drawn back and a key turning in the lock. The door opened a crack, spilling a slit of yellow light into the darkness. Aubrey's hand appeared with a large brown envelope.

'The formula is inside. Let the girls go.'

'Show me,' Henderson commanded. He made no move to accept the envelope which was being marked by spots of rain. He kept his gun trained on Lucy, and his other hand continued to grip Kitty's arm.

The slit of light grew wider as Aubrey opened the envelope and revealed the contents to Henderson.

'Seal it back up. Pass it to me and give me the keys to the laboratory.'

Aubrey froze for a moment and Henderson increased his grip on Kitty's arm, forcing her to cry out in pain. The sound was enough to galvanise Aubrey into action and he fumbled to obey. Henderson released Kitty just long enough to tuck the envelope inside his jacket, before slamming the door closed on Aubrey and locking it with the key. He paused to twist the barrel of the gun beneath the telephone cable that ran alongside the door frame, wrenching it away from the wall.

'Right, this way.' He stood behind the two girls and pushed Kitty in her back.

'Where are we going?' she asked as they stumbled forward once more.

She thought she caught a glimpse of movement in a group of bushes near the house and wondered if it could be Matt. Her hopes rose momentarily. Then again, it was so blustery, it might just have been the wind.

'You know they'll catch you. You'll hang for all this. You killed my poor Nanny Thoms and Viola. Why did you do it? They had done nothing to you. Nothing.' Lucy was openly sobbing, tears running down her cheeks as he forced them along at a rapid pace towards the side of the house.

'Ah, Miss Medford, your naivety is quite touching. They have to catch me first. Nanny Thoms saw me leaving the study after I'd taken the formula. And as for that mad foreign woman, she had discovered the wireless set I kept in the hut. I knew someone had been out that night and heard me broadcasting. She'd written it all down in that blasted book of hers.' He gave Lucy another push as she stumbled on a tussock of grass, snapping the heel from her shoe.

'These are my best shoes.' Lucy half hopped, half hobbled along.

They were almost at the edge of the terrace now and Kitty realised he was forcing them towards the side of the manor where the cars were parked at the back of the tennis court. Her uncle's Rolls Royce had gone to Newton St Cyres so there would only be the police car and Matt's motorcycle left on the gravel.

In the distance she heard Muffy barking at something. Light blazed from an uncurtained window that she realised must be Mrs Jenkinson's sitting room, where she allowed her fellow servants to sit after dinner was finished and the work was completed for the day. Surely now someone would look outside and see or hear them.

Henderson grabbed her arm once more and pulled her to a halt. 'Far enough for a moment. Miss Medford, we lose your company at this point, as you can be of no further assistance to me.'

Lucy's eyes widened in horror and Kitty wriggled in his grasp. Don't hurt her. She's done nothing to you.' Her struggle to free herself only resulted in a painful blow to her head that made her ears ring and her cousin gasp.

'Get the rope.' He indicated with the barrel of the gun and Kitty realised there was a coil of rope looped untidily by the wall. He must have placed it there earlier in the day, as she was certain her aunt's staff would never have left such a thing lying around the grounds.

He released her arm enough for her to collect the rope. 'Tie her up.' He kept his gun trained on them as Kitty struggled to make her stiff and wet fingers obey his instruction. Her vision was blurred from the blow he'd dealt her, and nausea made her weak.

'Pull that rope tighter. I don't want her going anywhere in a hurry,' he instructed as Kitty bound her cousin's hands together behind her back.

'I'm so sorry, Lucy,' she apologised as the rope bit into her cousin's skin and Lucy winced.

'Stop talking, we haven't much time. Now her feet.' He waved the gun once more and Kitty bent to loop the rope around Lucy's ankles.

'Good enough,' Henderson grunted. He pulled a handkerchief from his pocket and, balling it up, stuffed it into Lucy's mouth, causing her to gag. 'That should keep you quiet for a bit.' He gave Lucy a hard shove in her stomach and she doubled up in pain and toppled helplessly onto the hard gravel surface. He caught hold of Kitty's arm once more and she hissed with pain as he pulled her away from her cousin.

'That really wasn't necessary.' She could see Lucy was hurt and the white expression of pain on her cousin's face made bile rise in her gut. 'She couldn't put out her hands to save herself.'

'I decide what is necessary, and she's fortunate I let her live.' The cold steel barrel of the gun was poked against her ribs. 'Keep walking.'

'Where are we going?' Kitty asked again as he circled her away from the window, avoiding the light. She was relieved that her voice sounded clear, though she could feel her heart hammering in her chest. They headed away from the house back onto the grass towards the tennis court. Her hair was plastered to her head now and water had soaked the back of her dress.

'I am getting out of here. And you are my insurance to make certain they let me leave.'

'How far do you think you'll get? You must know Sir Horace has this place surrounded.' Her head ached and it was hard to find the words she wanted. Every step took her further away from the stream of light which promised people and safety.

'I have a way out.' He pushed her into a darker shadowy area beneath a tree as the sound of a twig snapping up ahead made Henderson pause.

They waited in the darkness. 'One word, one squeak, and you're dead,' he murmured in her ear. Her breath caught in her throat as they listened.

No further sounds reached them, and Henderson appeared to judge it safe enough for them to continue to move towards the vehicles parked beside the tennis court. One of the police cars stood next to Matt's motorcycle which was covered with a loose dark green tarpaulin.

He tightened his hold on her arm once more. 'Don't get any clever ideas about getting away. I'm a good shot and I have no compunction about using this gun.'

The chilling murmur of his voice in her ear made her heart race even faster. She could see no sign of movement near the cars and she wondered if she had imagined that snapping twig a few moments earlier.

Soaked to the skin now, Kitty doubted she could move very speedily even if she had the chance. The blow to her head had made her giddy and her legs were leaden beneath her. She tripped and sent a loose stone skittering across the ground towards the car. Her clumsiness was rewarded with another cuff to her head, dislodging her earring. She bit her lip and tasted the flat, metallic taste of her own blood.

'Be careful.' Henderson's words were barely audible but loaded with menace, his breath hot on her stinging ear.

He tugged her down, forcing her to crouch beside him as they neared the police car. Suddenly, Kitty spotted a shadow moving near the rhododendrons that grew alongside the court. A uniformed figure, probably one of the constables that Inspector Greville had set to keep watch. Her spirits rose; perhaps rescue might be at hand.

Henderson froze in place once more and she had no option but to watch and wait beside him. She knew that if she were to try and call a warning then both their lives would be forfeited. Instinctively, she prayed that the constable might notice them and raise the alarm somehow.

The constable moved, walking back and forth, swinging his arms. The moon slid briefly from behind a cloud and Kitty observed rain drip from the brim of the man's helmet onto his coat. The man drew out a pipe from the inner pocket of his coat and bowed his head as he concentrated on filling the bowl with tobacco.

Henderson moved more swiftly and silently than Kitty expected. The constable heard nothing until Henderson hit him on the back of the head with the gun, dislodging his helmet. The man fell forward onto his knees and Henderson administered another blow. Kitty winced and turned her head away. The speed and severity of Henderson's action rendered her unable to even scream.

She staggered upright and shook her head carefully in an attempt to clear her brain. Maybe while he was distracted she could make it to the safety of the house. Henderson was busy searching the unconscious man's pockets. She staggered forward a half step.

Henderson was back at her side before she had any opportunity to do more than try to collect her wits.

'Kitty!' Matt's voice.

She tried to turn in the direction of the shout, but Henderson was too quick for her. He wrenched her arm back, twisting it behind her and forcing her in front of him like a shield.

'Matt! Watch out, he's got a gun.'

'Stay back!' Henderson pointed the gun in the direction of Matt's voice.

Kitty peered into the darkness. Where was he? The moon had disappeared back into the clouds and the rain increased in intensity. Unable to free her hands to wipe her face, her vision was obscured.

Henderson pushed her towards the police car and wrenched the driver's door open. There was a movement from somewhere near the house and Henderson pulled the trigger. Kitty screamed and prayed that Matt had not been hit.

'Get in the car, passenger seat. Move it!' Henderson shoved her, sending her sprawling across the leather seats.

'Kitty!' Matt's voice sounded nearer.

She tried lifting her head to peer through the windshield. Thank heavens, he must have missed.

'Hurry up.' Henderson hit her again.

Suddenly, there was a flurry of barks and a small furry animal launched herself out of the rain at Henderson's ankles.

'What the devil? Get this dog away from me!' Henderson tried to dodge the excited Muffy as she danced and pranced around him.

Kitty seized her chance to scramble across the front seats to release the catch on the passenger door. She wriggled through and rolled out of the door, dropping on her knees onto the gravel. Behind her she heard a roar of rage, followed by a yip from Muffy. She half crawled, half rolled to shelter behind Matt's motorcycle.

The crack of another shot rent the air and she squeezed her eyes tight shut, anticipating that in a split second Henderson would find her and kill her. She hoped he wasn't aiming at Lucy's dog.

Then there came the roar of an engine and she realised that Henderson must have started the police car. She crawled to the end of the tarpaulin and peeped out to see the black police car reversing rapidly. Kitty ducked back out of sight as a spray of gravel pinged all around her as Henderson sped off along the drive.

'Kitty, are you all right?' Matt hauled her to her feet and began to tug the cover from his motorcycle. Rain streamed from his cap and the upturned collar of his raincoat.

'Yes. What are you doing?'

'If I head across the grass on the bike, I can cut him off before he leaves the grounds.' Matt jumped onto the cycle and fit the key in the ignition.

Kitty smoothed her drenched hair back from her face. 'Not on your own, you're not.' She hitched up the soaking wet skirt of her gown, slid onto the seat behind him and fastened her arms tight around his waist, his wiry, muscular frame a solid relief after the ordeal of the last half hour.

'What the hell are you doing?' Matt asked.

'Coming with you, of course. Come on, Matt, you're wasting time.' She was dimly aware that a crowd of servants had poured out of the back door of the manor. To her relief, she spotted Muffy sitting at Mr Harmon's feet and Alice's pale, anxious face as she huddled next to Cook.

'Have you ever ridden a motorcycle pillion before?'

'No, but I've ridden a donkey.' She gripped the leather seat between her knees and clung on to Matt. A fresh surge of adrenaline coursed through her veins.

He swore under his breath and gunned the engine. 'Hold tight.'

She buried her head against his back, the sodden cloth of his coat pressing against her cheek as they roared forward, sending another spray of gravel behind them. Her shrieks were drowned out by the noise of the engine as they bumped across the field in pursuit of the stolen police car.

The motorcycle headlamp cut through the dark, driving rain to illuminate the path ahead. Further on she could hear the police car roaring down the drive towards the gatehouse.

'Hang on.' Matt swung the bike at an angle and Kitty clung on for dear life as the bike skidded and slithered on the wet grass.

She squeezed her eyes tight shut as the roar and crack of another shot sounded somewhere in front of them. She muttered a prayer under her breath that no one else would be hurt. The motorcycle swerved again, making Kitty feel sick. Their speed started to drop and she tried to peer over Matt's shoulder.

They were almost at the gatehouse now and in the light from the police car's headlamps she could see that the vast wrought-iron gates were closed. Chinks of light shone through the gaps in the curtains of the house where the gatekeeper had drawn them against the night.

'He's not slowing down,' Kitty yelled. 'He'll hit the gates.'

Matt slowed right down. There was another loud crack and the police car swerved off the drive to bump across the grass away from the gates.

'He's going to crash.' She stared in horror as the car continued at full pelt before hitting the large oak tree near the lodge.

Matt had drawn the cycle to a halt as the sickening crunch of metal and glass was followed by a roar and a bang as the wrecked car burst into flames. He cut the engine as they stared at the fireball rapidly engulfing the base of the tree. There was a brief lull then a further explosion as the flames reached the fuel tank. Small branches further up the trunk of the tree caught alight before falling down onto the wreckage below.

People emerged from the lodge and rushed forward to form a small semicircle at a safe distance around the blazing car. The air filled with the stench of fuel and burning rubber. Further pops and bangs followed as the tyres exploded, sending sparks and pieces of debris into the night sky.

'I don't understand. What happened? Why did he swerve? I thought he was going to ram the gates.' Kitty shivered, the full horror of what she had witnessed beginning to sink into her consciousness. 'What was the shot?'

A male figure detached from the group around the car and began to stride across the dark field towards them. Matt slid from his seat and extended his hand to help her from her perch. Her legs trembled and refused to support her as she slid off the seat. He took off his coat and draped it gently around her shoulders as he steadied her.

'Captain Bryant!' Lord Medford approached them, his shotgun resting over his arm. 'Good Lord, Kitty, what are you doing here?'

'I take it Henderson did not escape?' Matt's expression was sombre. He kept his arm around Kitty who was shivering violently despite the welcome dry warmth of his coat.

A grim smile stretched her uncle's lips. 'Shot out his tyres, don't think Greville will be very pleased with the loss of a police car.'

Her knees sagged again, and she would have fallen if it hadn't been for Matt's support.

'Whatever has happened to you?' Her uncle frowned as he looked at her face and she guessed she didn't present a very pretty picture.

'Lucy, someone needs to find Lucy,' she struggled to get the words out.

'Come, my dear, my car is at the gates, let us take you back to the house. I should have told you of the change of plan but realised someone needed to secure the gatehouse exit to the estate.' Her uncle helped Matt to support her across the field and past the small knot of people who were working to extinguish the blaze.

'I'll see you back at the house. Don't worry, Lucy will be all right, we found her before we found you,' Matt said as her uncle climbed into the back of the Rolls next to her and gave his chauffeur the signal to drive off.

CHAPTER TWENTY-FIVE

Matt left the party from the lodge to finish extinguishing the blaze. From the moment the car had hit the tree he had seen there was no hope for Henderson to escape. But for Kitty's quick thinking back at the manor she would have been alongside him in the stolen car. She too could have died in that fiery blaze.

He returned to his motorcycle and climbed onto his seat. Trust Kitty to have insisted on riding pillion after Henderson, he thought. There had not been time to throw her off, which had been his first inclination. He fired up the engine and set off back towards the house, this time taking a slower pace off the grass until he reached the driveway.

Anger at her lack of thought for her own safety built within him. If she had seen what he had seen and suffered a loss like he had suffered, then she would not be so cavalier. It was those left behind who suffered, for they had to carry on living.

Dr Carter's sporty little car was parked on the gravel when he pulled up. Lord Medford had lost little time in summoning attention for his niece and presumably his daughter. Inspector Greville had asked the doctor to be on stand-by in case of casualties and it seemed his forethought had been a good call.

Kitty had already been whisked away by Alice and the doctor when he entered the hall.

'Captain Bryant, the very chap,' Lord Medford greeted him with a slap on the back and a hearty handshake. 'This way, my boy, a hot toddy is called for, methinks. Come, come, take that wet jacket off. Harmon!'

His host steered him into the study where a pale-faced Aubrey awaited him, accompanied by Sir Horace and Inspector Greville. Harmon hurried forward to peel his wet coat from his back and to hand him a blanket. The ride back without his great coat had ensured he was thoroughly soaked.

'Just managed to free young Aubrey and my constable from the laboratory,' Greville remarked, handing Matt a small glass of a steaming liquid.

'The man Henderson coshed by the tennis court, is he all right?' Matt asked.

'Sore head but alive, his helmet took the brunt of the first blow. He was lucky. They've carted him off to the infirmary at Exeter.' Lord Medford helped himself to a drink.

Matt took a cautious sip from his glass. 'And your daughter, sir? Is she safe?'

Lord Medford's expression sobered. 'Bruised and shaken, nasty rope burns to her wrists and ankles and grazes all down her legs. But typical Lucy, she's more relieved that her wretched dog is safe.'

'Doctor Carter has been busy. I've asked him to join us when he has finished with Miss Underhay. Mr Banks has also been taken to the hospital in Exeter, but I believe he should make a full recovery.' Inspector Greville's face brightened when the study door reopened and Mr Harmon appeared bearing a large silver platter of sandwiches.

'Cook sends her compliments, my lord. She thought some refreshments might be welcome.' He deposited the platter on the desk and returned a few seconds later to add another platter containing slices of pork pie and sausage rolls.

'Most excellent idea, please pass on our thanks, Harmon.' Lord Medford tucked into a sausage roll.

'What happened to Rupert?' Matt asked. He knew Lucy had been discovered bound and gagged before he had managed to track Kitty and Henderson, but this was the first he had heard of Rupert being injured.

'Henderson bashed him over the head with that billiard cue of his. Lucy thought he was dead. Poor girl was hysterical when we found her. She was convinced Banks was a goner and of course the bounder still had Kitty.' Lord Medford brushed pastry crumbs from his moustache.

'What about the formula, sir? Was it recovered?' Aubrey asked. He still appeared to be in shock.

'Miss Underhay worked out that Henderson had hidden it inside the handle of his billiards cue. Sure enough, when Lucy told us, and we took a look, there it was. Been right under our noses all the bally time.' Lord Medford reached for another sausage roll before Inspector Greville could empty the plate. 'Yes, the fake one burned in the car with Henderson, but the original was rolled up tight inside the cue.'

'So, the formula is quite safe?' Matt asked.

'Yes, I shall take it to London with me in a few hours' time. Our team of scientists are keen to develop it further,' Sir Horace said, patting his jacket pocket. 'In fact, if you will all excuse me, I have a car coming early this morning and I could use some sleep after tonight's adventure.'

As Sir Horace bade them good night, the cheery face of Doctor Carter appeared at the study door.

'Ah, Carter, come in. How are the patients?' Lord Medford indicated Sir Horace's recently vacated chair.

'Your daughter is resting comfortably, sir. I have administered a draught to her and to Miss Underhay. They both have cuts and bruises but nothing life-threatening.' He looked at Matt as he spoke. 'The constable has been sent to the hospital at Exeter to join Mr

Banks. I am hopeful that they will both be fit to be discharged by tomorrow.'

'Excellent news.' Lord Medford beamed. 'A small drink, doctor?'

'Thank you, but I must get off. Good shooting on your behalf, sir. Sorry to have missed the car chase. A good test for the motorcycle, eh? Isle of Man for you next year and the TT races, eh?' He clapped Matt on the shoulder and made his farewells.

With the last of the food safely inside Inspector Greville, the party broke up and Matt retired to bed still thinking of what might have happened to Kitty.

Kitty woke to pale, insipid sunlight streaming in through her bedroom window and the white, anxious face of Alice peering at her from across the room. She vaguely remembered being bundled into a warm bath, the kind, cheerful face of Doctor Carter and a drink of something that had tasted strange.

'Oh, Miss Kitty, thank goodness you're all right.' Alice bustled forward. 'Let me move the pillows for you. Your poor head, miss, and you lost one of them nice earrings what your aunt gave you.'

Kitty struggled to lift her head from the pillow, but a wave of nausea swept across her and she waved Alice away for a moment. 'Just a minute, Alice. I feel a little queer this morning.' Memories of the chase and the terrible ending flooded back. She licked her lips and touched the swollen area on her lower lip with her tongue.

'It's not morning, miss, it's nigh on teatime. You've been asleep all day. Captain Bryant has been up to ask after you several times and that nice Doctor Carter came and checked on you.'

Moving more cautiously, Kitty managed to raise her head sufficiently to take a peep at the clock. 'Good grief, I can't believe I've slept for so long.' She remembered being wrapped in Matt's coat,

he comforting smell of the material still warm from his body. He'd
been cross with her about something.

Alice carefully manoeuvred the pillows and straightened the
covers. 'Shall I get you a nice cup of tea, miss? And something
o eat?'

'Tea and maybe some toast please, Alice.' Her throat was dry
and perhaps nibbling a little toast might dispel the nausea she felt
whenever she moved her head. 'How is my cousin?'

'Miss Lucy is all right, miss. Very shook up and her arms and
egs is covered with bruises and scratches. Most cross about her
ruined gown and shoes.' Alice smiled and bustled away to fetch tea.

A knock came at her door shortly after she had departed.

'Come in.'

She wasn't too surprised when Matt popped his head around
he door. 'Alice said you were awake now. How's the head?'

'Sore.' She tentatively tried moving her arms and legs. 'A little
ike the rest of me.' She couldn't read his expression.

'Your uncle has recovered the papers; you were right, they were
concealed in the billiard cue. Sir Horace has taken them to London
by car this morning.'

She managed a weak smile. 'Good. I'm sure Aunt Hortense will
be pleased they are gone from the house. You can come in, you
know. Alice will be back in a minute with some tea, and as you
can see, I'm perfectly decent.'

He grinned and stepped into her room, closing the door behind
him. 'Lucy will probably be along to see you in a while. She's been
really worried about you.'

'Poor Lucy. I hated having to tie her up like that and then that
brute pushed her over when he knew she couldn't do anything to
save herself.' Unexpected tears welled in her eyes at the memory.
Parts of the ordeal began to come back more clearly to her.

Matt seated himself on the winged armchair near the fireplace and swivelled it around, moving it closer to her bedside so he could see her better. 'Rupert is conscious and doing well. He's at the infirmary in Exeter. Doctor Carter judged it a better place than the local cottage hospital. They want to keep him one more night to be on the safe side, apparently Henderson hit him with real force. Daisy and Aubrey have been to see him but were only allowed a few minutes.'

'And the police constable?' Kitty asked as she felt under her pillow for the pocket handkerchief she usually kept there.

'His helmet apparently saved him from the worst effects of the blows. He is expected out of hospital tomorrow too.'

Kitty retrieved her handkerchief and blew her nose. 'I'm so glad.'

Matt gave her a considered look. 'I was quite worried about you. When that car went up in flames, I kept thinking, what if you hadn't managed to get out when you did? It could have been you in that car.'

A delicate shudder ran along her spine. 'I asked myself the same thing. My guardian angel was clearly looking out for me.' She tried to keep her tone light. She knew all too well that their adventure could have ended very differently.

'The risks you took—'

She interrupted him. 'I knew those risks and took them willingly. I would do so again if it meant that a cruel and vicious murderer would be caught, and the security of my country could be ensured.'

He sighed and leaned forward in his seat. 'Kitty, you could have been killed.'

'Then at least I'd have lived first.'

'You are the most obstinate woman I have ever met, Kitty Underhay.'

'Then you need to meet more women.' A tear escaped onto her cheek and she dashed it away. 'I won't be shut away in a bandbox to be treated like a doll, just brought out on special occasions to perform a trick or to look pretty. I have as much right to live my life and choose the risks I wish to take as any man.'

'But you are not a man, Kitty. There are limits to what society accepts. I cannot talk to you when you are in this mood.'

'I am not in a mood. I am merely attempting to make you see how unreasonable you are being. If I were a man you would not be saying this to me.' She swallowed hard. She would not cry.

'That is unfair, Kitty.' His eyes sparked.

'Well, that is how I feel.' She clamped her lips together to stop them from quivering and fought back a wince at the sore spot.

He rose. 'Then there's nothing more to be said.'

Tears threatened to fall now like rain onto her pillow, but she turned her face away from him. 'No, nothing.'

There was a rattle of crockery at the door and Matt opened it to admit Alice and her tea tray.

'Oh, Captain Bryant, good thing I brought an extra cup.' She beamed at him as she entered and set the tray down on a small mahogany side table.

'It's quite all right, Alice. I'm not stopping.' He forced a grim smile, and after a last glance at Kitty, turned and left.

'Oh,' Alice started in surprise as the door banged shut behind him. 'What's got into him, then?'

Kitty let out a sob and Alice rushed to her side. 'Don't take on so, Miss Kitty. Is it your head? Shall I send for the doctor?'

'No, I'm just being silly.' She scrubbed her eyes with her handkerchief.

Alice frowned then went back to the tea tray. 'A nice cup of tea will see you right, and Cook has sent some honey for your toast.'

She suited her actions to her words and Kitty was soon propped up with a tray across her knees.

'Thank you, Alice.' She felt rather foolish and certainly not at all hungry. Although to appease the girl's feelings, she forced herself to eat a triangle of toast with a smear of honey.

Her maid returned the armchair to its usual position before the fireplace. She took up a basket of mending and perched on the seat. 'What was up with Captain Bryant then, miss?' Alice asked before sucking the end of a thread and poking it through the eye of a needle with an expert touch.

Kitty was not deceived by the innocent expression on her young maid's face. 'And is it any business of yours?' she asked, trying to sound reproving.

Alice's delicate features flushed right to the tips of her ears. 'I was just taking an interest, miss. I thought maybe it was a lovers' tiff like you see in the pictures with Gary Cooper and Helen Hayes. He's been proper mithered about you all day, he has.' She went off into a happy daydream.

'Matt is just a friend.' At least she had thought he was her friend and maybe could have become more than that. After their heated exchange of words, she was no longer sure that was still the case.

Alice merely continued to look smug.

'Life is not like the pictures.' Kitty tried glaring at an unrepentant Alice.

The maid continued to darn, a small smile playing on her lips.

There was another knock at the door and Lucy appeared, elegantly attired in peach silk pyjamas and robe, with Muffy at her heels. 'Kitty, darling, Alice said you were awake, so I had to come and see you.'

Kitty was pleased to see that apart from some bandaging on her wrists, her cousin appeared relatively unscathed by her ordeal.

'How are you?' She smoothed her bed covers to invite Lucy to sit with her. 'I see Muffy has recovered.'

Lucy laughed. 'Poor baby, she's been fêted as the hero of the hour after going for Henderson and allowing you to get free. She'll be as fat as a little pudding with all the treats.' Lucy perched on the end of the bed, Muffy at her feet.

'Lucy, I'm so sorry, I hated tying you up, and when that beast pushed you over...' Kitty blinked back the tears which threatened to reappear. The awful scene replayed in her head as she noticed a graze on her cousin's temple.

'Don't be silly. You had no choice. He would have shot you in an instant. He would have murdered both of us. You heard what he said about why he'd killed Viola and Nanny Thoms. I was convinced that Rupert was dead. Quite frankly I was more scared for you. Once he'd left me there trussed up like a chicken at least I knew I was safe. All I had to worry about was a ruined gown and breaking the heel on my favourite shoes. You, on the other hand, were still in danger.' Lucy patted her hand tenderly. 'Matt has been like a bear with a sore head all day today waiting for you to wake up.'

'Oh dear.' Kitty sighed. She wished she had been more temperate with her choice of words.

'What's wrong?' Lucy asked.

There was a clatter from Alice's direction as she dropped her scissors.

'We've just had a huge argument,' Kitty confessed.

Lucy blinked in surprise. 'Oh, darling, whatever for?'

'He didn't want me to assist Inspector Greville with capturing Mr Henderson. He thought it was too dangerous. He would rather I stayed in some safe, boring little life. Played the little woman and let the men take the risks.'

Her cousin sighed. 'Perhaps he's scared. After all, you could have been killed. He must care for you, darling, or he wouldn't feel so passionately about protecting you.'

Kitty knew her cousin had a point. She knew Matt's history, that the loss of his wife had deeply affected him. If he would only talk to her about what had happened to Edith then perhaps they wouldn't be quarrelling.

Alice coughed and pretended to be busy with her mending when the cousins looked in her direction.

'We are, or were, friends, Lucy. He's not my beau. He doesn't pay me compliments or bring me flowers or take me to the pictures.' Even if sometimes she had wondered what it might be like if they were to walk out together. When they had danced together, when he took her arm and when she'd clung on to him during that wild motorcycle ride.

'For a man who doesn't do any of those things, he seems to always notice when you enter the room. I've seen how he is around you, Kitty. He cares for you.'

'Then he has a queer way of showing it.' She conceded grudgingly. He did call and take her to tea, kiss her cheek when they met and there was some kind of connection between them. He was also the most complicated man she'd ever met.

'I'm sure that when you're feeling better you can talk to him and resolve your differences. Please don't worry, darling. It'll all be all right. The main thing is that you need to rest. Rupert should be allowed out of hospital tomorrow. He and Daisy are staying for another day or so then they are to return to London. He has the estate to sort out with his solicitors and some decisions he needs to make,' Lucy informed her.

'And you and Rupert...? Is there a you and Rupert?' Kitty asked. She knew her cousin cared more for Rupert than she had previously admitted. She'd seen her reaction when she'd thought he was dead.

Lucy fidgeted and blushed. 'I don't know. Rupert has a lot to think about. Inheriting a title and an estate has somewhat complicated his political ambitions.'

Kitty raised an eyebrow and winced as a sharp pain speared the back of her head. 'I'm sure Rupert will still find time for you.'

Her cousin's colour deepened. 'We'll see.' A small photograph on Kitty's dressing table caught her attention. 'Oh, is that a picture of your mother? She looks so much like you.' Lucy rose and picked up the picture, studying it carefully as she retook her seat.

'I like to keep it with me.'

The battered leather frame held a small photograph that must have been taken shortly before Elowed disappeared. Kitty only had a few photographs of her mother and until a few months ago, had had none of her father.

'Do you think you will ever find out what happened to her?' Lucy asked as she passed Kitty the photograph.

'I hope so. It's simply that the longer she is gone, the harder it seems to find new clues. I have so few memories of her and those grow weaker each year. And yet, sometimes it's as if she is very close to me. Does that sound odd?' She wished she could explain what she meant more clearly.

She could remember small things; the scent of her perfume, the sound of her laugh. Her mother allowing her to brush her long blonde hair in front of the mirror before bed. Yet sometimes it was difficult to recall her features, even though they were so like her own. She set the frame down on her bedside table.

'What will you do when you return home?' Lucy pleated the coverlet between her fingers.

'Aunt Livvy is returning to Scotland as soon as her ankle and shoulder are healed. I expect Grams will wish to accompany her for a while. I shall take over running the hotel again while she is away.' That dreadful, heavy feeling resurfaced inside her as if the responsibility of the Dolphin pressed against her chest. The weight of the ages pressing against her.

Kitty sighed. Despite the danger, the adrenaline rush of last night's events contrasted with the dreary repetitiveness of life as a hotelier.

'I admire you. You can do so much, be so independent. I shall be here with Mother and she will run me ragged, no doubt, since there will be no Nanny Thoms to fetch and carry for her. Daisy has invited me to stay with her soon so at least that may offer a small relief from the horticultural catalogues and talk of chemicals at the dinner table.' Lucy sighed.

'At least we can write to each other and telephone too. It will be so nice to have a friend.' Kitty reached out to hug her cousin, wincing as the movement made her injuries ache. Lucy was as constrained by her life and her parents' expectations of her as Kitty was by her duties at the hotel.

'Yes, that will be lovely, and I shall come to stay with you as we planned. You must tell me how your search for your mother goes on. Perhaps Uncle Edgar may be able to recall something more? I know Mother has finally talked to you about your mother's visit here so perhaps Matt will help you discover a clue.' Lucy's face brightened.

'Perhaps.' If he spoke to her again.

CHAPTER TWENTY-SIX

Matt left Kitty's room and headed for the terrace. He needed to get outside into the cooler air, freshened by the previous evening's rain. The argument with Kitty had upset and disturbed him in equal measures. He wished he could make her understand his concerns.

He strolled to the edge of the stone balustrade to look out over the rose garden and lit a cigarette. He knew even as he inhaled that he had smoked far too many cigarettes recently. Yet it was a reflex action that worked to clear his head, calm his thoughts and helped him to think more clearly. The one coping mechanism that always served him well.

Kitty's aunt came up the steps from the rose garden, a large wicker basket over her arm and a pair of secateurs in her hand. 'Captain Bryant, how is Kitty? I understand she is awake now.'

'She is recovering well, I believe, thank you.'

The older woman adjusted her basket. 'Such a relief, I must say. Poor Lucy is also recovering. One cannot believe the evil behaviour of that man. Mrs Jenkinson is still distraught. I understand he murdered her brother because he discovered the wireless set. To think I was so deceived in him. My husband tells me that Henderson was in the pay of some foreign power.'

'We were all deceived, Lady Medford. Henderson was a cunning and vicious man, not to mention a traitor to this country.' He took another draw on his cigarette.

Recovering the papers meant that the formula would not fall into the wrong hands, and should the worst happen in the future, many lives might be saved.

'Dreadful business. The newspapers are full of the story. I've telephoned Mrs Treadwell and appraised her of Kitty's condition. I have assured her the girl is quite safe. Such a worry for her and as her aunt I feel horribly responsible.'

A pang of guilt mixed afresh with anger speared Matt. 'Since the loss of her daughter, Kitty is extra precious to her grandmother.'

'Quite so.' Lady Medford looked at her basket and sighed. 'I was cutting some roses for Nanny Thoms and Frau Fiser's funerals. I do hope it won't all become something of a circus. Poor Viola had no family and Nanny Thoms only has an elderly sister who has been in a nursing home for a number of years so there is no one there either, really.'

'It's very good of Lord Medford to take on organising Viola's funeral,' Matt said.

'Well, it's the least we could do under the circumstances. There's not exactly a social protocol for when one's employees and guests are murdered in one's home.'

Matt extinguished his cigarette. 'I have been very grateful for your hospitality despite, as you said, the unfortunate circumstances, however I must head home, I'm afraid.' The argument with Kitty had made up his mind. He needed space and time to think about things. It worried him that his concern for Kitty had been so great and the reasons for their quarrel troubled him.

'You are, of course, very welcome to stay longer. I'm sure my niece would enjoy your company while she recovers.' His hostess eyed him keenly.

'That's very hospitable of you, but unfortunately business calls. I'm sure Kitty will understand.' Actually, he wasn't terribly certain that she would understand but it had to be better if there was some space between them for a little while. Perhaps when they had both had time to reflect they might manage to find a way through their differing points of view.

'Of course. I think Kitty's grandmother is anxious for her return so I expect she will return to Dartmouth herself in the next few days.'

He had no doubt that Kitty's grandmother would want her back as soon as possible; Kitty was everything to her. Lady Medford carried on inside the house. Matt spent a few more minutes looking out over the garden before going to pack his bag.

Kitty and Alice returned to Dartmouth a few days later. Lord Medford insisted that his chauffeur drive them back to the Dolphin Hotel in his car. When Kitty had learned that Matt had returned home without speaking to her, she had tried to shrug it off even though she had felt hurt and disappointed. She had written to her father, telling him all she'd learned of her mother's visit to Enderley and she hoped he would reply soon. If he could recall the names and addresses of his acquaintances in Exeter before the war, especially Dawkins, then it might give a lead to her mother. And failing that, perhaps she could write to someone at the estate in Ireland to see if they knew anything.

Lucy had seemed sensitive to her feelings regarding Matt and refrained from asking about the situation. It had been nice to see Rupert and Daisy again before they had left for London, and without any suspicions clouding the air between them. Rupert's head had been bandaged and he had appeared pale but otherwise in good spirits.

She was quietly pleased to see the relationship rebuilding between Lucy and Rupert. It amused her that her aunt and uncle regarded a potential match with a friendlier eye since Rupert's recent upturn in fortunes.

'It'll be funny to be back at the hotel, won't it, miss?' Alice gazed out of the side window of the Rolls with every appearance of enjoyment.

'Yes. I'm afraid you might find it rather dull after this last week.' Kitty knew she would find it dull herself. And if Matt were no longer her friend then life would be very dull indeed. It was a little scary to realise how quickly she had come to look forward to talking and sharing time with him.

'I expects Mrs Homer will have plenty of work for me, and me mum will be glad to see me to help with the little ones.'

'You have been an absolutely splendid lady's maid, Alice. When Lucy comes to visit later this year, I shall make sure you are lady's maid to her during her stay.'

The girl's thin face brightened. 'That'll be nice. Miss Lucy is a proper posh lady. She has some lovely things.'

Kitty's grandmother and her great aunt were waiting for them on their arrival at the hotel, looking out of the large leaded-pane window of her grandmother's salon above the main entrance. Her heart twinged at the sight of their dear, familiar faces and she immediately felt guilty that she wished so much to be elsewhere. An image of Matt's face crossed her mind and she blinked back the tears that unexpectedly prickled her lashes.

Mickey, the maintenance man, came out to assist Alice with their bags. 'Good to have you back, Miss Kitty.'

Kitty surveyed the ancient half-timbered walls of the hotel, the hand-painted sign of the Dolphin creaking gently above her head in the soft breeze from the river. She took a last look at the sunlight sparkling on the water and followed Alice inside.

'Welcome back to the Dolphin.'

A LETTER FROM HELENA

want to say thank you for choosing to read *Murder at Enderley Hall*. If you enjoyed it and want to keep up to date with all my atest releases, just sign up at the following link. Your email address vill never be shared and you can unsubscribe at any time.

www.bookouture.com/helena-dixon

If you read the first book in the series, *Murder at the Dolphin Hotel*, you can find out how Kitty and Matt first met. I always enjoy meeting characters again as a series reader which is why I love writing his series so much. I hope you enjoy their adventures as much as love creating them. The next book continues Kitty and Matt's mysteries and I hope you'll enjoy reading more of their exploits.

I hope you loved *Murder at Enderley Hall* and if you did, I would e very grateful if you could write a review. I'd love to hear what ou think, and it makes such a difference helping new readers to iscover one of my books for the first time.

I love hearing from my readers – you can get in touch on my acebook page, through Twitter, Goodreads or my website.

Thanks,
Helena Dixon

 nelldixonauthor

 @NellDixon

 www.nelldixon.com

ACKNOWLEDGEMENTS

I would like to once again thank the people of Dartmouth for a
their kind and generous assistance in providing information an
allowing me to fictionalise parts of their beautiful town.

I would like to thank everyone at the Beer Engine pub a
Newton St Cyres for all their expertise and assistance. Originall
called the Railway Engine, it is now a fabulous micro-brewer
serving wonderful food and great beers. It was established in th
late 1800s and sits alongside the railway so was perfect for inclusio
in *Murder at Enderley Hall*.

I would also like to thank the staff at the National Motorcycl
Museum for their advice and information.

The British Communist Party archives were also extremel
helpful.

Murder at Enderley Hall wouldn't exist without the suppo
of the Coffee Crew, aka my wonderful author friends, Elizabet
Hanbury and Phillipa Ashley.

Of course, it goes without saying that I need to thank m
husband, David, who is also my research assistant, and my daughter
Robyn, Corinne and Alannah, who are my cheer squad. Last bu
not least, everyone at Bookouture for their hard work and expertise
my lovely editor, Emily Gowers, and my brilliant agent, Kate Nash

Printed in Great Britain
by Amazon

23659637R00148